And Then He Kissed Me

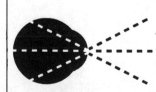
This Large Print Book carries the
Seal of Approval of N.A.V.H.

And Then He Kissed Me

Patti Berg

Thorndike Press • Waterville, Maine

Published in 2004 by arrangement with Avon Books, an imprint of HarperCollins Publishers, Inc.

Thorndike Press® Large Print Core.

The tree indicium is a trademark of Thorndike Press.

The text of this Large Print edition is unabridged. Other aspects of the book may vary from the original edition.

Set in 16 pt. Plantin.

Printed in the United States on permanent paper.

Library of Congress Control Number: 2003111812
ISBN 0-7862-6074-2 (lg. print : hc : alk. paper)

When I'm good I'm very, very good,
but when I'm bad, I'm better.

MAE WEST

As the Founder/CEO of NAVH, the only national health agency solely devoted to those who, although not totally blind, have an eye disease which could lead to serious visual impairment, I am pleased to recognize Thorndike Press★ as one of the leading publishers in the large print field.

Founded in 1954 in San Francisco to prepare large print textbooks for partially seeing children, NAVH became the pioneer and standard setting agency in the preparation of large type.

Today, those publishers who meet our standards carry the prestigious "Seal of Approval" indicating high quality large print. We are delighted that Thorndike Press is one of the publishers whose titles meet these standards. We are also pleased to recognize the significant contribution Thorndike Press is making in this important and growing field.

Lorraine H. Marchi, L.H.D.
Founder/CEO
NAVH

★ Thorndike Press encompasses the following imprints: Thorndike, Wheeler, Walker and Large Print Press.

Prologue

Without a doubt, Juliet Bridger had lost her mind. The shocking yet fascinating details of her tumble into the depths of madness hadn't yet hit the tabloids, but they would soon enough. And sure as shooting, the headline would read:

BLOND BOMBSHELL
GOES BANANAS

With any luck, the sleazy account would make note of the fact that Juliet went berserk in the grandest of style.

It began on the Fourth of July at one of her extravagant parties. To mark the occasion, fireworks splattered across the nighttime sky, Pacific Ocean waves lapped gently against the rocky Carmel coast, and considering all the luminaries in attendance, paparazzi almost certainly hid in Juliet's prize-winning rhododendrons to photograph anything remotely indecent.

Strange as it seemed, it was the caviar that pushed Juliet over the edge. Not Garrett Pierce, her billionaire ex-husband who'd tried to drag her down with him when he went to prison for seven years. Not the menacing phone calls he'd plagued her with for the past six months. Not the gossip that she'd played a role in Garrett's fraudulent business deals or the fact that far too many of her former so-called friends had the audacity to believe it was true.

It wasn't the nasty whispers that she was as big a bimbo as she was a bombshell. It wasn't even the rotund Italian tenor who'd been hitting on her all evening, kissing her hand, admiring her décolletage and dishing out synthetic adulation.

No, it was definitely the fish eggs. Nasty, vile little things that she detested.

Wrinkling her nose — a faux pas in polite society yet perfectly acceptable to the middle-class world in which she'd grown up — Juliet reluctantly lifted toward her mouth the puff-pastry star smeared with crème fraîche and sprinkled with beluga. It reeked of high-class elegance, like everything else at the party she was throwing for two hundred jet-setting acquaintances who weren't worried — *yet* — that being seen in her company would tarnish their reputations.

According to her ex, eating caviar was *de rigueur,* a must-do, at any social event. Juliet hadn't forgotten a thing Garrett Pierce had drummed into her head during their eight years of marriage. Like Henry Higgins, he'd instructed her on the right way to walk, to talk, to sit and stand. He'd taught her how to buy and sell stock, to pick the best diamonds, the finest wines, and the most influential friends.

Garrett had known everyone who was anyone. He'd made billions developing video games and computer software, and even though she was a fresh-faced twenty-two-year-old when they met and he was twenty-seven years her senior, the charming and oh-so-handsome man had swept her off her feet with flowers and smiles and long, soul-searching walks on the beach.

And what a knight in shining armor he'd been, rescuing her from the long-term movie contract she'd gullibly signed when a two-bit producer lured her away from college with promises of making her rich and famous. Instead he'd made her the dumb sex-kitten blonde who was the first to get slashed by the depraved psycho in seven of his *Slash McCall* flicks.

Garrett, of course, had his own plans for making her rich and famous, and she'd wanted stardom so badly that she'd bought into his carefully calculated strategy. First, he'd used her face and form when developing the jungle-goddess heroine in *Amazonia 2807*, which had become a series of mega-selling video games. Not long after that she was starring as Amazonia on TV, traipsing around in nothing more than a bikini made of leathery leaves and frolicking with two lean and powerful jaguars.

Garrett's plan hadn't ended there. Oh, no. She rode on floats in New Year's parades, she dished out food to the homeless on Thanksgiving and during Christmas, and, with her trusty jaguars at her leafy-bikini-clad side, she stood in the cold and collected coats and toys for needy children.

Garrett made her a household name, taking full advantage of every photo op, and ever so slowly, right before the public eye, transformed the queen of the rain forest into one classy dame who knew how to look beautiful, entertain well, and make millions writing mysteries.

Once upon a time she'd loved him. Once upon a time she'd believed that fame and fortune could make her exceedingly happy. Then the fairytale had shattered and blown apart — when Juliet caught her husband in bed with the newest starlet he'd taken under his wings.

That nasty night two years ago had ripped her heart to shreds. Now Garrett was in prison, the starlet was a has-been, and Juliet was still living in Garrett's overpowering shadow, not sure how much of his fairytale world she loved and how much of it she put up with because he'd convinced her it was *de rigueur.*

At the moment, the only thing she knew for sure was that she didn't *want* to eat the beluga sitting atop the stylish canapé she'd been staring at while Paolo Benedetti's voice droned on in her ear. Instead, she wanted creamy potato salad drenched with mayo and chock-full of sweet Vidalia onions, just like her dad had made when she was a kid. She wanted a hot dog, with the wiener roasted over an open fire, its skin charred and juices dripping through the cracks. She wanted it slathered with relish, good old-fashioned mustard and catsup — so much relish, catsup, and mustard that the mix of red, yellow, and green would ooze from the bun and slither over her fingers.

She wanted the warmth and tenderness she'd known as a child, she wanted . . .

"Are you all right, Juliet?" A voice echoed in her ear. A cool hand rested on her bare arm. "You look a bit pale."

Juliet raised her eyes. Nicole Palisade, the woman who'd been her trusty sidekick in "Amazonia 2807" and who had given up a dismal film career to become her assistant a few years later, was little more than a blur in a swirl of faces, all of them gawking as if Juliet had dribbled champagne down her chin.

"I'm fine," Juliet lied, laughing lightly. "But I've come to the conclusion that I detest caviar."

Nicole's eyes narrowed in disbelief, or was it fear that made her frown, worry that Juliet had flipped her lid, because only yesterday she'd been concerned that the specially ordered beluga wouldn't arrive on time.

Another hand clutched her arm. The clammy fingers belonged to the silky-voiced yet smarmy tenor who hovered much too close, looking like a killer whale in a tux, all black and white and blubbery.

"Would you like to lie down?" Nicole asked.

"No, no, I'm all right."

But the crush of people milling about on the veranda seemed to strangle her. In spite of the ocean breeze, she felt hot and sticky. She wanted to run and hide.

Another burst of fiery fantasy shot into the sky, the thunderous boom and crackling of a million sparks raising goose bumps on her arms. The exotic scents of frangipani, ginger, and gardenia that she'd asked the florist to decorate with assailed her. The hodgepodge of spicy fragrances was far too overpowering, and she longed for the unpretentious perfume of sweet peas and roses that she remembered from the garden she'd tended with her dad — the blue-collar worker who'd raised her on his own after her mother skipped town and shacked up with another man; the guy whose potato salad was voted the absolute best by Juliet's Girl Scout troop; the dad who'd disowned her when she'd run away from college, and had died before she could get to his bedside to say, *I'm sorry I disappointed you.*

She looked around her for some of the old-fashioned comfort she remembered from the days when she and her dad had been the best of friends — the picnic blanket spread on the lawn, someone churning a wooden ice cream freezer, children waving sparklers. Instead, guests in Armani, Hugo Boss, and Carolina Herrera laughed, sipped champagne, nibbled at hors d'oeuvres, and gossiped about the high-society elite they'd hobnobbed with yesterday and the day before, in places like Rio and Milan, Positano and Saint-Tropez.

An hour ago she'd been gossiping, too . . . and then she saw the beluga.

A waiter passed by and Juliet dropped her canapé on his tray. She turned to Paolo Benedetti, who hungrily eyed her uneaten tidbit in much the same way he'd been ogling her breasts, and in an attempt to look fully rational, she fastened a quasi smile on her face. *"Ciao,* Paolo!"

The tenor's brow furrowed as she tore out of his grasp. And then she ran, the scarlet silk of her svelte and revealing vintage thirties gown trailing behind her as she skirted past two Oscar winners, a prima ballerina, an Indy 500 champ, a pious judge, and a not-so-pious ex-president. She raced into the kitchen, around the chef who was shouting orders at his minions, through the dining room, to her expansive bedroom with a wall of windows that overlooked the rugged Carmel coastline and windblown Monterey pines.

Juliet slammed the door behind her and clapped a hand over the Harry Winston diamonds and rubies dangling down her chest. Her heart pounded hard and fast. The room spun and she knew in an instant that she had to get away from this Alice in Wonderland world and back to reality.

She wanted to be the girl she used to be, the girl who'd dressed in nothing but hot pink in high school, chewed Dubble Bubble, wore her hair in an Annette Funicello beehive, and bebopped to the oldies when all of her friends were plastering Duran Duran posters on their bedroom walls.

If she could turn back the clock or travel through time . . .

"Is something wrong, Juliet?"

Juliet spun around. Nicole's high heels clicked on the hand-painted Mexican tiles as she walked into the room, tall, far too slender, but stylishly perfect in a silver-metallic Oscar de la Renta.

"Tonight's party is all wrong." Juliet pushed her hair aside and unlatched the heavy necklace. "I should have served potato salad instead of caviar. I should have draped the deck in red, white, and blue. I should have . . ." Juliet sighed as she set the necklace on her dresser. "I should have stayed in college, become a teacher like my dad wanted, gotten married at twenty-five, and made peanut butter and jelly sandwiches for the two-point-five children running around my little tract house."

"You would have been miserable." Nicole smiled at Juliet's reflection in the mirror. "No Manolo Blahnik, no Kate Spade —"

"And no more paparazzi trying to catch me at my worst." Juliet pulled a dangly diamond and ruby earring from her ear. "I'm tired of the hype. Tired of being on all the time and tired of trying to be perfect because that's what's expected of me."

"Couldn't you get tired of everything tomorrow?" Nicole asked, not a speck of humor in her voice. "You have nearly two hundred guests outside. Paolo Benedetti's upset that you deserted him and refuses to sing unless you come back, and —"

"I'm not going back. The jewels are off, my party smile is off, and as soon as I pack a few things, I'm off."

"But —"

"No buts, Nicole. I need to get out of here."

Juliet crossed the room, lifted the cumbersome dome lid on an antique Spanish trunk and dug deep for the battered backpack her father had given her right before she'd left for college. As she touched the still soft leather, she could see the proud smile on his face when she'd unwrapped his gift, and the even bigger smile when, at the very bottom of the box, she found the keys to the pink Mustang she'd always wanted.

He'd had such high hopes for her, and she'd tried to live up to his expectations, but then she met that sweet-talking producer who'd put stars in her eyes. She bailed out of college, she went to Hollywood, and when her dad got wind of what she'd done, said he never wanted to see or speak to her again, claiming she'd deserted him and his ideals just as her mother had. She'd been hurt by his stubborn pride. She'd cried for weeks on end, and when he had a heart attack and died not more than six months later, she wanted to crawl into bed and never get up again.

But she did, and she threw herself into her work with a vengeance, trying to prove to herself — and to her dad — that she'd made the right choice.

Success had rained down on her, but so had gossip and innuendo. Even her painful divorce had been played out in the papers for all to see. Success was squeezing the life out of her, and even though she'd just turned thirty-two, she felt as if she'd lived a billion years.

It was time to escape.

Dropping the trunk's lid, Juliet stuffed a few changes of underwear into the leather bag, then went to her bedside and packed the ornate silver picture frame that held the photo she'd taken of her dad waving good-bye as she climbed into her Mustang and left for UCLA.

She grabbed the empty journal that sat beside her dad's photo and dropped that into the bag, as well as the pen Nicole reluctantly held out to her.

"You can't be serious about leaving?" Agitation rang in Nicole's voice as Juliet zipped up her backpack. "What about your guests?"

"They won't miss me."

Latching on to the crystal-beaded purse that matched her gown, Juliet breezed toward the hallway.

Nicole's stilettos clattered on the floor as she rushed after Juliet. "You do plan on coming back, don't you?"

"Sooner or later — maybe." Juliet snatched a set of car keys as she whisked out of the house, through the breezeway, and threw open the door to the garage.

"Couldn't you give me a more definitive

answer? What am I going to tell people if they ask when you'll be back? How can I schedule anything?"

"Just take messages." Juliet strolled across the garage, ignoring her Mercedes, her custom-made Bentley, and her Lamborghini, cars Garrett had handpicked because they, too, were *de rigueur,* and ripped the dusty cover off of the rarely driven pink Mustang. "I'll call you in a couple of days. Maybe then I'll have more answers for you."

Nicole grasped the top of the car's door when Juliet flung it open and tossed her bags inside. "At least tell me where you're going."

"I don't have the faintest idea. I just want to get in my car and drive."

"That's ridiculous, Juliet, not to mention totally irrational."

"Maybe, but I need to get away, go someplace where no one knows me."

"Where? Timbuktu? Have you forgotten that your face is on the backs of millions of books? You're in *People* magazine every time I turn around. And then there's the fact that little boys — and big boys — stare at a digitized jungle goddess who looks exactly like you every time they play Amazonia 2807. You might want to hide,

Juliet, but the truth of the matter is — you can't."

"I can and I will." Juliet twisted the key in the ignition and the engine roared to life. "Trust me, Nic, this time tomorrow, no one will recognize me."

Nicole stood alone in the moonlight, watching the Mustang's taillights turn onto the road and disappear from sight. Her lips tilted in an ever so slight smile. "Run all you want," she whispered into the gentle breeze, "but you can't hide, Juliet. Not from me."

Out of the corner of her eye Nicole saw the rhododendron bushes trembling. She heard the rustle of leathery leaves and twisted to face the shrubbery lining the drive. A cluster of electric blue blossoms broke from one of the branches and tumbled to the ground as the shadowy figure of a man slipped from his hiding place and strolled toward her.

"Got some great pictures, Nic." The man smiled victoriously. "Even got one of the ex-prez groping that ballerina's butt."

The ex-prez was old news and the ballerina was a nobody. The people who bought the tabloids could care less about their not-so-subtle dalliance, but it was hard to find fault with the blunders made by her brown-eyed he-man.

When Ben stepped behind her, Nicole leaned into his hard, Herculean body, closing her eyes as warm fingers slid beneath the metallic fabric of her gown. He clutched her breasts, knowing how much pressure she liked — how much pain. She allowed herself a moment of sheer, unadulterated pleasure before she stilled his hands. "Later, baby. You've more important things to tend to first."

Hot breath whispered against her ear. "What do you want, Nic? Just tell me and I'll do it."

"Follow Juliet's every move."

She turned in Ben's arms and kissed the taut skin at the base of his throat. "Go. Now." She pushed Ben away without hesitation. "Don't let Juliet get too far from your camera's lens. If all goes well, I can finally get even with that woman who claims to be my friend."

Chapter 1

Cole Sheridan speared his fingers through his hair, but it had a mind of its own and tumbled back over his heated brow. He looked like hell. He felt like shit. But who wouldn't after what he'd gone through the past eight hours? He'd had his hands and arms up the backside of a mare half the night in an attempt to save her foal. In the end the little guy didn't make it. Neither did the mare.

If only he'd been called earlier. If only Jim Foley, the mare's owner, hadn't thought he could handle the difficult birth on his own. If only Jim's ranch had been closer to Cole's place. So many "if onlys," but in the end Cole had arrived too late, a cesarean had been out of the question, and he'd known at the outset that things didn't look bad — they looked fatal.

The last thing he wanted at ten-twenty-two this morning, when he was already out of sorts, was the sun beating through the windshield of his pickup and the guy on the radio telling him something he already knew. It was hot enough outside to fry Rocky Mountain oysters on the pavement. Definitely too damn hot for Plentiful, Wyoming, which was supposed to peak somewhere in the low 80s when July rolled around. Today they predicted it would hit 102, breaking the town's record by a blasted eight degrees.

The deodorant he'd put on yesterday morning had worn off hours ago, he had to pick up supplies before heading home, his stomach had growled continuously for the past two hours, and Jim Foley had been so pissed about losing his horses that he hadn't offered Cole coffee or even a day-old donut, only a string of swear words and a threat to sue.

Something told him this wasn't going to be the best of days.

The cell phone rang and Cole's jaw clenched. *What now?* He needed a shower before handling another emergency. He needed to shave. He needed caffeine.

Or a few hours of sleep.

Doubting he'd get any of those things in the immediate future, he grabbed the phone from beside him on the bench seat.

23

"Doc Sheridan," he barked.

"This is Twyla Lewellyn."

Fear kicked him in the gut when he heard the nanny's voice. "Is something wrong?"

"You're darn right something's wrong. I quit."

Cole glared into the sun, focusing on what he could see of the road, while panic about his kids' safety turned to cold, hard irritation. "You can't quit. You just started yesterday."

"You didn't tell me there were five of them," Twyla harped. "You didn't tell me they're monsters, and you also neglected to mention that three of them are in diapers."

Cole's fingers tightened on the steering wheel. "Look, Twyla, you wouldn't have taken the job if I'd told you the truth. I interviewed seven women and two men last week and all of them declined the job when I told them I have five kids."

"That's not my problem."

"Yeah, I know, and I should have told you the truth, but I'm a busy man and I need someone to take care of them."

"I'm not changing my mind. I'm quitting. *Now.*"

"I'm twenty miles out of town, thirty

24

from home. I've got groceries to buy, mail to pick up —"

"Two hours. That's all the longer I'll give you because that's all the longer I can put up with those heathens of yours."

"Give me three."

"Two and a half."

Cole's eyes narrowed. He gritted his teeth. "You were hired to do a job and I'm holding you to it. So help me, you walk out that door and leave those kids alone even one second before I get there to watch them myself, and I'll have every law enforcement officer in Wyoming hot on your trail. I'll have you arrested for child endangerment and anything else I can pin on you. Do you understand?"

"Just get here quick, because if I get kicked in the shins one more time or find one more rabbit turd in my iced tea, I'll sue you for every penny you're worth."

Twyla slammed the phone in his ear.

Shit.

Through the heat waves bouncing up from the asphalt, Cole spotted a rattler sunning itself on the pavement and swerved out of its way. Most other men would have run over the blasted serpent. Considering his present state of mind, Cole was surprised he hadn't done it himself just to be ornery. But saving creatures, whether they hopped, trotted, crept or slithered was his lot in life; not killing them.

At the moment, however, he didn't have much compassion for creatures that walked upright, especially nannies, particularly Twyla Lewellyn, Nanny #13. He should have known a woman who looked like Frankenstein's monster and sounded like Peter Lorre would bring him bad luck.

He shoved his foot down on the accelerator and watched the speedometer climb from sixty to eighty. If he hurried he could tick off a few of the things he'd had on his to-do list for the day. He needed to get to the grocery store and buy at least a week's worth of food. He needed to stop at the farm supply to pick up grain for the horses, goat chow for the pygmies, and new leather work gloves on the off chance he could find time to mend the fence in his south pasture.

The haircut that had been on his list for two months would have to wait. So would chowing down on a decent cheeseburger and slugging down a cold beer at the Misty Moon.

So much for plans.

A scrawny jackrabbit dashed across the

road, just beating the thick tread of his tires. A moose poked its head out of a stand of bright green willows, stared at his dusty and loud diesel-engine truck, and as if bored with what it saw, went back into hiding. And up ahead, if the blaring sun hadn't distorted his vision, Cole could swear a shapely, very feminine butt in tight black spandex was sticking out from under the hood of a car, waving at him like a distress flag.

Shit.

He didn't have time to handle another emergency. He had shopping to do, a temporary baby-sitter to find, a nanny to hire, kids to feed and entertain, not to mention dirty diapers to change. On top of that, God knows how many dogs and cats and turtles and hedgehogs he'd have to treat for some ailment or another during the day.

He'd nearly forgotten what normal was like, but damn if he didn't want that uncomplicated and orderly life back again.

He slowed to forty-five as he passed the disabled car. The woman attached to the fine derrière was leaning over and staring at the engine. She had on hot pink stilettos. She had longer than long legs encased in skin-tight capris.

Her butt wiggled.

Shit.

Cole slammed on his brakes and pulled to the side of the road. Dust billowed around his big blue Ford, and when it cleared he threw open his door, swung out of the cab, and strolled toward the classic pink Mustang.

Nice car. The woman was pretty spectacular, too, with a chassis even sweeter than the Mustang's. Great thighs, great butt, and when she stood, there was no missing the most fabulous set of breasts he'd ever set eyes on.

Cole swallowed hard as he tore his gaze from her luscious curves and focused on the pink bubble she was blowing through pink puckered lips. Slowly, as if she'd just realized he was standing in front of her and ogling her body, she pushed her pink sunglasses to the tip of her nose and in the harsh sunlight glared at him over the top. An instant later, her violet eyes widened in downright terror, as if he were Hannibal Lecter licking his chops.

The big pink bubble popped. She sucked the gum back into her mouth, backed up fast, wiggled her butt into the driver's seat of her Mustang, and slammed the door. For good measure, she locked herself inside.

Cole shook his head at her display of out and out fear, although there was no denying that he looked like a disreputable cur. There was also no denying the fact that she had one hell of a killer physique that he wouldn't mind getting to know a little better, but he didn't have time to get to know her at all.

Closing in on her car, he set his hands lightly on top the sizzling fender, and took a peek under the hood. No steam; no smoke; clean engine, but he couldn't miss the gaping crack in the radiator hose.

Cole went to the passenger door, rested on his haunches, and peered at the black-haired beauty through the window. "Hate to tell you this, but you've got a busted radiator hose."

"Thanks for the diagnosis, and thanks for stopping," she said, scooting as far away from the window as humanly possible, as if she thought he might punch his fist through the glass, latch on to her, and drag her out through the jagged shards — then eat her alive. "But if you don't mind, I'd appreciate it if you'd go away."

Ungrateful female.

"You gonna fix the car yourself?"

"That's highly unlikely."

Suddenly she didn't look so enticing; she looked like one more irritation in a day full of irritations. "You expecting a miracle? A heavenly light to shine down on your vehicle and make it start?"

"I expect no such thing." She sighed heavily. "Look, you could be the nicest guy on the face of the earth; then again, you could be Ted Bundy's clone —"

"I'm neither," Cole bit out, his annoyance and her frostiness getting the better of him.

"Okay, so you're not nice; so you're not a serial killer, but my dad taught me not to talk to strangers and, believe you me, I've watched enough episodes of 'Unsolved Mysteries' and 'America's Most Wanted' to know not to accept help from people I know nothing about. Therefore, I wish you'd go away."

That would be the smart thing to do. Get the hell home before Nanny #13 walked off the job, but he couldn't leave the woman in the middle of nowhere, alone and stranded. Not in this heat.

"Look, lady, this hasn't been the best of days, my frame of mind sucks, and I'm in a hurry. Trust me, killing you doesn't fit into my schedule."

"All it takes is one quick jab with a knife

or an itchy trigger finger and I could be history."

"I haven't got a knife; haven't got a gun; and I'm almost out of patience. If you want a ride into town so you can get a new radiator hose, get out of your car and let's go."

Even through her sunglasses, he could see her eyes narrow. "Thanks for the offer, but since you're in a hurry and I'm not" — she attempted to shoo him away with a brush of her hand — "I'll wait for the cops to come by and help me."

Damn fool woman. "This isn't the main road and it isn't traveled all that often. If I leave, you could sit here for a day or two before someone else passes by."

She glared at his unkempt hair, at the stubble on his face, at his grubby white T-shirt. "I'll take my chances."

"You always this stubborn?"

"I'm cautious."

"Foolish is more —"

"Do you have a cell phone?" she interrupted, holding her thumb to her ear, her little finger to her mouth, as if he were some country bumpkin who needed sign language to understand the word phone.

"Yeah. Why?"

"Because the battery died on mine and

I'd appreciate it if you could call a tow truck."

"This isn't the big city, it's the middle of nowhere. There's one tow truck in town and it could be hours before Joe can get away from his gas station to help you."

"I'll wait."

"It's gonna be 102 degrees by noon. You sit in your car for a couple of hours, you just might die."

"I get out of my car — I might die anyway."

He didn't have time for this. "Fine. Suit yourself."

Cole shoved away from the Mustang. Getting as far from the paranoid woman as he possibly could was the smartest thing to do. As bad as this day had been, he was sure it could get far worse if he stuck around her any longer.

He threw open the door to his truck and the annoying woman honked her horn. The squeaky beep sounded like a chicken blowing its nose and the ghastly noise rang out four times before he turned. The con-founded woman wiggled her index finger at him from behind her bug-spattered windshield, beckoning him back.

Shit.

Cole glared at his watch. He glared at

the woman, then, shaking his head, he strolled back toward the car and stared down at the face peering through the window. His jaw had tightened but he managed to bark, "What?"

She smiled. It had to be the prettiest smile he'd seen in his whole miserable life — but it was also the phoniest. "You *will* call a tow truck, won't you?"

Leave it to a woman to use her feminine wiles to get what she wanted. Leave it to a woman to be a pain in the butt.

"Yeah, I'll call." He turned on his heel and headed back to his truck. "Not that it'll do any good," he added for good measure.

Cole gunned the engine not two seconds after he climbed into the truck, peeled out of the dirt and onto the road. The sooner he got away from the woman the better.

Grabbing his cell phone, he searched through the numbers he'd programmed into it and called Joe at the gas station. From experience, he knew it would take at least fifteen rings before Joe bothered to answer, busy or not. Then, even if Joe knew he had a disabled vehicle to get to, he'd make a pit stop at the Elk Horn Café to fill up on Mountain Dew and chocolate cream pie to boost his energy. Filling gas tanks and towing cars was hard work, and Joe made sure everyone in town knew it.

On the second ring, Cole looked in his rearview mirror and could just barely see the woman climb out of her car. He slowed the truck to a crawl as the phone continued to ring. The woman bent over to peek under the hood. Her derrière wiggled again.

Shit.

Stabbing the end button, Cole tossed the phone back on the seat and made a screeching U-turn on the two-lane highway. The second he swung the truck in front of the woman's car, she again scrambled for safety behind locked doors.

Keeping his annoyance at a minimum, Cole climbed out of the cab, dug around in the chrome box in the bed of his truck, and dragged out a length of good strong chain.

The woman was going with him whether she wanted to or not.

Cole rigged the chain to his truck's trailer hitch, slammed the hood down on the Mustang, and hollered at the woman peering at him over lowered sunglasses.

"It's twenty miles to town and I've got a hell of a lot more important things to do right now than tow some hardheaded woman in a broken-down Mustang. But it's too damn hot for you to stay out here until someone else comes to help you, so don't give me any more grief."

Cole crouched down on the blistering hot dirt, worked his head and shoulders under the car, and secured the chain. Dirty, sweaty, and stinking like a dog that had tangled with a skunk, he shoved out from under the Mustang and took one step toward his truck.

The blasted woman again beeped her blasted horn.

Cole's eyes narrowed. He twisted his head to stare at the woman over his shoulder. "What?"

"Do I just sit here?" she hollered through the windshield. "Do I steer the car?"

"Put it in neutral, release the emergency brake, and roll down the window so you don't bake. And yeah, steer the blasted thing so it goes the same direction I'm going, and use the brake so you don't plow under my truck and get your head ripped off."

"All right," she said contritely. And then she smiled again. Not a fake, half-assed smile, but a big one. A damn pretty one. "Thank you."

An ounce or so of anger and pent-up

frustration washed away when he saw that smile, and somehow he managed to mutter, "You're welcome."

It was quarter after eleven in the morning. He had errands to run, a heap of work to do, five children needing attention, and Nanny #14 to hire, hopefully someone who looked more like Mary Poppins than Frankenstein's monster.

Except for the woman's smile, it had been a pretty shitty day. One of these days things would get better. They had to, because they sure as hell couldn't get worse.

Chapter 2

"So, what do you think, Nic?" Ben's voice echoed through the speaker phone, almost drowning out Paolo Benedetti's luscious, perfectly pitched high C as Puccini's "Nessun Dorma" flowed through the hidden speakers in Juliet's office. "Pretty good stuff I sent you, huh?"

Nicole wadded the FedEx envelope into a ball as she stared at the photographs spread across Juliet's desk. "They're worthless, Ben. What on earth am I going to do with sickly sweet pictures of Juliet sipping a chocolate malt at an old-fashioned soda fountain or giving a homeless guy a bag of food from McDonald's? If I'd wanted nice, I could have hired a photographer who snaps kiddy pictures at Wal-Mart."

"You didn't hire anyone, Nic. You asked me to *help* you, in the same way I've been helping you for the past eight years, and what I sent you is the best you're gonna get."

"I need something more."

"I'm in Wyoming, for God's sake, following a pink Mustang that's being towed down a lonely stretch of highway. Yesterday I followed Juliet across eastern Oregon and southern Idaho, where the only things to photograph are dirt and sagebrush. Hell, Nic, if you want pictures of Juliet having sex with an arms dealer or lying naked on the deck of a yacht she purchased with ill-gotten money, I'll have to hire a yacht and a fake arms dealer and a Juliet Bridger look-alike, because the real Juliet Bridger hasn't done much more than get her hair dyed black at the Ritzy Glitzy Salon in Winnemucca, Nevada, and buy a bunch of pink clothes from some fly-by-night place called Gaudy Galore."

"Okay, so maybe she hasn't done anything sinful or sleazy or even remotely dishonest, but that doesn't mean we can't make people believe she has. I just need the right pictures; the right headline and story." Nicole aimed the controller at the CD player and turned down the volume. "Unfortunately, your yacht idea might be a little too simplistic. I mean, who wants to see another picture of Juliet sunbathing in the nude? On the other hand, I like your arms dealer idea."

"I was joking, Nic."

"Well it's the best joke you've told in a long time. If you can dummy up some pictures of Juliet cavorting with a nefarious arms dealer and giving him a wad of cash —"

"You don't need fabricated photos. All you have to do is use the ones I sent you."

"And write a story about Juliet's ten thousand-calorie-a-day milkshake diet and the distinct possibility that she'll soon balloon into an Anna Nicole clone?"

"No, damn it, you can play off the fact that Juliet's changed her appearance. That she's dyed her blond hair black, and that she's hiding behind pink sunglasses. You can make up a story about Juliet being on the run from some Jersey wise guys who are pissed because she and Garrett put the screws to them. Or better yet" — Ben sighed heavily — "you can forget about getting even with her."

Every muscle in Nicole's body knotted with bitterness. "Forget that Juliet stole Garrett away from me? Forget that I was going to be Amazonia before Juliet twisted Garrett around her little finger and sweet-talked him into giving her the job? Forget that I was supposed to be a star and ended up playing Juliet's half-woman, half-lizard sidekick?"

"Yeah, Nic, I want you to forget all of that crap, especially the shit about you and Garrett."

"I can't." Nicole leaned back into the plush comfort of Juliet's amber-colored leather chair and stared at the intricate Aztec sun stone carved into the plaster ceiling. "Juliet ruined my life and I'm going to ruin hers."

At the other end of the phone Ben was quiet, too quiet, and then she heard the unmistakable sound of him taking a drag off of his cigarette, heard him blowing out slowly, and imagined the smoke swirling about the phone, about his face, just barely masking the hurt in his eyes.

If Garrett were at the other end of the phone, instead of Ben, she would have heard anger, not silence. But Ben was as different from Garrett as night was from day. When she'd met him, he didn't have a penny to his name, while Garrett had been a billionaire. Ben looked like a bald G.I. Joe with a scar slashed across his face, while Garrett looked like Cary Grant. When they were together, Ben held her all night long, as if he were afraid to let go,

40

while Garrett had screwed her, got out of bed for a Scotch on the rocks, then spent the rest of the night playing with his computers.

Ben loved her; Garrett loved himself.

Naturally she turned to Ben. They needed each other, and they'd been through a lot together in the last eight years. She'd helped Ben get exclusive photos of stars who didn't like having their privacy invaded. She'd anonymously written stories to accompany the photos he sold to the tabloids. She'd shown him how to invest his money.

And she'd stayed by his hospital bed after he'd been beaten into a coma while snapping photos of a riot, then helped him through his rehabilitation.

In turn, he'd supported her emotionally when Juliet torpedoed her acting career. He did anything and everything she asked him to do, and he didn't walk away on those occasions when she made the mistake of bringing up her past with Garrett.

He'd always be there for her — no matter what.

"I'm sorry, Ben," she whispered into the phone. "It's been a rough couple of days taking care of all the emergencies that have cropped up since Juliet left. I didn't mean to take it out on you."

"You want me to come home?"

"No, baby, I want you to stay close to Juliet."

"I'd rather be close to you, Nic. Real close, taking your mind off of Juliet and making you think about no one but me."

"I'd like that, too. But not now, baby. Not now," she whispered, closing her eyes and imagining the heat of his fingers skimming over her body and the warmth of his lips kissing the curve of her throat.

He was her lover, her friend, and her secret, a part of her life she didn't share with anyone, especially Juliet, because God knows that bitch would steal him away just as she'd stolen everything else Nicole had ever wanted or had.

She would never tell Juliet about Ben, but someday, when the timing was right, she'd let Juliet know that the only reason she'd wanted to work as her assistant was to have access to all of her secrets. She despised the woman, but had pulled the wool over Juliet's gullible, be-kind-to-everyone eyes. She knew Juliet believed they'd become more than assistant and employer, that they'd become friends. Juliet confided in her, relied on her.

What a fool Juliet was, letting her trusted

assistant know every last detail about her income, the ins and outs of her novels, not to mention the juicy facts about her life with Garrett — all of which Nicole dished out in the stories she anonymously wrote for *Buzz*.

One of these days, when Juliet was at her lowest, when Juliet's career and her popularity were ruined, she'd tell Juliet the truth, that she'd been behind the rumors, behind the scandalous photos.

God, it was going to be fun seeing the shock and unbelievable pain in Juliet's face.

Nicole leaned forward in the chair, and as Ben caressed her with whispered words, she ripped one photo of Juliet after another in half and tossed the pieces into the trash.

Revenge was infinitely sweet.

Chapter 3

Juliet sat ramrod straight in the Mustang's driver's seat, hands gripped around the steering wheel and eyes focused on the big blue truck as the stranger towed her — *hopefully* — toward the nearest town. It seemed utterly ridiculous to think he had something other than rescuing her on his mind, but she'd been the dumb blonde victim in far too many *Slash McCall* blood-bath flicks, not to mention the author of a whole lot of mysterious tales about the unsuspecting prey of murderers and madmen, to sit back, file her nails, and pretend that everything was peachy-keen when she might very well be at death's door.

She didn't want to worry, but there was always the possibility that the stranger was taking her to some despicable hovel in the middle of the woods where he planned to do lewd, lascivious and diabolical things to her.

One look at the man was enough for anyone to wonder what he was up to. After all, his hair and clothing were littered with bits of straw, as if he'd been in a barnyard brawl, and there were those dark stains on his shirt and jeans that, to her mystery-writer's eye, looked exactly like blood.

He was definitely a man to be wary of.

Juliet's foot shot to the brake pedal when she saw the truck's bright red brake lights flash. Her heart drummed heavily in her chest, and she hoped against hope that the stranger wouldn't turn off the highway onto a lonely road. She thought about bolting from the car and running for her life, but the thumping of her heart slacked off when the truck followed the signs leading toward Plentiful, a town described in her Wyoming tour guide as "a bit of the Old West with a touch of class".

Juliet's fingers eased up on the wheel when the craggy mountains they'd spent the past twenty minutes winding through flattened into ranchland. Majestic log homes began to peek through stands of aspen and pine and seemingly endless white wooden fences stretched around fields of tall emerald grass where horses and an occasional goat and cow grazed in the sun.

They crossed a meandering, rock-strewn stream, passed a small white church with a steeple that stretched halfway to heaven, and at last drove under an archway built of thousands of twisting elk horns, with a sign dangling beneath it that read, "Welcome to Plentiful."

Juliet's neck and shoulder muscles relaxed as they circled a park where children did cartwheels on the lawn, dogs chased Frisbees, and a teenaged boy and girl necked in the shade of a spreading cottonwood.

Duffy's Ice Cream Parlor, its clapboard panels painted a multitude of pastels, sat on one corner of Main. Across from that was the Mischievous Moose Emporium, where a tall, gangly bronze moose with a dubious grin lazed just outside the entry.

Tourists with cameras slung around their necks walked up and down the boardwalk. A lean and lanky cowboy shoved through the swinging doors of the Misty Moon Saloon, and through her car's open window Juliet caught the heavenly scent of hamburgers and steaks grilling over mesquite.

Her stomach growled as the truck towed her past the Plentiful Bank and Trust, Teton Outfitters, several jewelry and clothing shops, a toy store, and a lovely old salmon-and-teal colored Victorian with A STUDY IN SCARLETT — MYSTERY BOOK AND TEA SHOPPE painted blood red on the window.

A mangy black cat raced across the street, barely beating the truck's wheels, and brushed against the legs of a tall dark-haired guy dressed all in black, who clutched the hand of a petite and pregnant redhead standing just outside the bookshop's door.

Not far away, three elderly ladies stood near an old-fashioned wrought-iron streetlamp, shading their eyes to gape at the car being towed through town. Juliet waved. The women smiled back, then huddled together to gossip about the sight they'd just witnessed.

Downtown Plentiful wasn't classy. It wasn't lined with the fancy boutiques and designer shops Juliet frequented on Fifth Avenue or Rodeo Drive. It wasn't the same caliber as Aspen, either. No, Plentiful looked as if it had been inked and water-colored by Walt Disney, the kind of place where everyone in town gathered together on the Fourth of July to sing "God Bless America" with the high school band playing in the background, shot off Red Devil fireworks in the street, spread picnic blankets on the grass, and kicked back to eat potato salad and hot dogs.

Plentiful was exactly the kind of town she'd been searching for as she'd driven north. Small and unpretentious; quaint and homey. And, with any luck, not an ounce of beluga could be found anywhere near.

The Mustang bumped through a rut in the road, and, all too soon, the water-colored buildings became nothing but a blur in her rearview mirror.

Pastels changed to lackluster browns and grays as they cruised by a motel that could have been ripped straight out of *Psycho*, and past a gigantic tan and black concrete cowboy boot that had obviously been a fast food joint before it was boarded up and left to crumble.

Juliet sighed as her starry-eyed vision of Plentiful dimmed. The town wasn't perfect after all; then again, she was awfully tired of everything — including herself — having to be perfect.

Joe's Gas and Bait, the service station where the guy in the big blue truck chose to stop, was anything but perfect. Juliet glared through her open window at the cinderblock building, which had once been painted white but now was a dingy, weather-stained gray. The office door was covered in black fingerprints. Two large freezers marked BAIT stood in front of the windows, their white paint chipped away to reveal red and blackish brown rust.

A pile of tires, hubcaps, and miscellaneous auto parts spilled across the asphalt on one side of the garage. Parked on the other side was a mud-encrusted yellow tow truck, which almost blocked the open door to the restroom marked "Men or Women — get key from office."

The Walt Disney fantasy town was fading fast.

And now she had to get out of her car and face the cantankerous, disheveled, and dangerous-looking guy who'd come to her rescue.

Juliet opened her car door and slid her sweaty bottom out of the driver's seat. She pressed her hands against the small of her back to work the kinks out of her joints, then peeled her pink lacy stretch top from her hot and sticky skin.

Checking her do in the passenger door window, she fluffed some life back into her Annette Funicello beehive. If her hair dresser could see what Rita at the Ritzy Glitzy Salon in Winnemucca, Nevada, had done to her hair, he'd have a catatonic fit. Her new coif wasn't chic enough for his tastes. It didn't reek of rich and famous. Neither did the hot pink polish Rita had swirled on Juliet's fingernails and toes, the pretty-in-pink duds Juliet had picked up at Gaudy Galore, or the violet contact lenses Rita told her were all the rage.

But her disguise was foolproof, part kitschy, part the girl she'd been before she'd run off to see the world. Still, the pink Kate Spade sunglasses, pink Jimmy Choos, and pink flamingo Isabella Fiore tote she'd picked up at Neiman Marcus in San Francisco as she ran away from Wonderland let her retain a part of what she'd been for most of her adult life.

She no longer looked like the dumb blonde sex kitten who continually got sliced and diced on the big screen, the jungle goddess in a leafy bikini from TV shows and video games, or the stylish mystery novelist-slash-ex-wife of a fabulously wealthy yet imprisoned conman.

She'd successfully escaped her former life — at least for a while. She blew a big pink bubble and decided that freedom from paparazzi, from Garrett's phone calls, and from the life that had been crushing her felt awfully good.

Of course, the scorching blacktop burning through the soles of her stilettos didn't feel quite as nice. She thought about climbing back into the car so her feet could cool off — until the hint of a breeze fluttered around the garage. It carried with it the scent of grease and gasoline, but it blew through her lacy top and offered much-needed relief from the stifling day.

It whipped around the man who'd rescued her, too, tossing his sun-streaked dark blond hair about as he climbed from his truck. The gust disappeared as quickly as it came, leaving a sand-colored lock dangling over his brow.

How odd. He no longer looked like the scary stranger who'd frightened her out on the highway. Truth be told, except for his grungy clothes, he looked rather good, kind of like the body-builder pool boy she'd eyeballed once or twice after she'd kicked Garrett out of the house.

Blowing another Dubble Bubble bubble, she watched her rescuer plow strong fingers through his wavy mop, but the unruly lock tumbled back over his brow as he ambled toward her, lingering traces of a frown dulling what could have been sparkling blue eyes.

He leaned against the tailgate of his truck, folded his arms over his chest and glared at her bubble, at her pink sun-

51

glasses, then shook his head as if she'd caused him endless amounts of trouble.

"So," he said, an ominous beginning to a conversation, "are you going to hop back in your car and lock the door again, or have you come to the conclusion that I'm not Ted Bundy?"

She sucked the bubble back between her lips. "I suppose I might have overreacted a bit."

One of his brows rose. "A bit?"

"Okay, a lot, but in case you haven't peered in the mirror recently, you look as if you just escaped from Devil's Island, which would — or should — make any woman question your motives for stopping on a deserted road to lend a hand. And then" — she pointed a finger straight at his chest — "there's the fact that you've got what looks to be blood on your clothes."

He tugged on his shirt and stared at the stains. "Yeah, I guess I do."

She frowned. Her muscles tensed again. "Human?"

"Equine," he said gruffly. "The mare died. Her foal died." Everything about him was rough, but she could almost feel the raw, agonizing emotion seething beneath his hard exterior.

"I'm sorry."

"Yeah, me too." He pushed away from his truck. "It was one hell of a night, the morning hasn't been much better, and now that you're safe and sound, I've gotta get going."

Juliet glanced at the grimy garage, at its mucky windows, at the freezers that were supposed to contain bait but could easily hide a body — or would if they'd been written into one of her mysteries — and decided she'd rather not be unhitched too soon.

"I hate to ask this, but do you think you could tow me to a different gas station?"

"Sorry, but like I told you before, I'm in a hurry. It's Joe's Gas and Bait or nothing."

"But this place looks —"

"Like hell. Yeah, I know." He dropped down on the sizzling pavement and ducked under the car to retrieve the chain. "Joe might not have the cleanest place around," he said, his voice muffled, "but he's the best mechanic in this part of the state."

"Damn right."

Juliet's head jerked toward the garage as a grizzled fellow with an immense pot belly walked out from behind a dusty black van, wiping oily hands on an equally oily towel. He gave Juliet only a moment's notice before his gaze shot toward the blue jean—

clad legs sticking out from under the Mustang. "What's goin' on, Cole?"

At least she now knew the stranger's name.

"The lady's got a busted radiator hose," Cole hollered from under the car. "Figured you might be able to replace it."

"Maybe." Joe — his name was embroidered on his greasy olive green shirt — gave Juliet a quick nod before scrutinizing the exterior of her car. "Nice Mustang. Sixty-five?"

"Sixty-four and a half. One of the first off the assembly line," Juliet answered, scooting away from Cole's long, muscular legs when they accidentally brushed against hers, and away from Joe who smelled like he bathed in axle grease.

Joe scratched the stubble on his face. "Think I got some Mustang parts around here somewhere. Can't be a hundred percent positive on that; can't be a hundred percent positive on anything no more, but I'll take a look."

"What if you don't have the part?"

"Don't you go worryin' that pretty head of yours. If I ain't got the part, someone else in town will."

"So it shouldn't take all that long to fix?"

"If I don't find any other problems once

I look under the hood, it shouldn't take much more than an hour at the most." Joe shoved the oily towel into his back pocket. "You do want me to check everything, don't you? Give it a thorough going through so you don't break down again?"

She wasn't too sure she wanted him touching her little pink car, but what choice did she have? "Well . . . yes, I suppose that might be a good idea."

"Then I'll get to it after lunch." Joe patted the Mustang's hood. "Right now I'm headin' over to the Elk Horn Café. It's chicken fried steak day. Chocolate cream pie day, too. Shouldn't be there more than a few hours."

"Couldn't you do it *before* lunch?"

"Could . . . but then I'd miss out on the chicken fried steak, and I'd hate for that to happen." Joe took off his greasy baseball cap and slicked back his sparse gray hair. "I'm meetin' Betty Sue Horner for lunch, same as I do every day. You're welcome to join us if you want something to do while you're waiting, and like I said, the chicken fried steak's —"

"I don't think she wants chicken fried steak," Cole interrupted, climbing out from under the Mustang with one end of the tow chain in his hands. "I've got the feeling she's in a hurry — kind of like me."

"Too many people in a gall-darned hurry. Not me. Nosiree." Joe hit Juliet with a false-teeth smile as he tugged his hat back on his head. "I'll be back around two or three. There's an old Coke machine out back, only thirty-five cents a can or free if you kick it in the right place, and the office is unlocked if you want to go inside, plop your butt in my chair and twiddle your thumbs."

"What I'd really like —"

"Tell me later," Joe said, grabbing the key from the Mustang's ignition. "Betty Sue don't like me bein' late and I'm already runnin' behind."

Joe strolled toward the road. When he tucked his hands in his pockets and started whistling like Andy Griffith, Juliet turned narrowed eyes on Cole. "I thought you said he was the best mechanic around."

Cole shrugged. "I never said he was fast. But he is the best. Of course, if you're in a hurry —"

"I'm not, but what if I was?"

"Then you could head over to Harry's Auto Parts, see if he has a radiator hose, and come back here and fix the thing yourself."

"I barely know where the dipstick is."

"Then you have two choices: take a quick course in auto mechanics or cool your heels until Joe gets his fill of chicken fried steak, chocolate cream pie, and Betty Sue Horner."

Cole tossed the chain in the back of the truck and dismissing her as if she were nothing more than a spot of grease on the pavement below his feet, walked toward the cab of his truck.

"You aren't leaving, are you?" Juliet called out.

Cole stopped next to the pickup's door. His shoulder muscles tensed beneath his T-shirt and he turned slowly. "That was my plan."

Juliet's eyes narrowed at his curt reply. "You were just going to walk off without saying good-bye?"

He sighed heavily. "As much as I'd like to be Mister Nice Guy, as much as I'd like to stand around here all day chitchatting, I've got a lot on my mind, I'm in a hurry —"

"So you've said a time or two. Of course, if you'd just been polite, shook my hand and said good-bye, you could have been long gone by now."

"And if I hadn't stopped to help you I'd be home."

"But you did and I'm extremely thankful, so if you'll give me another moment or two of your precious time, I'll get my wallet and pay you for your trouble."

"You think I helped you because I wanted money?"

The man was extremely pigheaded and she had no idea why she was bothering with him. "Doesn't everyone expect to be paid for services rendered?"

"Look, lady, I don't know where you come from —"

"California," she said, then chomped on her tongue to keep from admitting more.

"Well, in California people might expect payment for helping someone stranded on the highway, but here in Wyoming we usually do it out of the goodness of our hearts. And before you tell me you seriously doubt I have a heart —"

"I would never be that rude. If you'll remember correctly, I'm the one who thought we should part company with a friendly handshake, a polite good-bye, and maybe a token of appreciation, yet you insist on arguing."

He folded his arms over his chest. "You really want to give me a token of appreciation?"

"Of course I do." She reached into the

Mustang, pulled out her flamingo tote, and extracted her wallet. "How about twenty dollars?"

He shook his head far too slowly for comfort. "That's not nearly enough."

She rubbed two bills between her fingers. "Forty?"

A slight grin tilted his mouth. "Obviously you've got no idea how much trouble you've been."

Her jaw tightened. "Fifty, but not a penny more."

"Still not enough." He moved toward her, his blue-eyed gaze burning over her Jimmy Choos, her black spandex capris, her pink lacy stretch top, and right through her sunglasses.

A lump caught in her throat. "Obviously you overestimate how much your services are worth."

"I haven't overestimated a thing."

His big, strong hand swept around the curve of her back. He tugged her hard against his chest and held her there tightly.

Juliet sucked in a deep breath as her breasts flattened against his dirty white T-shirt. He smelled like oil and asphalt. Like fresh hay and sweat. And was that a lingering whiff of Obsession wafting around him that was making her awfully dizzy?

Not that it mattered, of course. She didn't want to be in his arms, didn't want to be so close she could almost count the number of dark blond whiskers on his cheeks. She struggled against him, slapping both hands against his very broad shoulders and attempting to push, desperately trying to get away from all the testosterone oozing from his pores.

When that didn't work, she stared fiercely into his eyes. "Look, Cole, I don't know what you've got in mind, but all I wanted was a simple handshake and goodbye, not . . ."

Firm lips slanted over her mouth and cut off her protest. She would have fought back, but, heaven forbid, his unyielding embrace made her feel incredibly weak. Helpless. Vulnerable. A surprisingly delicious warmth rippled through her insides. My, oh my, she'd never been kissed by a real live brute. Never been manhandled except on the big and small screens, and she'd giggled through take after take because the guys doing the manhandling were totally inept.

But Cole's kiss was masterful. Sheer perfection. Absolutely, amazingly wicked.

And since she was never going to see the gorgeous beast again, she decided to enjoy his kiss for as long as it lasted.

Her arms stretched up and around his neck. Her fingers wove into unbelievably soft blond hair that was thick, wavy, a tad too long, and felt like millions of strands of fine silk thread. Her toes tingled as if they'd been asleep for a billion years and were just now waking up. Her heart thudded out of control.

And he pushed her away.

Damn!

Juliet wobbled on her Jimmy Choos. When she had enough control to pop open her eyes, Cole had a silly-ass grin on his face. Then the bully had the audacity to wink. "Thanks for the payment. It doesn't come anywhere close to calling us even, but" — he shrugged — "I haven't got time for more."

"You're going to force your kiss on me and then just walk away?"

"Damn right."

Fire flared in Juliet's cheeks as he marched toward his truck. "Of all the smug, overconfident, pigheaded bores."

"Yeah, that fits me to a tee." He climbed into the cab, slammed the door behind him, and turned the key in the ignition. The engine rumbled, and without a wave or even a quick peek at her through the rearview mirror, the truck tore away from the gas station and up the highway, leaving a trail of dust in its wake.

How dare he kiss her and dump her in the space of thirty seconds? She wasn't used to being treated that way.

And if she ever saw the devilishly handsome lout again, she'd give him a piece of her mind.

But she wouldn't be seeing him again. So what if he'd kissed her? So what if he'd nearly knocked her off her hot pink stilettos? He was much too bold and the mere fact that he was nothing like any of the men she'd ever known made him much too tempting, an irrepressible distraction she didn't want coming between her and her newfound freedom.

No way. No how.

Never.

She spun around on her Jimmy Choos, ready to hit the road for parts unknown, far, far away from Cole with the steely blue eyes and the lusty kiss, but a dusty and disabled vehicle stared her right in the face.

Damn it all. Her pretty pink Mustang wasn't going anywhere for a while — and neither was she.

Chapter 4

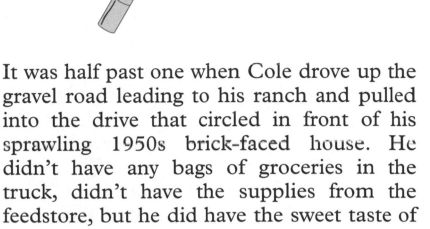

It was half past one when Cole drove up the gravel road leading to his ranch and pulled into the drive that circled in front of his sprawling 1950s brick-faced house. He didn't have any bags of groceries in the truck, didn't have the supplies from the feedstore, but he did have the sweet taste of pink bubble gum on his lips, the damn fine memory of a soft and luscious body pressed against his, and the lingering sense of fingers inching their way into his hair and trying to pull him even closer.

Who knows where that kiss would have taken them if he hadn't been in a hurry.

But he had been, damn it all.

And now he was late, but in spite of his tardiness, Nanny #13's black Toyota was still parked in the carport. Frankenstein's Monster hadn't deserted the girls, but there was no doubt she was in a hurry to get away. The car's trunk was open wide and two beige vinyl suitcases had been dumped haphazardly inside, as if Ms. Lewellyn had gotten sidetracked while packing to leave. God knows the girls had sidetracked him a time or two in the past six months.

Hell, his whole life had been sidetracked. His goals for the future had been put on hold. His plans for expanding his clinic, for opening a few emergency hospitals in western Wyoming, and for making his name synonymous with the ultimate in veterinary care had taken a backseat to caring for the girls.

He hadn't had any choice about being their guardian. His free-spirited sister had died. She didn't have a husband, her adopted daughters and the triplets she'd given birth to didn't have a father, and Cole's parents — who'd be hippies till their dying day — couldn't take them off his hands until they returned from their year-long mystical retreat in Tibet.

He laughed to himself. Handing the girls over to his parents, in spite of their non-conformist ways, had been the original plan. He hadn't wanted to be saddled with children at the age of thirty-four, and they'd certainly put a crimp in his plans; but his feelings had changed, and it would be a

64

cold day in hell before he'd let them go.

Shutting off the engine, Cole shoved out of the truck and strolled up the half-finished redbrick walk he'd been laying the day a drunk driver plowed into his sister's VW bus and cut off her life, turning his own perfectly organized existence into one that was now a chaotic challenge.

A little girl's pink bicycle lay on its side atop the lawn that needed mowing, a ripped-open box of Jell-O lay in the middle of the walk, its powdery orange insides drizzled across bricks and mortar, and Barbie and Ken sprawled naked in the once well-groomed flower beds that now served as a makeshift fort, dollhouse, and weed farm.

He needed to hire a gardener because he no longer had time to do the work himself. He needed to hire a cook and a house-keeper and another nanny. Hell, maybe he needed a wife, but getting married hadn't been one of his immediate goals. He'd hoped to put that off until he turned forty. He still had six years of bachelorhood to look forward to. Six years of sex with whomever he wanted, whenever he wanted — but in the past six months he'd had none at all.

Instead he had five little girls who'd

wormed their way into his heart; and when his folks showed up in a few weeks, he was going to have one hell of a fight on his hands.

Plowing his fingers through his hair, Cole pushed thoughts of arguing with his parents out of his mind and walked into the house to see what kind of trouble the girls had gotten into today.

Good luck had finally smiled down on him. Nanny #13 hadn't been killed or maimed. She wasn't even tied up and being fed rabbit turd. She was, however, sitting on the black leather sofa, her lips pursed as she shot daggers at him through tight, narrowed eyes.

Lugosi, Karloff, and Rathbone, Cole's Great Danes, stood on guard in front of the nanny. Across the room, five giggling girls sketched a Crayola landscape on the once-white wall.

Cole cleared his throat and five wide-eyed little faces swiveled toward him.

"Uh-oh." Five-year-old Jade threw her hands behind her back as if she thought she could hide the crayons and her colorful handiwork. The little minx smiled sweetly. "Hi, Uncle Cole."

Cole's left brow rose. "Having fun?"

The twenty-two-month-old blond-haired

triplets giggled as they scampered across the room and tackled his legs. He boosted Chloe — at least he thought it was Chloe — onto his shoulders. She wrapped warm little fingers around his forehead as he scooped Caitlin and Carly into his arms.

Six months ago he got his exercise by lifting weights instead of little girls; now the weights were buried deep in the garage. His weight room had been turned into a frilly bedroom, where Ballerina Barbie pirouetted across curtains and bedspreads.

Through all the hands and cheeks and lips vying for his attention, he managed to spot Holly's dark brown eyes widening in something close to fear, as if she thought a spanking was on its way. It looked like it was high time for another heart-to-heart talk about spankings. That may have been her foster mom's favorite choice of punishment, but it hadn't been his sister's. It definitely wasn't his.

Jade's foster care experience was just the opposite of Holly's. The precocious little girl was always happy and carefree. Even now Jade smiled up at him while doing her best Vanna White impression, elegantly pointing out the rainbow of colors on the wall. "Isn't it pretty, Uncle Cole?"

"Beautiful," he said, trying his damnedest to keep a straight face.

"I wanted to draw zebras and tigers like the toys Grandma and Grandpa sent us," Holly whispered, "but Jade thought flowers would be better —"

"And easier," Jade interrupted. "Chloe, Carly, and Caitlin tried to draw flowers, too, but they're much better at scribbles."

Cole nodded sagely as he studied the zigzags scrawled from one side of the wall to the other. "So I see."

"Are you gonna cut a switch off a tree and spank us until our bottoms are blood red?" Holly asked, her hands flying behind her to cover her derrière.

"You know I don't believe in spankings."

"You should," Nanny #13 snapped. "That's what they deserve for being bad little girls. Now, if you don't mind, would you call off your hounds so I can leave."

Lugosi and Karloff, the pitch-black Danes, growled. Rathbone, the harlequin, stared the woman straight in the eyes, his massive white-with-black-patches body itching to swallow her whole if Cole gave the order. The words "Sic her" were on the tip of Cole's tongue, but he held his temper. Damn, he'd made a mistake hiring Ms. Lewellyn.

Karloff had growled at the woman while

she was being interviewed. Cole should have known right then and there that she wouldn't fit into their life. But after twelve other nannies, a host of friends and neighbors filling in when there was no one else to care for the girls while he worked, he'd been desperate to hire someone.

Next time he'd listen to the dogs.

Cole whistled once, shrill and short. The Danes rushed toward him, begging to have their ears scratched, but he had something more immediate on his mind.

"Not now, boys." He set the triplets back on the floor and leveled his gaze on the girls. "Why don't the five of you go play in Jade and Holly's room while I say goodbye to Ms. Lewellyn."

"Do we have to?" Jade hit Cole with heart-tugging dark brown eyes that on most occasions were hard to say no to.

"Yeah, you do," Cole said flatly. "And stay out of trouble — if possible."

Holly ran down the hall, the triplets toddled after her, and Jade aimed her manipulative smile at Cole. "I haven't finished coloring my petunia. Don't you think I should do that before I go play?"

"Nope, I don't."

"You're sure?"

"Positive."

"Oh, all right." Jade's lips puckered into a pout, she dropped her crayon into the bucket full of broken Crayolas, and with shoulders slumped, made a slow, overly dramatic exit with the Danes dutifully following behind.

"Those are the most overindulged, spoiled-rotten children I've ever encountered." Nanny #13 lumbered out of the soft, plump sofa and grabbed the suitcase sitting on the floor. "If you ask me —"

"Obviously I made a mistake in not asking you a lot of things before hiring you." Cole grabbed the woman's bag from her hand and headed for the door. "Now, if you don't mind, I want you out of my house."

"I'm not leaving until I get the money you owe me. Two weeks' salary."

"You were here one blasted day!"

"Which felt like a year."

Cole's jaw tightened. "Fine. I'll get you a check and you can be on your way."

Cole stalked out of the living room, heading for the kitchen. He grabbed a checkbook from the desk he'd built into the oak-and-granite-topped counter and scribbled out two weeks' worth of salary, a tidy sum, he thought, that once would have been slated for some newfangled piece of laboratory equipment or another full-time vet to help him out.

He still wanted it all — but he couldn't do everything on his own. Getting married was an option half of the older — and younger — women in town had mentioned once or twice. Raven, the nineteen-year-old too-bright-for-her-own-good receptionist who pretty much ran his clinic, had brought the subject of marriage up at least once a day.

But marriage wasn't in his game plan.

Not until he turned forty.

Behind him he heard the scrunch of crepe-soled footsteps on the tile floor. "If you've finished writing that check, I'd like to get going."

Cole turned around and slapped the check into the nanny's outstretched hand, latched on to her suitcase once again, and ushered the woman out of the house, straight to her car. He pushed the case in, shoving all of her luggage deeper into the trunk, then slammed the lid, thrust his thumbs into his back pockets, and stood back, waiting for her to start the engine and leave.

There were no good-byes, no I'll-see-you-laters, just a small cloud of dust behind Nanny #13's tires as her car chugged up the drive and out of sight.

Good riddance.

As happy as he was to see her go, he didn't like the idea of calling the nanny agency . . . again. Thirteen women had up and quit on him and the girls in the past six months, which meant there was a damn good possibility they wouldn't send him anymore résumés to review.

Maybe marriage wasn't such a bad idea after all.

Gracie Griffin the park ranger came to mind. She was pretty enough and curvy enough, but, hell, he'd learned on their first date that she aspired to be a taxidermist. She'd even asked him — on the sly — if he could send a few euthanized animals her way so she could practice the fine art of stuffing and mounting.

Scratch Gracie.

Of course, there was always Miranda Green, the supermodel who lived in Plentiful when she wasn't traipsing around the world. But he had a thing for breasts and butts and Miranda had neither. Nor did she have a sense of humor. After their last date she'd told him in no uncertain terms that she never wanted to see him again, all because he'd dragged five little girls along with them to dinner, and Chloe vomited pizza all over Miranda's cashmere sweater.

Scratch Miranda.

Scratch marriage.

Cole headed back into the house, putting together a mental list of all the things he had to do.

Change diapers — more than likely.

Fix peanut butter and jelly sandwiches for lunch.

Clean peanut butter and jelly smears off floors, tables, and walls — or not.

Remind girls that nannies are not to be tortured.

Remind dogs that nannies are not chew toys.

Take girls to clinic and let Raven watch them while frazzled vet neuters amorous tomcat.

Listen to Raven's demand for pay increase because she's a receptionist . . . not a receptionist *and* a baby-sitter.

Find temporary baby-sitter.

Find new nanny.

Think about having sex with long-legged, feisty, and gorgeous female — preferably one with black hair, pink sunglasses, and great breasts and butt.

Take cold shower because long-legged, feisty, and gorgeous female with black hair, pink sunglasses, and great breasts and butt was just a brief but sizzling hot diversion who would soon be heading on her way to who-knows-where, and he'd never see her again.

A scream ripped Cole away from his "to-do" list. His muscles tensed, and he ran toward Holly and Jade's bedroom. The screaming intensified. Dogs barked madly.

Cole twisted the knob and threw open the door.

Carly — at least he thought the identical triplet was Carly — was lying sound asleep on the floor, her curly blond head resting on Karloff's neck. Caitlin and Chloe were jumping up and down on Jade's bed, Rathbone and Lugosi were barking in time with their bounces, and Holly and Jade, at opposite sides of the room with their mouths open wide, were in mid-scream.

Cole dragged in a deep, calming breath as the deafening shrieks died a slow death. "Mind telling me what's going on?"

Jade shrugged her little shoulders. "We were practicing."

"Practicing what?"

"How to scream," Jade announced.

"I gathered that much. Mind telling me why?"

Holly swung her arms back and forth. "That's what girls do in scary movies and

74

we want to be movie stars."

Cole frowned. "Please don't tell me you sneaked into my den and watched one of my scary movies when I told you that stuff is off limits until you're a lot older."

"Actually," Jade said, sounding a whole lot wiser than she should sound at five, "the nanny sneaked in there when she thought we were taking a nap, and we sneaked in after her —"

"To make sure she didn't steal any of your stuff."

"And she was watching *Frankenstein*."

"It wasn't *Frankenstein*, it was *Crash McCoy*."

"Not *Crash McCoy*! *Slash McCall*."

"And there was this blond girl, and she was covered with make-believe blood, and she was screaming."

"And we screamed too."

"But we weren't scared."

"Heck no, we screamed because it was fun."

"And we scared the nanny and she yelled at us."

"And we don't want any more nannies."

"Especially mean ones."

"Or ugly ones."

"Or ones that don't like snakes."

Cole shoved his fingers through his hair,

his gaze bobbing from one side of the room to the other as Holly and Jade went into a long dissertation on the merits of screaming and scaring nannies, while Caitlin and Chloe jumped up and down on the bed, Karloff and Carly snored soundly on the floor, and Rathbone and Lugosi barked and howled.

Cole added one more item to his list:

Take aspirin and keep a bottle handy for at least the next sixteen to eighteen years.

Chapter 5

Ben hid in the dim alleyway next to the ice cream shop, ignoring the scents of rotten bananas and sour milk emanating from the Dumpster he'd been standing behind for the past fifteen minutes. With his camera balanced on the top corner of the trash bin, he snapped photos of the people walking up and down Plentiful's boardwalk.

Pivoting his camera to the left, he caught sight of Juliet sitting on a wooden bench in front of the Mischievous Moose Emporium, legs crossed demurely, one pink stiletto dangling from her toes, doing the same thing he was doing — studying the people passing by.

He zoomed in on Juliet's sunglasses, trying to catch the different emotions she tried to hide behind her disguise. Looking through the viewfinder, everything around her — the red and white geraniums spilling out of old oak barrels, an American flag waving over her head, and the grin on the gangly bronze moose — became a blur, but that's what he was shooting for. The focal point of the photo he was setting up was Juliet and the loneliness drawn on her face, the resolve to find something that had been missing in her life, and the determination to keep those emotions from showing.

Nicole wanted him to snap nonexistent shots of scandal and intrigue, but he'd deal with getting those photos later, whether they were fabricated or real. For now, he concentrated on taking the kind of pictures that intrigued him: catching a person's vulnerability, their deepest emotions — when they thought no one was watching.

Three days ago he'd snapped pictures of Juliet standing on a deserted stretch of beach, not far from her Carmel home, still wearing the scarlet gown she'd had on the night before at her Fourth of July party. She'd done nothing but stare out across the water while the frothy waves rolled over her toes and her dress billowed behind her.

He'd captured desperation on film that morning: overwhelming doubt and sadness occupied her face. But, finally, grit and tenacity seemed to conquer the things that plagued her.

He'd known those emotions himself. There had been too many years after the riot, after he'd been beaten into a coma, after surgery to relieve pressure on his brain, when he could barely hold a camera, when he couldn't string together a sentence of more than three or four words.

There had been too many days when he'd thought life as he'd always known it was over, that he'd never be whole again. But Nic had been there for him. Nic had helped him through everything, standing at his bedside day after day as he held on to the threads of life, comforting him when he seethed with anger, massaging his muscles and supporting him through months of agonizing recovery.

She'd been his rock; and he'd been hers.

Now they seemed more business partners than anything else.

Ben took a drag off of his cigarette, thinking back to the day when he'd chosen to take photos of Nicole Palisade instead of Juliet Bridger. Other photographers had clamored to get shots of Amazonia, queen of the rain forest, her fabulous body barely covered by a leaf here, a leaf there; her pale blond tresses shimmering in the sunlight filtering through the trees, and two powerful jaguars — one black, one spotted —

purring as they rubbed against her thighs.

Nicole was standing in the background, covered in rubbery green lizard scales strategically applied and swirling over tantalizing parts of her body. Contact lenses tinted her eyes a fiery red, and clawlike nails curled from the end of each finger. No one seemed to notice her in the shadows; no one but him. Everyone else was oblivious to the all-encompassing passion in Nicole's narrowed eyes. No one else sensed that Nicole wished she could dig her claws into Juliet and rip her to shreds.

He'd clicked away with his camera, taking one shot after another of Nicole as he hid in the fabricated Hollywood jungle, congratulating himself on the money he'd make from the photos. After all, the tabloids would have a field day with his pictures and the story of the jealous — never the bride, always the bridesmaid — starlet.

And then Nicole spotted him. Her red eyes burned through the leaves of the trees and nearly singed the finger with which he snapped her picture. She slipped away from the director as all of the action focused on Juliet and the jaguars; she moved toward him, silent and unseen — except through the lens of his camera.

Nicole sidled up to him, grazing his cheek and nearly drawing blood with one of her curled claws. She smiled ever so slightly, and then she kissed him. Even now he remembered the cinnamon taste of the Red Hots she'd been sucking on, remembered the teasing way she'd nipped his lips, the erotic sting of long, thick nails trailing down his back.

When she had him completely mesmerized, she plucked the camera from his hands and ripped out his film, dangled it before his face. Then she dropped it at her feet.

Later that night, she danced for him, slow and easy, wearing nothing but skin. She told him that Juliet had wrapped billionaire Garrett Pierce around her little finger and planned to marry him — for his money of course, because Juliet Bridger used people. She always had; she always would.

That night Nicole had lowered her sizzling body onto his, made love to him as no other woman ever had, told him she could help him get the hottest pictures of his career, could help him write the most scandalous stories — all he had to do was help her get even with Juliet Bridger. She wasn't out to ruin Juliet, Nicole had told him. She just wanted her to suffer as she had suffered . . . one humiliation, one indignity at a time.

Jealousy and revenge were ugly — but he would have done anything for Nicole after that night, and he pretty much had.

She in turn had taken care of him, in more ways than he could ever imagine. She'd made it easy for him to conquer his demons. He only wished he could help her conquer hers.

And then there was Juliet. She had no one to help her. She'd been surrounded by hangers-on — and one woman out to get even.

Minutes passed and he concentrated on Juliet again, snapping her picture as she strolled through town. He left his hiding place but kept his distance, staying out of sight while she went to the bank and withdrew money from the ATM — a smart move because using a credit card would reveal her identity.

Three hours went by. She strolled from store to store, tall, voluptuous and beautiful, swinging a flamingo-speckled totebag where she stuffed souvenirs. She drank a mocha at the Java Shop, bought pink jelly beans at the candy store, and even said hello to him as he held open the door for her when she ducked inside the Misty Moon Saloon.

Little did she know that he'd watched her for years; that he was her assistant's lover — and well-kept secret.

He followed Juliet into the bar, pocketing the wallet he'd unobtrusively slipped from her bag. It was a hasty maneuver; one that wasn't even well thought out. But Juliet's lack of money, credit cards, and I.D. could cause her untold complications — and, thereby help him to get the compromising photos Nicole wanted.

Taking a seat at the far end of the bar, he ordered a whiskey and looked like any other patron in a saloon full of people drinking beer, tossing darts, playing pool, and listening to the oldies on a jukebox.

He slugged down a long, cool swallow of Jim Beam on the rocks and watched Juliet over the top of his glass. She had a nice laugh. She gave handouts to homeless people, she was loyal to her friends, and had an uncanny knack for rising to the top in everything she ever did — in spite of rumors, innuendo, and downright jealousy.

He had the feeling he knew her better than anyone, because he'd watched her for so many years. "Stay away from her," Nicole had said, and he had. But a camera could detect a person's moods and their frame of mind better than the naked eye. And what he saw when he looked at photos of Juliet was a woman who could be anything anyone wanted her to be, but didn't know what she wanted for herself.

He lit up a cigarette and through the smoke he watched her smile at people passing by. He liked her, but God he wished he didn't. If he could despise her, even feel the least bit of hatred, it would be a damn sight easier to help Nicole make the woman's life a living hell.

Chapter 6

Juliet sat alone in one of the red vinyl booths at the Misty Moon Saloon, sipping on a cold bottle of the owner's home-brewed Moose Jaw beer, feasting on a double-decker cheeseburger, spicy fries, and peanuts while watching the promenade of people who moseyed about a bar where it seemed everybody knew everybody else's name and business.

No one knew her, of course, but that's exactly what she wanted. Freedom from gossip and from the stares of people who knew her blond-bombshell image far too well.

Popping a peppery fry into her mouth, she kept her eyes on a tall, middle-aged woman feeding a couple of coins into the now quiet jukebox, her behind wiggling to music only she could hear. The brightly lit Wurlitzer whirred, a CD dropped, and the whine of a guitar wailed through the saloon.

Seconds later Gene Pitney sang about Liberty Valance riding into town, the words and music so vivid the cowboys tromping through the bar seemed to transform right before her eyes into Lee Marvin, John Wayne, and Jimmy Stewart slugging it out, breaking bottles and mirrors and wooden chairs.

She hadn't listened to the oldies since her father had passed away. Suddenly, she vividly remembered her dad driving her to and from high school in the '57 Chevy he'd restored, the radio cranked up so loud the dashboard vibrated while he sang "Back in the U.S.S.R." and "Surfin' U.S.A."

In the evenings he'd put a stack of albums on the stereo and croon "Sugar Shack" and the "Duke of Earl" while fixing creamed tuna on toast for dinner, washing piles of laundry, dusting and ironing.

Juliet's only job was to go to school, slave over piles of homework, get involved in every extracurricular activity known to man, and bring home straight As. She'd done it all, which made Sam Bridger a very proud man. Heaven forbid that his daughter should turn out like her mom, a two-timing trollop who ran off with a long-haul trucker and was never seen again, or like himself, a blue-collar warehouse worker with a tenth-grade education.

Sam Bridger could have brooded over his misfortune when his wife left. Instead, he spent every ounce of his energy turning Juliet into the perfect daughter. He loved her so darn much, and she was so afraid of breaking his heart that she never told him she wanted to give acting a shot. Never told him she wrote ghastly mystery stories late at night and would someday like to see them published. How could she when he wanted desperately for her to be a doctor, a lawyer, a scientist or teacher?

For eighteen years she did everything he asked of her — and then she disappointed him, broke his heart, by turning away from his dream, only to find that her own dream wasn't all she'd hoped it would be.

She wondered how many other people sitting here in the saloon also had failed dreams.

At the far end of the knotty-pine paneled room, past the hanging copper lamps and the mounted heads of moose, antelope, mountain goat, and black bear, a loud-mouthed skinny guy and a big burly fellow tossed darts, swigged beer, and belched. She imagined their dreams consisted of nothing more than getting laid, and she had the sneaking suspicion they ended each night frustrated and horny.

Straight across from her, a man, whose butt drooped over the sides and back of his barstool, picked peanuts from a dish, cracked them open, and tossed the shells over his shoulder. No doubt the Misty Moon was the place where he spent most every night. He probably had a job he despised, a too-hefty mortgage, and a wife he'd grown tired of — but he no longer had the energy to make changes.

Not everyone could run away as she had. It took guts, or money, or both. Or maybe it just took a moment's insanity.

Taking another sip of her beer, Juliet watched the saloon doors swing open and the three elderly women she'd waved to as she was being towed through town shuffled inside and meandered past her table. One looked like a cross between Annie Oakley and Oprah Winfrey, another was the spitting image of Elton John, right down to the chartreuse pantsuit and pancake-sized rhinestone glasses, and the third could pass for anyone's gray-haired, bun-wearing grandmother, circa 1950.

The ladies gave Juliet a blatant once-over, then did a quick U-turn and, chatting madly to one another in hushed tones, boosted their derrières onto barstools and sneaked peeks at Juliet when they weren't busy gabbing.

Meddling busybodies, no doubt, but sweet as sugar and willing to do anything to help a friend. They were the kind of women who made their own dreams come true, and to hell with anyone who objected.

And then there was the big, bald-headed guy sitting at the far end of the bar drinking whiskey. He had a camera slung around his neck, but he didn't look like a tourist, more like a photojournalist on a mission. With a scar slashed down his forehead, over his left eye, and across his nose, he reminded Juliet of the straight-razor killer in her book *Seven Sins*.

Of all the people in the bar she found him the most intriguing, maybe because underneath the rough exterior lay a man who was lonely, a guy who had a dream just like hers, but too many obligations kept him from making it a reality.

At least that's what she imagined.

Juliet continued to watch him over the top of her beer bottle. He shared a laugh or two with the bartender, then plunked his glass down on the copper-topped bar, lifted a cigarette from the ash tray, and took a long drag, turning to stare at Juliet through the smoke billowing out his nostrils.

His glare sent a shiver up her spine and she averted her gaze, looking at a wall of snapshots, photos of some of the Misty Moon's patrons with their arms slung around Molly, the saloon's kilt-and-neon-Nike-wearing owner.

And right in the center she saw a photo of Cole in full-blown living color, a dark blond lock of hair falling over his brow, wearing a button-down white shirt with the sleeves rolled up on his forearms and well-fitting faded jeans.

Now, there was a man who made her shiver, but not out of dread, out of desire. Especially after that kiss.

"Excuse me." The whispery voice and the knuckles rapping on the table tore Juliet back to reality, just in time to see the grandmotherly lady who'd been checking her out a few minutes before scoot into the booth across from her. "Sorry to bother you." The woman smiled sweetly. "I'm Mildred — Mildred McWhinnie. My friends and I couldn't help but notice that you're all alone, and we were wondering if we could join you?"

Juliet barely had the words "I'd love it"

90

out of her mouth before Mildred's friends scuttled off of their barstools, shuffled across the room with their drinks and outfit-coordinated purses in tow, and wiggled their behinds into the shiny red half-circle booth.

Two hands — of differing sizes, colors, and wrinkle formations — flew across the table. The Oprah-slash-Annie Oakley lookalike grabbed Juliet's hand first and pumped it up and down three times. "I'm Ida Mae Peel."

"And I'm Lillian Rafferty." Elton John's quasi-clone pushed at her immense rhinestone glasses to keep them from sliding off of her nose, and offered Juliet a featherlike handshake that was as meek as her voice.

"We're pleased as punch to meet you." Mildred set her iced tea glass and her white patent-leather handbag on the tabletop. "The moment we saw you and your pretty pink Mustang being towed through town I said to myself, 'I've just got to meet that lady.'"

"Quit beating around the bush, Mildred." Ida Mae leaned forward, her ample breasts and the fringe on her purple and white cowgirl shirt crumpling against the edge of the table. "Tell us, dear, because we're just dying to know the truth. Are you really on the run from some Tony Soprano wannabe?"

"Me?" Juliet frowned in stunned disbelief. "What on earth makes you think that?"

Mildred clanked the long silver spoon around inside her iced tea glass. "It's all the talk around town."

At least everyone in town wasn't wondering if she was Juliet Bridger in disguise.

"I've only been in town a few hours," Juliet said. "I'm surprised people are talking about me at all."

"You're not exactly the kind of woman who walks around town without being noticed," Ida Mae said, giving Juliet's beehive and her tight pink top an unabashed exam. "And it doesn't take long for word to spread about here, especially when Joe from Joe's Gas and Bait starts mixing Mountain Dew with chocolate cream pie over at the Elk Horn. Poor man gets drunk as a skunk on that concoction, and then his lips let loose."

"And he was telling some whoppers at lunchtime." Mildred leaned forward and whispered. "Why, I'll have you know that man not only told everyone at the Elk Horn about your car breaking down, but he also told anyone in spitting distance" — Mildred gazed about, as if she wanted to make sure only the people sitting at the booth could hear — "that you've got the finest pair of knockers he's ever set eyes on."

Juliet choked on her beer. "He didn't?"

"Of course he did," Lillian said in her sweet and mild voice. "But don't fret, hon, Joe has a tendency to say that about all the girls he runs into. Once upon a time he even made comments like that about me, but —"

"That's history, Lillian." Ida Mae plucked a peanut from the bowl in the center of the table, turning her frustrated gaze from Lillian back to Juliet. "So, you aren't on the lam from anyone?"

Juliet shook her head. "Not the mob, not the cops, not a former lover." She didn't bother to tell the ladies that she was on the run from the paparazzi, from gossip, and from the life she'd been living.

"Well, that's good to hear," Mildred said, "but on the off chance you're going to be in town awhile and find yourself in need of help — with the law, a lover, or anyone — Ida Mae, Lillian and I have a certain skill at undercover work. It wasn't all that long ago that we put the screws to a serial killer — just as he was getting ready to strike again."

"And don't forget how we solved the case of the mysterious woman who dropped dead at the bookstore," Lillian added. "It was as if one of those delightful cozies we like to read came to life, and we were the protagonists."

"You know," Mildred said, her iced tea glass poised close to her mouth, "if you're going to be in town awhile, and if you like to read mysteries, you could join our Tuesday Morning Sleuth Society."

"It's a small reader's group," Lillian explained, "just the three of us — people in town call us the Sleuths — and Scarlett Wolfe, too, since she's the owner of A Study in Scarlett, the bookstore where we get together."

"We've been meeting every Tuesday morning for nearly ten years," Mildred said, "and I imagine there isn't a mystery that the four of us haven't read. Why, everything we know about sleuthing we've learned from cozies and 'Murder, She Wrote.'"

"Don't forget the forensic knowledge we've gotten from Jayne Mansfield-Smythe." Lillian pushed her glasses up the bridge of her nose. "Have you ever read her?"

Read her? She'd created the gum-chewing forensic pathologist in her very first book, but she couldn't pass on that little tidbit. Instead, she said, "I've read every single one. Some two or three times."

"Jayne Mansfield-Smythe is nothing but a blond bimbo created by a blond bimbo." Ida Mae tsked as she shook her head. "For the life of me, I don't understand what anyone sees in the claptrap written by Juliet Bridger."

Lovely, just lovely. A few hours in town and she was already hearing the dreaded voice of her critics.

"I hate to disagree with you, and you know darn good and well that Scarlett would *strongly* disagree," Mildred declared. "No one writes mystery novels as well as Juliet Bridger. Unfortunately, she's not writing as fast as I'd like her to."

A fan, thank goodness!

"That's because she's too busy fighting off the tabloids." Ida Mae tsked yet again. "You did hear those stories about her being just as involved in that corporate scam as her ex?"

Mildred plunked her iced tea glass on the table. "Heard it; don't believe it."

"I don't believe it either," Juliet added, coming quickly to her own defense, a no-no in normal circumstances, but considering her disguise, it was fairly simple to stick up for herself. "From what I've read in legitimate papers and have seen on network news, Juliet Bridger's completely innocent. She didn't know her husband was pulling a fast one on his partners, his employees, his friends . . . or her."

"Just as I said," Ida Mae declared, "Juliet Bridger's a blond bimbo, as gullible as the day is long."

"Maybe she loved him," Juliet said, remembering that once upon a time she'd worshipped the ground Garrett had walked on. "Maybe she was afraid to believe the worst about him, and felt betrayed and hurt when all of his dirty laundry was exposed."

"Exactly." Mildred took a sip of her iced tea. "God knows, it's easy to be fooled by people. Why, most everyone in this town was fooled by our former chief of police. Now *there* was a scandal."

"And don't forget that shyster Brace Harrington." Lillian sighed, a faraway smile touching her lips. "My word, but that man looked nice, but tried selling people a load of . . . well . . ."

"If you can't spit it out, Lillian, I most certainly can." Ida Mae shook her head. "Crap. That's what he tried to sell all of us.

His name was really Bill Deal, and I swear the people around here would have tarred and feathered him if the police chief hadn't clapped him behind bars first. The citizens in Plentiful don't take kindly to people trying to pull a fast one on them."

Juliet chuckled weakly, then bit into her cheeseburger to conceal her anxiety. Hopefully no one would find out that she was disguising her real identity behind black hair and pink sunglasses, because being tarred and feathered didn't rank high on her list of fun and games.

"You know," Mildred said, plucking a peanut from the bowl as she stared at Juliet, "we've spent all of this time talking about shysters and mobsters, but we still don't know a thing about you. Not your name. Nothing."

Name? Why on earth hadn't she come up with a name when she'd come up with her Annette Funicello does *Beach Blanket Bingo* disguise? She couldn't spit out Juliet Bridger, or she'd be shunned, maybe even tarred and feathered by her delightful yet eccentric companions.

Thinking quickly, Juliet whipped out the moniker of a character she'd dreamed up once upon a time but hadn't yet stuck into the pages of a book. "How rude of me."

Juliet smiled behind the french fry she held to her lips. "I'm Autumn Leeves. That's two Es in Leeves, not an E and an A as in the leaves on a tree."

"Autumn Leeves," Mildred repeated. "What an absolutely lovely name."

Lovely, yes, but Autumn Leeves was a fictional copper-haired hooker who, according to Juliet's notes for her next novel, sliced the throat and removed the private parts from each of the johns she screwed on the 8th, 18th, and 28th of each month.

Autumn Leeves was certifiably insane.

Juliet was beginning to think she'd honestly and truly flipped her lid, too, because she was digging herself into a hole that had every possibility of getting deeper.

"Are you on vacation?" Lillian asked. "Or thinking about settling here in Plentiful?"

"On vacation. Just driving around the country; seeing the sights."

Mildred brushed a few peanut crumbs onto the shell-strewn wooden floor. "And what do you do when you're not on vacation?"

"Teach kindergarten." The lie rolled far too easily off of Juliet's tongue.

One of Ida Mae's gray eyebrows rose. "Really?"

Oh, Lord, now she had to explain. She dug deep into the recesses of her memory to pull out bits and pieces of the decent characteristics she'd developed for her hooker-slash-killer-slash-teacher. "I may not look like the stereotypical kindergarten teacher —"

"I don't believe there's a right or wrong on how a kindergarten teacher should look," Ida Mae interrupted. "The important thing is how much that teacher loves children." She leaned against the table, and whispered. "You do love children, don't you?"

"Of course I do." At least she was sure she would if she'd ever been around any children.

"A very dear friend of ours — Doc Sheridan — absolutely loves children, too." Ida Mae flashed a wide grin at her friends, as if sharing some kind of private joke, then turned back to Juliet. "It's certainly a shame that you're leaving town because when two people have something like that in common, they really should get to know each other."

"That is so terribly true, Ida Mae." Mildred nodded her utmost agreement. "And Doc Sheridan is such a dear."

"And handsome." Lillian patted her

heart. "The man simply takes my breath away."

Juliet laughed uneasily. "If you're trying to play matchmaker —"

"Oh, no, nothing of the sort." Ida Mae shook her head. "It's just that poor old Doc Sheridan has seen more than his fair share of troubles lately, and he needs a . . . a temporary . . . housekeeper."

"Terrible housekeeper, that man," Mildred added. "So disorganized."

"In spite of being so handsome." Lillian sighed dreamily.

"It would be ever so nice if you could stay in town for a week or two," Mildred said. "We could get to know you better, and it would be lovely if you could help the Doc. Why just this afternoon he called to tell me how desperately he needed someone."

"And when he called *me* to talk about it and mentioned the salary he's offering, I could hardly believe what I was hearing. The amount just staggers the imagination," Ida Mae added. "And of course, room and board come with the job."

"It sounds like a great position," Juliet fibbed, something she was becoming quite adept at, "but taking care of children is my specialty, not housekeeping. And to be perfectly honest, I've really been looking forward to this vacation."

Mildred sighed heavily. "I suppose it was a bit much to ask of you, since you're a stranger in town and just passing through, but we do like to take care of good people like Doc Sheridan."

"That they do." Molly sashayed up to the booth, her kilt swishing as she walked. She shot a wry smile at Juliet. "They'll take care of anyone, given half the chance. In fact, you stick around town long enough and they'll have you serving meals at the senior center, shelving books at the library, *and* singing in the choir at Saint John's Episcopal."

Actually, that didn't sound all that bad, but Ida Mae had already made it clear she didn't like Juliet Bridger, and she and the other ladies gathered around the table would detest her if they found out they'd spent the past half hour chatting with the famous author — and she'd been lying through her teeth.

"You know," Juliet said, "as much as I'd love to stick around Plentiful, I need to get back on the road again."

"Such a shame." Mildred shook her head. "But if you can't stay, you can't stay."

"Can I talk you into a piece of apple pie before you go?" Molly asked. "It's the best this side of heaven, loaded with cinnamon and brown sugar, and I'll throw in a dollop of homemade vanilla ice cream for free."

"Sounds nice, thank you," Juliet said, wishing she could stay and knowing she couldn't, "but I left my car at Joe's Gas and Bait and I should pick it up before he closes."

"Suit yourself, hon." Molly pulled a stubby pencil out of the wispy grayish-black bun haphazardly pinned on top of her head, scribbled out a check, and slapped the bill on the table.

Juliet grabbed her tote and dug inside for her pink-and-green Kate Spade wallet. She pushed aside lipstick, mascara, and other odds and ends, but her wallet and all of her I.D., her cash, and her credit cards were gone.

Looking up nervously, Juliet spotted Molly's suspicious eyes focusing narrowly on her frantic movements. A hint of perspiration broke out on Juliet's brow and she reached under her heavily lacquered but drooping bangs to wipe it away.

Molly's bulky arms crossed irately over her generous bosom. "Lose something?"

Juliet smiled halfheartedly. "My wallet."

She poked her head under the table to see if it might have fallen out, but she saw only one smashed french fry, one pair of old lady shoes, Lillian's glittering tennies, Ida Mae's purple and white cowgirl boots, and her own hot pink Jimmy Choos.

Sitting up again, Juliet flashed Molly one more smile. "It's not under the table either."

"I gathered that."

"Obviously I've lost it. Or someone took it."

"Don't even mention stolen wallets," Mildred said, clapping a hand over her bosom. "We had a lady drop dead last year — and her wallet was missing. I'd hate for you to drop dead, too."

"She's not going to drop dead, she's going to spend the rest of the day washing the pile of dishes in the kitchen and then she can scrub the bathrooms" — one of Molly's bushy eyebrows rose as she gave Juliet the evil eye — "unless you have a friend who'll loan you some money."

She had friends. Well . . . so-called friends. But she wasn't going to call anyone to bail her out of this. First off, news of her dilemma would somehow end up on the front page of *Buzz*. Second, she didn't want her friends, her acquaintances, her business associates, or anyone else to know where she was.

Juliet studied her fingernails. The pretty pink swirls wouldn't survive hot soapy water, and she didn't know if she'd survive sticking her hand into a dirty toilet. "You know, Molly, I'm not all that good at washing dishes or cleaning toilets, but I make a damn good Manhattan and could work behind the bar for a couple of hours."

"Sorry, hon, but we don't serve those wishy-washy 'Sex In the City' drinks here. It's the dishes and toilets or —"

"I could tend bar for *two* days and not just one."

Molly's eyes narrowed. "I thought you were a vacationing kindergarten teacher, and now you're telling me you're a bartender?"

"I put myself through college tending bar." Another lie; the devil would surely rise up and snatch her if she kept this up. "It's been awhile, but some things you just don't forget." Juliet slipped out of the booth, skirted past Molly, and ducked behind the bar, refusing to give Molly a moment to protest. "So, what'll you have? Name a drink and I'll fix it right up."

"Any drink?" Molly asked, depositing her kilt-covered tush onto a barstool, with

Lillian, Mildred, and Ida Mae lumbering onto stools beside her.

"Any drink," Juliet responded. "You name it, and it's yours."

"All right. A Rattlesnake."

"Easy enough, Molly my dear, just let me get my bearings and in two shakes of a lamb's tail you'll be sipping on the finest Rattlesnake you ever tasted."

It had been a long time since she'd stood behind a bar or fixed a drink, and she'd done that only for research, but her fictional heroine Jayne Mansfield-Smythe did it quite often. All Juliet had to do now was summon up an ounce of Jayne's moxie, and she'd have Molly eating out of her hands.

She spent a few seconds checking the layout of the bar, then went to work. Grabbing a lemon, Juliet tossed it into the air and stabbed it with an ice pick on its way back down, just as Jayne had done in *Two Murders Are Better Than One*, although the ice pick Juliet used wasn't dripping with blood.

Squeezing about a teaspoon of juice into a shaker, she snatched an egg from the small fridge tucked under the bar and cracked and separated it with one hand, surprising Molly and herself. After dumping the yolk in an extra cup and the shell in the trash, she tossed the egg white on top of the lemon, added an estimated ounce-and-a-half of Chivas, spooned in a dab of powdered sugar, a few dashes of Pernod, then shook it with some ice and strained the concoction into an old-fashion glass she found chilling in the fridge.

Smiling triumphantly, Juliet slapped a cocktail napkin on the copper bar and placed the drink squarely in front of Molly. "Give that a try and see if it meets the Misty Moon standard of best this side of heaven."

Molly's eyes narrowed as she cautiously lifted the glass, but there was no mistaking the admiration in the grin that sneaked onto her face after she tested the drink. "Not bad." She sipped a little more. "Can you make anything else?"

"You want a Creole Mama or a Daisy Duke, I can do it." Juliet brazenly popped the top on a Moose Jaw and took a swallow. "I can whip up a Dingo Salad if you want or a Beaver's Beard, not to mention a Purple Gecko or a Waikiki Woo-Woo." She winked at Molly. "So what do you think? Wouldn't I be much more beneficial to you as a bartender than a scullery maid?"

Molly grabbed the pencil from behind her ear, shoved it under her bun and scratched her head. "I suppose I could use a little help behind the bar, considering that it's the peak of tourist season."

"You won't regret this," Juliet said, smiling weakly. She hoped she wouldn't regret it, either.

"Now that that's settled," Mildred said, eyeing the bottles of booze lined up in front of the mirror on the back wall, "you can start your new job by making me one of those Purple Geckos."

"I'll take a Waikiki Woo-Woo." Lillian giggled.

"And" — Ida Mae shook her head and tsked — "I'll be the designated driver."

Joe from Joe's Gas and Bait sidled up to the bar, bringing with him the definite scent of grease and gasoline. "You can make mine a Moose Jaw."

As if she'd worked at the Misty Moon forever, Juliet dragged another bottle of beer out of the fridge and set it in front of Joe. "How was lunch at the Elk Horn?"

"Best chicken fried steak I ever tasted. Of course, after I saw you peeking at me through the window half a dozen times I cut my lunch short so I could get to that car of yours."

"Then it's ready to go?"

"Yep. Good as the day she rolled off the assembly line. New hoses, new belts. I even vacuumed the insides, and when I heard through the grapevine you was hanging out at the Misty Moon, figured I'd stop by and give you the bill." He slapped Juliet's key on the copper-topped bar and shoved a grease-speckled invoice under her hand.

Juliet nervously picked up the bill and stared at the total scribbled on the bottom. Slowly her gaze raised toward Joe. "You didn't by any chance find a pink and green wallet while you were vacuuming, did you?"

His eyes narrowed beneath the brim of his baseball cap. "Nope, no wallet, no loose change — inside *or* out."

"Then we have a slight problem."

"You mean to tell me you can't pay for the repairs?"

Juliet smiled weakly. "That seems to be the gist of the problem."

Joe smacked a hand over her car key. "No money, no car."

How was she possibly going to get out of this mess? Think fast.

"You know, Joe, Molly's been kind enough to let me work off the debt I owe

108

her, so maybe I could work off what I owe you, too."

"You don't look like no grease monkey."

"No, but I've got a prize-winning green thumb."

"What do I need with a green thumb?"

"Beauty, Joe. Sheer beauty." Juliet hit him with her most charming smile. "Can't you just picture your office decked out with a few ficus trees and some feathery ferns in hanging baskets? And I could stuff those empty brick planters out by the street with sweet alyssum, some daisies and marigolds and maybe a little purple aster."

Joe looked skeptical. "I'm not into sissy things."

"Of course you're not, and I'd never give the station a snooty look. I was thinking something a little more outdoors-ish and wild."

"Yeah, well, I suppose it wouldn't hurt, but" — he rubbed his stubbled jaw — "you any good at painting? That old cinderblock building of mine hasn't been touched in a long time."

"Give me a brush and a bucket of paint and I can do wonders with those greasy walls."

Joe took off his cap and slicked a hand over his sparse gray hair. "All right, give me a few days worth of work starting to-morrow morning, and we've got a deal."

There was no telling how late she'd have to work tonight, and she really did need a little beauty sleep. "Could we make it in the afternoon?"

"All right. Afternoon." Joe turned on his heavy black boots and headed for the swinging doors. "See you tomorrow at one."

"Wait," Juliet hollered from behind the bar.

Joe turned slowly. His eyes narrowed. "You trying to con me out of something else?"

Juliet hit him with a smile much bigger and much brighter than her charming smile. "Any chance you could trust me with the keys *and* my car?"

Any hint of niceness drained from Joe's face. "And let you run out of town without beautifying my place or giving me cold hard cash for my parts and labor?"

"Ah, get off your high horse," Molly ordered, smacking Joe across the arm with her ever-present towel. "Autumn's not going to skip town."

Joe's jaw tightened as he walked toward the bar and slapped the key in Juliet's out-stretched hand. "That pretty pink Mustang of yours is parked right outside. You make sure you show up tomorrow, or" — he grinned — "I'll sic the cops on you."

"I'll be there, don't you worry."

The swinging doors clapped back and forth after Joe beat a path from the Misty Moon. A shaft of late afternoon sunshine shot into the saloon and struck Juliet in the eyes, but she couldn't miss the frown on Molly's face as she wiped a water spot off of the copper-topped bar. "So, Autumn, if you're gonna work for Joe in the afternoon, when do you plan to pay off your debt to me?"

"I was thinking nine till closing. Does that work?" Juliet asked as she set two glasses on the bar and started to mix the drinks Lillian and Mildred had requested.

"Suppose." Molly swept a pile of peanut shells onto the floor. "But what are you going to do between now and then? Not run off, I hope."

"Of course not. I've got to retrace my steps and see if I can find my missing wallet, call my credit card company if the wallet doesn't turn up, find a place to stay and . . ." Juliet frowned. She drummed her fingers on the bar. "Finding a place to stay might be rather difficult since I don't have any money, so" — she shrugged — "I guess I'll have to spend the night in my car."

"You couldn't possibly spend the night all scrunched up in your car." Mildred scooted off her barstool, her white patent-leather purse clutched tightly in her hands. "Why, that would be an absolute outrage when Doc Sheridan is willing to give his new . . . housekeeper free room and board. If Molly will let me use the phone in her back room, I'll give him a call right now."

"All I need is a place to sleep," Juliet stammered. "I couldn't possibly take on a housekeeping job in addition to everything else."

"Don't worry your pretty little head." Mildred said, scuttling toward Molly's office. "Taking care of Doc Sheridan's house won't be any trouble at all."

Chapter 7

"Housekeeper? Are you crazy, Doc?" Raven Walkowicz, the best and youngest receptionist Cole had ever employed, glared at him in staggering disbelief.

"Probably, but sometimes a man's gotta do what he's gotta do."

Cole shoved through the clinic door with Raven traipsing behind, her short legs taking three strides to keep up with every one of his. He stalked past the corral, where the girls were tormenting a couple of black-and-white pygmy goats, up the drive to his house, and took stock of the mess out front.

Raven finally stepped in front of him, fisted hands on her hips. "You've got to tell the truth."

"Yeah, I should, but I'm not going to, at least not during the interview."

Cole rescued Barbie and Ken from an overgrown flower bed, grabbed Holly's bicycle from the lawn, and headed for the garage. Rathbone, Karloff, and Lugosi romped around him wanting to play, but he didn't have time, not when a kindergarten teacher would be arriving in half an hour to discuss his "housekeeper" position.

"God, Doc, how can you be so dense. If this Autumn Leeves person thinks she's here to interview for a 'housekeeper' job, she's going to want to see the inside of the house, not just the outside."

"And your point is?"

"You may be able to hide the mess out here, but how do you plan to keep her from seeing the dolls, the high chairs, the triple stroller, and five frilly bedroom sets?"

Cole contemplated Raven's question as he dumped an armload of little-girl junk behind the jet ski he hadn't used since last summer. "I'll take her through the side door and interview her in the den."

Black-haired Raven with five eyebrow rings, a diamond in her right nostril, an ugly silver stud sticking through her tongue, and God knows how many hidden piercings, stepped in front of him again, determined to get her point across. "You take her into that house of horrors den of

114

yours and she's going to pee her pants. You'd be better off telling her about the girls."

"Okay, so I'll interview her at the clinic, but I'm feeling her out before I tell her I have five kids." Cole brushed past Raven and headed for the pasture to collect another bike, a host of Tonka Toys — his choice for playthings, not the girls' — a couple of wagons, and a pink frilly fairy costume.

"Have you forgotten that a nanny quit this morning because you lied to her."

"I didn't lie. I just left out a few details."

"So this time you plan to leave out *all* the details pertaining to children and pretend you're hiring a housekeeper?"

"Sounds crazy, but that's the idea."

"And Mildred dreamed this up on her own?"

"With a little help from Ida Mae and Lillian." Cole swept an overturned tricycle out of the dirt, fought Rathbone for possession of Ballerina Barbie, and came away with everything but the doll's head.

"Only a brainless idiot or a shifty, underhanded jerk would follow through with a devious plan like this."

"All right, so I'm a shifty, underhanded jerk, but I'm the one who's had thirteen nannies quit in the last six months. This time — if the dogs don't growl at the woman and she meets all of my requirements, and she should, because the Sleuths told me they've never met anyone more perfect — I'm going to unleash the girls slowly, make sure they do all the right things."

"No more rabbit turd in the iced tea?"

Cole shook his head. "And if those girls even think about taking Squeeze out of her enclosure and letting her loose in the kitchen while the nanny's cooking breakfast, I'll . . ." Cole shoved his fingers through his hair. "Hell, if this woman doesn't work out, I don't know what I'll do."

"I hate to tell you this, Cole, but your plan's gonna backfire and I don't want to be here when it happens."

"You won't be here and neither will the girls." Cole reached into the pocket of his jeans and pulled out a wad of cash and the keys to the Suburban he'd bought to haul his expanded family around in. "I want you to take the kids into town and buy them dinner. Pizza, ice cream, the whole nine yards. And then I want them to spend the night at your place. In fact, I've already packed their things."

Raven's eyes narrowed. "I'm your recep-tionist. I like dogs and cats and snakes and an occasional rodent. Not once did I sign on to be a baby-sitter."

"Yeah, well, I didn't have five kids when I hired you, but I distinctly remember you begging for this job and telling me you'd do anything to work for me."

"Anything related to your veterinary practice."

"The way I see it, baby-sitting my girls is related, because if I don't have someone to watch them, I can't do my job."

Raven folded her arms over her chest. "I want a raise."

Cole had expected that. "Fine."

"Fifty dollars a week."

He'd expected her to ask for a hundred. "Fine."

"And a bonus at Christmas."

"I already give you a bonus."

"I want a bigger one. Plus a turkey and a Christmas tree."

"You're pushing your luck."

"Which is exactly what you're doing by not telling this Leeves woman the truth."

"If I hire her, I'll tell her tomorrow, after the kids greet her with smiles and fresh flowers — ones that aren't crawling with ants — and show her how sweet they can be."

Raven raised a skeptical be-ringed eyebrow. "You going to show her how sweet you can be, too?"

Cole shrugged. "You ever known me to be sweet?"

"Only when you're kissing a dog."

"For all I know," Cole chuckled, "Ms. Leeves might be the homeliest dog I've ever seen."

Juliet twisted the rearview mirror toward her and, keeping one hand on the steering wheel and one eye on the highway as the Mustang whizzed northward, puckered her lips and painted them a hot passionate pink, hoping to make a good impression on Doc Sheridan.

What a field day *Buzz* would have if they caught wind of her latest escapade. She could see the headline now . . .

BLOND BOMBSHELL
FLAT BUSTED

Scratch that. *Buzz* had gone that route once before, when they ran a story about her breast implants. Of course, she didn't have breast implants; every speck of her body was 100 percent natural, but a ravenous public would devour any bit of gossip, and word that she'd had double-D saline bags stitched inside her double-A boobs had set tongues a wagging.

They'd even printed trumped up BEFORE and AFTER pictures of her decked out in a clinging and very revealing gold Versace gown. What a sight she had been. Her phone had rung for weeks after because her so-called friends with their inquiring minds just *had* to know the truth.

This time, if *Buzz* knew where she'd run off to, they might be able to get photos of her scrubbing urinals. Ah, now there was a headline . . .

BLOND BOMBSHELL
WITHOUT A POT TO PEE IN

Oddly enough, being flat busted and without a pot to pee in didn't feel all that bad. It felt rather liberating, like starting life all over again.

Maybe she could do it better this time around.

Then, again, maybe she should put pedal to the metal, drive right on out of Plentiful and never come back. Everyone in town believed she was Autumn Leeves, a blackhaired kindergarten teacher from California, and they just might tar and feather

her if they learned the truth.

Skipping out on her debts would be easy and possibly life-saving, because no one could ever track her down. But she'd skipped out of one life already. She wasn't going to skip out on this one, too. Besides, an old and troubled doctor needed her.

As the wind blowing through the open windows tossed her beehive about, Juliet pictured the man she'd soon be meeting. A widower, no doubt, somewhere in his mid to late seventies, with a shock of white hair, a lined yet kindly face, and a spine that was tired and bowed from fifty years of bending over patients, listening to their hearts, treating their wounds, and consoling them in times of grief.

The Sleuths never said why he needed a housekeeper, but Juliet guessed that the good doctor's wife had died sometime within the past year, he was weary of his own cooking, and since the little lady was no longer around, needed someone to pick up his medical texts, the Robin Cook and Michael Crichton novels he devoured, and the Sunday *Times* with the crossword puzzle only half completed.

Doc Sheridan was looking for a little companionship, a friendly word here and there, and someone to send him off to bed when his snoring got so loud the pictures on the living room walls began to shimmy.

Working for Doc Sheridan a few hours a day — until all her debts could be paid off — would be a piece of cake, and it would also give her a much-needed place to sleep.

Twenty miles from town and only half an hour late for her interview, Juliet spotted Snowbird Lane and turned into the aspen- and evergreen-lined gravel drive that wound its way toward the base of the still snowcapped Tetons. Doc Sheridan, Mildred had told her, would be waiting outside by the paddock — leaning on his cane, Juliet imagined, eyes nearly hidden behind Coke bottle–thick glasses, an arthritic cocker spaniel beside him, both of them eagerly anticipating her arrival.

Zipping up the lane, dust flying behind her, she had the sense that she was driving through heaven. An Appaloosa, a roan, and two dappled grays with black silky manes grazed in the pasture to the south of the drive. Beyond the aspens, nearly hidden in a stand of pine, were llamas of varying colors and sizes, with two black-and-white pygmy goats frolicking around them. And if she wasn't mistaken, she saw a couple of woolly buffalo beside a pond, standing solemn guard on their small patch of land.

To the north was another pasture where a three-legged elk and a swaybacked white mare with barely any meat covering her ribs stood near the white rail fencing and watched Juliet drive by.

At last, the brick-faced ranch-style home Mildred had described came into view. Old and sprawling, it was surrounded by over-grown flower beds in desperate need of a gardener. A three-car garage sat at the far end of the house, separated by a breezeway dotted with big clay pots that had scraggly red and white geraniums spilling over the sides.

Was the doctor in dire financial straits? Too poor to hire a gardener? Or was he de-pressed and lonely, a man who'd lost in-terest in something that had once been his pride and joy?

Could she possibly help him?

The entry door opened as she neared the front of the house, and three massive dogs burst from inside, long legs kicking up grass and gravel, barking madly as they ran toward the Mustang. Juliet slammed on the brakes and stared through the open window at the Great Danes, two of them solid black, one white with black patches. They stood guard, pointed ears perked, tails motionless instead of doing a friendly wag, daring her to set foot out of her vehicle.

Where was the half-blind cocker spaniel?

Where was the kindly old doctor who set Lillian's heart aflutter?

Another figure stepped out of the house. No cane. No hunched spine. No shock of white hair.

And the face was anything but kind. In fact, the man wore an unquestionably smug grin on his undeniably gorgeous — and familiar — face.

What was *he* doing here?

Juliet killed the engine and the dogs stopped their incessant barking. All was silent except for the babble of water in a brook and unseen birds chirping in the aspen trees, until Cole's shrill whistle rent the air. Without hesitation, the Danes bounded to Cole's side. Their tails wagged as they looked up at the man, obediently waiting for his next order. But Cole didn't say a word. Instead, he strolled toward the Mustang, gravel crunching beneath his boots, with three powerful sentries marching at his side.

Blowing a big pink bubble, Juliet tilted her sunglasses to catch a better look at Cole over the top. A white polo shirt stretched across a deeply bronzed upper body built to bench-press fillies — equine or human. Faded blue jeans slung low on his hips and stacked over dun-colored cowhide boots. Sun sparkled in his sandy blond hair.

He'd cleaned up nicely. Too nicely, and she had the wildly incredible feeling he once again had something other than offering a polite hello and handshake on his mind.

She sucked the bubble back between her lips and leaned her forearm on the open window. "If you're thinking about kissing me again, now that you no longer appear in an all-fired hurry to get somewhere," she said bravely, "you'd better readjust your thinking."

He stopped not much more than a yard from her car and folded his arms across his chest. "You mean you didn't come out here to work off a little more of your debt?"

"I considered that paid in full the second you drove off without saying good-bye."

"I was in a hurry, or I would have stayed longer." An off-kilter grin tilted his lips. "I might have kissed you longer, too."

"Then it's a good thing you had to rush off, or I might have had to slap you for taking liberties without my permission."

"If I remember correctly, you seemed to enjoy it."

"Obviously I was suffering from heat-stroke." She smiled wryly, not about to let him know his kiss had nearly knocked her off her Jimmy Choos. "The temperature's cooled down since that regrettable incident at Joe's Gas and Bait, and I'm thinking much more clearly."

"I take it that means you wouldn't enjoy my kiss as much the second time around?"

"We'll never know, will we?"

He shrugged slightly. "That remains to be seen."

He swept a twig up from the gravel drive and tossed it into the corral, muscles flexing in his shoulders and arms. The dogs dashed after the stick, slipped under the bottom rail on the fence and tore through the grass in search of their quarry.

Cole leaned casually against the driver's door of the Mustang and watched the Danes play keep-away with their newfound toy, pretty much ignoring the fact that she was still seated in the car and he was blocking her exit and most of her view.

She stared at the round-headed rivets that studded his jeans, at the W stitched on the pockets, at the back of a perfectly formed behind resting just inches from her fingers.

"So," he said offhandedly, as if speaking to the wind, "did you come out here for a reason?"

Still studying the intricacies of Cole's tush, she managed to utter, "To see Doctor Sheridan."

Cole turned and she took in the entire slow-motion view. His jeans buttoned up the front instead of zipped. He wore a bronze buckle with the bust of a mighty elk etched in the metal. She tried not to stare, but he was so close, so big, that not staring was an impossibility.

Resting his hands on the windowsill, he leaned down and peered at her through the opening. His furrowed brow was nearly hidden behind the dark blond hair that tumbled over his forehead. Steel blue eyes roamed over her pink sunglasses, her passionate pink lips, and the cleavage not completely covered by her stretchy lace top.

His gaze once again settled on her eyes. "You're not Autumn Leeves, are you?"

"I'd be lying if I said I was someone else." She craned her neck to look past Cole, hoping the lonely old doctor she'd come to visit would show up soon, before temptation made her do something foolish.

"Looking for someone?" Cole asked.

"Doc Sheridan."

"I see."

She was seeing quite a lot, too. The deep tan of his skin, a tiny scar just over his right eyebrow, dimples on either side of his mouth.

The man was too gorgeous for words.

She struggled for something halfway intelligent to say. "So . . . do you work for the doctor?"

"You could say that."

Avoiding his irresistible grin, she peeked around him again and took stock of the enormity of the house and the garage, as well as the charm hidden behind overgrown shrubs and trees. "He's got a nice place."

"Yeah, he does."

Her gaze swept over the corrals, the myriad animals, and the assortment of wooden birdhouses hanging in the aspens and pines. "He must like animals."

"Uh-huh."

Looking back at Cole, she couldn't miss the way his long, strong fingers stroked the regal head of the white-and-black Dane that had pranced back to his side, or the way his blue eyes twinkled in the last of the fading sun. "You like animals, too?"

"Uh-huh."

He had a lot of nice qualities, ones she never would have expected when they'd met out on the highway, but — unfortunately — she hadn't come here to see Cole.

"Would you by any chance know if the doctor's here? We have an appointment."

Cole looked at his watch. "The doc was expecting you half an hour ago."

"Yes, well, I had a little trouble getting out of town."

His eyebrow rose. "Car break down again?"

"In a manner of speaking." Juliet shifted her Dubble Bubble from one side of her mouth to the other. "I had the misfortune of running out of gas." Plus the tough job of convincing Joe to put a can of gas on her already hefty tab. "And before you suggest I take a course in how to read gas gauges, this incident wasn't my fault."

"No?"

"No. It just so happens the gauge has gone on the fritz. And to make a long and exceedingly boring story short, I had to walk back into town, which isn't all that easy to do on scalding hot pavement when you're wearing four-inch Jimmy Choos, and then I had to lug the gas can all the way back to my car and, well I've finally arrived. I'll apologize to the doctor when I see him. So" — again Juliet looked past Cole toward the house — "is he here?"

"He's around."

"And he'll be here shortly?"

"More than likely."

Cole crouched down next to Juliet's window. Two Great Danes now flanked his right side; one flanked his left. "I had the feeling you were just passing through town," he said, "but rumor has it you took a bartender job at the Misty Moon."

"That's another long story."

"I'm no longer in a hurry." His voice was deep, mesmerizing, and she found herself wanting to . . . to kiss him again. Of course, the last thing she needed was more trouble in her life.

"I seem to have misplaced my wallet," she said, opting for words instead of kisses, "which leaves me totally broke, and I'm not about to call anyone to bail me out because, well, just because. So Molly gave me a job working as a bartender tonight, and tomorrow night to pay her for all the food I ate before I realized I had no money."

"No money? No credit cards?" His eyes narrowed. "How'd you manage to pay Joe for the car repairs?"

"I promised to beautify the gas station — you know, plant a few flowers, paint the walls."

Cole shook his head and chuckled. "You get in this much trouble everywhere you go?"

"Of course not. It's just been one of those days."

"You think this string of bad luck is over?"

With all the lies she'd told, she doubted it. "I hope so."

"But you're not sure?"

"The only thing I'm sure of is the fact that I need a place to sleep until I can afford a motel room, and I was told Doc Sheridan was offering —"

"You're going to sleep with Doc Sheridan?"

She ignored Cole's shameless interruption and shot a quick look at the outside of the doctor's homey yet unkempt house. "I'm going to weed his flower beds, finish the walk leading up to his house before someone trips over a brick and flies into the door, and —"

"Can you cook?"

"Of course I can." She'd watched her dad and her personal chef do it for years.

"Give me five pounds of potatoes, a couple of Vidalia onions, and a jar of mayonnaise and I'll whip up the best potato salad you ever tasted. I can impale wieners on a stick and roast them over an open fire, and when I was in fifth grade my sugar cookies took first prize in my Girl Scout troop's holiday bake-off." Her dad had, of course, done the baking. "But shouldn't I be telling all of this to Doc Sheridan? Or" — she frowned — "did he send you out here to check me out? To make sure I'm not a flake or a thief or too old and crotchety to take care of him?"

"In a manner of speaking."

"You're not big on giving definitive answers, are you?"

"You want a definitive answer?"

"Of course I do, to any and all questions."

"All right then, before you waste any more time here, let me just tell you that the doc is looking for a more mature, grandmotherly type . . . housekeeper."

"Don't you think Doc Sheridan should be telling me what he wants and what he doesn't want?"

"Yeah."

"Then, if you don't mind" — she adjusted the rearview mirror again and peeked at her lipstick and hair — "could you tell him I'm here?"

"He already knows."

Juliet turned slowly, once more greeted by Cole's smug expression. "So why hasn't he come out to meet me?"

"He has."

Juliet crooked her neck to peer around Cole. There wasn't a soul in sight except — Her eyes narrowed. She jerked her head back toward Cole. "Please don't tell me *you're* Doc Sheridan?"

"Who did you think I was?"

"I don't know. Cole Somebody. The hired help. A stableboy, maybe."

"No, just Doc Sheridan."

Annoyance seethed inside her. "I can't believe you let me go on and on about staying here with the doctor, and cooking for the doctor, and taking care of the doctor without telling me that *you're* the doctor."

"You'd already assumed I was a ranch hand, just like you'd assumed earlier today that I was Hannibal Lecter —"

"Ted Bundy."

"Whatever, but" — his smartassed grin returned — "as much as you want to sleep with me —"

"I *don't* want to sleep with you, I want to

132

sleep in your bed." She seethed over her poor choice of words. "Damn it, I want to sleep in one of your *extra* beds."

"Doesn't matter what you want. You're all wrong for the job."

"Mind telling me why?"

"Because you get into trouble at the drop of a hat."

"You know nothing about me, and the problems I've had today have been nothing more than unfortunate and one-time-only occurrences."

"All right, then. You say you can cook but for some peculiar reason, I don't think you can."

"Try me."

"I would, but whether you can cook or not doesn't concern me as much as your inability to be punctual."

"I ran out of gas, for heaven's sake."

"Okay, so you're a lousy planner, which, I'm sorry to say, makes you a lousy house-keeper candidate."

"You're just looking for excuses because . . . because you're afraid if you hire me you might want to kiss me again."

He gripped the edge of the open window and leaned close, so close she could almost feel the heat of his smoldering blue eyes. "I'm not the least bit afraid of you, *or* of kissing you. In fact, if I wanted to, I'd kiss you right this moment, but I've got more important things on my mind like hiring a housekeeper — and like I said before, you're not what I'm looking for."

He shoved away from the car, turned his back, and stalked toward the house, the dogs strutting at his side.

If he thought he could walk away from her again without saying good-bye or thanks for coming or anything remotely polite, he had another think coming.

Throwing open the car door, Juliet marched after Cole, the heels of her Jimmy Choos sinking in the gravel. "Could you please slow down a bit?"

He stopped at the door. The muscles in his back bunched. He tilted his head and looked at her over his shoulder. "You still here?"

"Yes, and I'm not leaving." She slipped off her stilettos and hobbled through the gravel on bare feet. "I came here to get a job —"

"You came here to get a bed to sleep in."

"All right, so my motives might be a little skewed, but I'm willing to work for the right to sleep in that bed." She swept a crushed box of orange Jell-O off of the unfinished brick walkway. "And from the looks of things around here, you're in desperate need of someone to work for you."

"Yeah, I am. But not you."

God, the man was maddening.

"Look, Cole, you may think you don't want me, but I can cook. I've got a green thumb. And the way I see it, if I'm good enough to kiss, I'm good enough to clean your toilets."

She swept a Barbie-doll head out of a pile of dirt and stared at it. She rolled it around in the palm of her hand. She frowned as her gaze rose to meet Cole's blue-eyed glare. "You wouldn't by any chance be a pediatrician, would you?"

He shook his head. "A veterinarian."

Juliet blew a quick pink bubble as she tried to size up the situation. "You have children of your own?"

He sighed heavily, as if he'd wanted to hide the fact. "Yeah, I've got a few kids."

The talk in the bar about her loving children and the doc loving children was finally making sense.

"Let me see if I've got this right. You need a baby-sitter, not a housekeeper?"

Cole shoved open the front door and the Danes pranced inside. "I need a nanny-*slash*-housekeeper."

"What about your wife?"

"If I was married, I wouldn't have kissed you."

Cole marched into the house. Juliet quickly slipped her stilettos back on and followed, listening to his bootheels and the narrow tips of her heels thud and click on the redbrick entry floor.

"So, are you divorced?" Juliet asked, catching up with Cole and checking out his comfy yet masculine black leather furniture, sinking into the plush silvery blue carpeting, as they made their way into a big country kitchen.

"No."

"Widowed?"

"No."

"Are you going to explain, or do you plan on uttering no to all of my questions?"

He pulled open the refrigerator door, grabbed two bottles of beer, and set them on the smoky blue granite counter. "They're my sister's." He popped the lids off of both bottles, handed Juliet one and leaned against the white oak cabinets. "I've had custody since she died six months ago."

"I'm sorry."

"Yeah, me too." Cole took a long sip of the icy cold beer. "She was too young to

136

die and I wasn't ready to be a dad, but I'm managing."

"There was no one else to help you?"

"Let's just say I was the only one ready, willing, and able to do it at the time."

He didn't sound angry. Annoyed, maybe. Or disappointed that no one else had cared enough to step up to the plate and lend a hand. She wanted to ask him more, but right now she had to work on getting Cole to hire her.

Juliet wandered around his kitchen, with Cole watching her every move as she checked out the jelly fingerprints on an old oak kitchen table that looked as if a thousand children had banged forks and spoons on top, and the Crayola drawings stuck to the refrigerator. "Cute pictures."

Cole chuckled lightly. "You should see the mural on the living room wall."

She turned in time to catch his smile. "I take it the mural wasn't part of the room's original decorating scheme?"

He shrugged. "I used to like stark white walls. Now I'm into pastels." His gaze roamed from her Jimmy Choos to the sunglasses stuck on the top of her head. "If I'm not mistaken, you do, too. Particularly pink."

"You're very observant."

"I do my best."

Juliet had the feeling Cole did his best at everything, and she tried not to think about what he was best at. Instead, she took a sip of beer and worked her way around the kitchen.

While Cole watched her, she studied the framed and titled To-Do list mounted over a built-in desk cluttered with a computer and endless stacks of paper. "Interesting list, but I take it you're not yet forty-two?"

"Thirty-four. Why?"

She traced a finger across one of the boldly typed lines. "It says right here that you'll start raising a family at forty-two." It also said he'd get married at forty, and she wondered if he'd hold out that long, now that he had children.

Juliet heard his boots behind her. Felt his body when it pressed lightly against her back as he peered over her shoulder. From the corner of her eye, she saw the smoothness of his freshly shaved cheek — and inhaled the spiciness of his aftershave.

"I've been too busy to revise it," he explained, "but those had been my goals once upon a time."

She turned, resting her hip against his desk. One of her knees accidentally brushed against his inner thigh, sending a ripple of heat to every sensitive point on her body, and places in between.

Working for Cole could be dangerous. Still, she wanted to take a chance.

After all, it was for only a couple of days.

"I gather the kids take up a lot of your time?" she asked, again concentrating on his children, in spite of the fact that her knee was still touching his leg.

"*Most* of my time, especially when they don't have a nanny."

"Do you resent it?"

"I resent the fact that I've had to put some of my dreams on hold. I resent the fact that I've hired and fired — or lost — thirteen nannies in the past six months. But I don't resent having the girls in my life."

Her eyes narrowed in astonishment. "You've had thirteen nannies?"

"Number thirteen quit this morning, right before I stopped on the highway to give you a hand."

"Are you that difficult to work for?" she teased.

"I've got rules and regulations that no one wants to follow. I believe in punctuality. Dependability."

"So you've said."

"I need a nanny who's strict but understanding. Someone calm and . . . *grand-motherly*." He took another swallow of beer. "I hate to break this to you, Autumn, but you're not exactly the grandmotherly type."

She was going to rot in hell for saying this, but . . . "I may not be old and gray, but I *am* a kindergarten teacher. I take care of children all day long, nine months out of the year."

"Yeah, but mine can be little hellions. That's why they're staying with my assistant tonight. That's part of the reason why I've had thirteen nannies. And that's part of the reason Mildred thought it might be a good idea for you to come here under false pretenses."

"If you're trying to frighten me into leaving, I should let you know that I don't scare off easily."

"Unless you think you're about to be accosted by Ted Bundy."

"That was an entirely different situation."

She skirted around him and crossed the room. She set her bottle of beer on the countertop. "Look, Cole, I can understand you wanting a grandmotherly nanny." She plugged the sink, turned on the hot water, and squirted a healthy amount of blue detergent inside, as if she did menial labor every day of the week. "I can understand you not wanting to hire me when you know absolutely nothing about me other than the fact that I'm a teacher." She turned to face him, hoping the lie didn't show in her face. "But if you don't give me this job and a place to sleep, I may end up spending the next couple of nights in my car."

"It's summertime." He grinned lightly. "At least you won't freeze."

"Damn it, Cole. You need me as much as I need you, and believe you me, this isn't anything permanent."

"I need permanent. I'm tired of having a nanny a day here and a day there."

"Well, right now you don't have anyone unless you hire me. So give me the job *and* a place to sleep until I can pay off my debts, and as soon as you can find a nanny who fits all your requirements, I'll get out of your hair."

He studied her eyes. She studied his. He was just as unsure of hiring her as she was determined to get the job.

Reaching around her, Cole turned off the water. They stood much too close and she knew that staying under his roof was going to be one whopping big mistake.

"You're sure?" he asked.

"Positive."

"Don't you want to know something about the girls first?"

"I already told you I'd take the job no matter what, but sure. How old are they?"

His grin returned. "Six, five and almost two. All girls."

Three? And one was only two which sounded like an ominous prospect. "Tell me more about the two-year-old. Is she potty trained?"

"No."

She swallowed uncomfortably. "All right, I'll have to work on that."

"Others have tried."

Juliet twisted around, trying to hide the discomfort that had to be radiating in her eyes, and sank a few dirty glasses and bowls into the soapy water. "How hard could it be to potty train one little girl?"

"I never said there was just *one* little girl."

Not good. She rinsed the glass and turned it upside-down in the drainer. "Twins?"

Cole leaned against the cabinet, and she could see him shaking his head far too slowly.

"Three?" Her voice cracked.

"Chloe, Caitlin, and Carly." His eyes twinkled. "My sister's artificial insemination went a little better than expected."

Juliet blew a fat pink bubble and sucked it back between her lips. She had no idea how to handle children, but she didn't see that as her biggest problem. Handling Cole, and her overwhelming desire to kiss him again and feel his touch, was her immediate concern.

And then there was the fact that she desperately needed a bed to sleep in — all by herself.

"If you think I'm going to back away from my generous offer to take care of your girls, just because they're . . . hellions, you're wrong."

"I can be hell to live with, too."

"I'd assumed that the moment I met you, but I know how to deal with hellish men."

"How?"

How, indeed, could she deal with a man like Cole? She could easily give in to her feelings, but she wasn't going to be here long and she didn't believe in quickies with anyone, let alone men with five children.

Grabbing a towel that had been tossed haphazardly on the countertop, Juliet dried her hands, and kept on drying them until she had an answer.

"There's a lock on the nanny's bedroom door, isn't there?"

Cole chuckled as he nodded his head. "There's a private entrance, a private bathroom, and a lock I installed when Nanny #7 came to stay for all of three days."

"Good." She tossed the towel back on the counter. "Just give me all the keys so I can lock out unwanted intruders, and I'm sure we'll get along perfectly fine."

Chapter 8

Juliet shifted from one pained and tired foot to another, her peach-blossom pink Ferragamo sling-back stilettos a tad too precarious for standing behind the bar and waiting tables for close to five hours.

The Misty Moon had buzzed with activity until nearly one A.M., but for the past hour it had been quiet, empty except for herself and the bald-headed guy with the scar slashed across his face who'd sat at the end of the bar most of the evening nursing a whiskey on the rocks and now nursing coffee. Even Molly had gone home, far too easily entrusting the keys to Juliet, when this was her first night on the job, telling her to lock up at the stroke of two.

She'd been given three different jobs today, all without anyone asking for I.D. or a résumé. She'd never known people so trusting, or so brutally honest, and it was nice to feel as if she fit right in. Of course, fitting in at Cole Sheridan's place might not be as easy, she thought, wiping the inside of a martini glass she'd just washed.

God, what had she gotten herself into? She'd never changed a diaper. Hadn't prepared a meal in twenty-some-odd years. But damn it all, Cole didn't think she had what it took to be a housekeeper *or* a babysitter, and that made her all the more determined to prove to him, and herself, that she'd been born to change a diaper with one hand while gripping a frying pan in the other.

Taking care of little girls and preparing meals, however, was a far cry from living under the same roof with a virtual stranger, especially a good-looking virtual stranger who had brought back feelings in her that she'd thought would never return.

For the first time in a very long time, she found herself wanting to touch a man, wanting to be held by a man, wanting to crawl into a man's bed and feel the weight of him stretched over her.

But not just any man — just Cole Sheridan. He intrigued her; he excited her.

And then, of course, he'd kissed her.

Her muscles tightened as she remembered the faint scents of amber and clove emanating from his body, the feel of silky hair and warm lips and a broad hand pressed against the small of her back, tugging her toward him, holding her tightly, while steel blue eyes pierced through her resistance.

Even now, thinking about that kiss while washing dishes and crunching peanut shells beneath her shoes, heat slithered through her body, settling deep in the pit of her stomach, and lower still.

Juliet squeezed the towel in her hands, willing herself to think of anything but Cole's kiss. Willing herself to keep from wanting another, because as much as she wanted to touch Cole, as much as she wanted Cole to touch her, she had to keep him at arm's length — because she was living a lie.

If they got too close — not that that would happen, but it could — she'd have to tell him the truth, and then he'd despise her, the same way she'd despised Garrett when she learned about his deceit.

She could never hurt someone in the same way she'd been hurt.

Sighing heavily, she positioned the martini glass on the shelving behind the bar, making sure it was perfectly aligned with all of the other glasses, then grabbed the pot of coffee and refilled the scar-faced man's midnight blue mug.

"Long day?" he asked, lifting the steaming cup to his lips and slugging down a hefty swallow of the blistering hot brew, as if it were nothing more than a sip of cool water.

"Very long day." Juliet dumped the cigarette butts out of his ashtray and wiped it clean. "How about you?"

"Every day's a long day, but I'm not complaining."

He tapped a cigarette out of the pack of Marlboros sitting beside his coffee cup and pulled a silver lighter from the breast pocket of his black polo shirt. Moments later, smoke curled out of his nostrils.

"Not that it's any of my business," Juliet said, drying a margarita glass and putting it away, "but those things are going to kill you."

"Yeah," he said, shrugging as he took another drag, "but it tastes damn good and no matter how much I want to shake the habit, I can't seem to give it up."

Kind of like an ex-husband she'd once had. Out of eight years of marriage, two had been good — at least she thought they'd been good; six had been miserable, yet she'd put up with Garrett because —

she laughed to herself — she'd thought she'd been in love.

"You been tending bar long?" Scarface asked, his cigarette poised near his lips, ready to swallow another deadly gulp of smoke.

"A while." Sometimes noncommittal answers were the best when speaking to someone you didn't know.

Grabbing a clean towel, Juliet swirled it over the copper-topped bar, rubbing away all the water spots. "Are you a professional photographer, or a tourist with really good camera equipment?"

"Professional."

She flicked a peanut shell onto the floor. "Are you working on something particular right now?"

"A photo shoot for *National Geographic*, traveling from small town to small town, taking candid shots of people from all walks of life."

"Get anything interesting today?"

"A few shots I think I'll like; my editor might not be quite as impressed."

Juliet laughed lightly, knowing that feeling all too well. "You have different ideas about the tone of the piece?"

"She wants the edgy stuff, but I've had my fill of that over the years."

"Sounds like you're ready for a change."

He smashed the butt of his cigarette in the ashtray. "The job and my editor are kind of like this other bad habit of mine. Too hard to give up."

Reaching across the bar, he held out a hand. "I'm Ben Monroe."

Juliet tossed the towel over her shoulder. "Autumn Leeves," she said as easily as if it were her real name, and shook his hand.

"Nice to meet you." He shoved out of his barstool, slapped a twenty on the bar, and headed for the swinging doors. "See you tomorrow . . . maybe."

He was nicer than she'd imagined earlier today. This time he hadn't sent a shiver of dread up her spine, he'd merely made her want to know more about him. He was troubled, but not one to bare his soul. Of course she didn't bare her soul to anyone either. At least she hadn't in the past.

But she was starting all over again. Anything was possible.

Juliet glanced at the clock. The big hand had just clicked past twelve; the little hand rested over the two. She wasted no time locking the doors, wiping down the bar, sweeping the floor, and giving the bathrooms the dreaded once-over. At quarter after, she grabbed her tote from under the bar, flipped off all but the neon lights that Molly told her to leave on overnight, and headed for the back door.

The ring of the telephone stopped her.

Juliet yawned. Ignore it, she told herself, then dutifully headed back to the bar and picked up the phone.

"Misty Moon," she answered, only to be met with silence. Too damn much silence. And then the breathing.

She gripped the edge of the bar, the copper cold beneath her warm, nervous fingers, and waited for what she was sure would come next.

Laughter peeled through the phone. A mocking chuckle vibrated in her ear, loud and oppressive, like a demonized mannequin in a B-rated horror flick.

The cackle went on and on. No words this time. No whispered threat. Just Garrett's unbearable laugh.

"Damn it, Garrett. Leave me alone."

Silence again. Unbearable silence.

"Please, Garrett." Juliet sighed. "Don't do this to me."

The dial tone rang in her ear. Only then did she tremble, putting the phone down and slumping against the edge of the bar.

She'd thought she could run away. Thought she could hide from everything that had been making her life miserable, but obviously she'd been wrong.

Her life had caught up with her even here in the seemingly magical town of Plentiful — and so had Garrett.

Nicole sat cross-legged atop the red satin sheets on Juliet's custom-made king-sized bed. She sipped some of Juliet's best Dom Perignon out of a fine eighteenth-century crystal champagne glass, part of Juliet's extravagant and priceless collection of antique stemware.

Juliet had so much. Far too much.

"All of this should have been mine," Nicole whispered to herself. "The house, the bed, the wine cellar. Garrett, too. Especially Garrett."

Nicole stretched a hand toward the tape recorder and punched the Rewind button, listening to the long, drawn-out whir and finally the click when the tape stopped at the very beginning. She pressed the Play button, and when Garrett's insidious laughter echoed through Juliet's bedroom, she smiled with deep satisfaction.

Who would have thought three years ago when she'd begun secretly taping Juliet's friends, acquaintances, and even her soon-to-be ex-husband, that she'd be able to put the recordings to such good use.

Obviously it paid to be prepared for anything and everything.

Obviously it also paid to have Ben on her side, taking photos of Juliet, tracing her footsteps, keeping track of where she was at all times, even getting phone numbers so the woman he loved could have her fun.

It was amazing what a person would do in the name of love.

Nicole thumbed through the box where she kept all of her Garrett Pierce recordings. Once upon a time she'd bugged his homes, his phones, even his hotel rooms. She'd taped business meetings, casual luncheon conversations, and intimate pillow talk with the bimbos he'd trifled with. Garrett had thought no one was listening; he'd been wrong.

She'd even taped Garrett in the courtroom the day his guilty verdict was read. He'd been so calm, so quiet, until Juliet looked at him with those sorrow-filled eyes, crushed that he could deceive others as despicably as he'd deceived her.

He'd yelled at her across the courtroom. He'd called her an ungrateful bitch. That's when he said he'd get even — and Nicole had every juicy word on tape.

How funny it was that Garrett thought

his ex-wife had turned him into the feds. Spurned lovers, he should have known, could be far more vindictive than spurned wives.

Put-upon assistants could be vindictive, too.

For six months now she'd been playing little bits and pieces of the Garrett tapes for Juliet's listening pleasure. Sometimes she strung words from one conversation together with words from another to create exactly the right phrase she needed to drive Juliet out of her mind.

Before tonight, the calls had made Juliet angry, but she'd pushed them aside as just another lousy part of Garrett's true character. Tonight, however, there had been fear in Juliet's voice.

Nicole smiled. She was one step closer to ruining Juliet Bridger. And in the next few days, as soon as Juliet got wind of the newest bit of gossip in *Buzz*, the screws would grind a little more deeply into Juliet's hide.

Chapter 9

Cole poked his head into the examining room where Chuck Shayne, the semi-retired vet who helped him out when an animal needed twenty-four-hour care, slouched in an easy chair flipping through the pages of the *Sports Illustrated* swimsuit issue.

"How's it going?" Cole asked, leaning against the doorjamb.

Chuck peered over the top of the magazine, then looked at his watch. "It's two-thirty in the morning. What are you doing up?"

"House is too quiet to sleep. Figured I'd check on the Newf."

Chuck's gaze shot back to the magazine's centerfold. "She's sleeping soundly for a change so whatever you do, don't wake her."

Leaving Chuck to his daydreams about sexy women who were a good fifty years younger than him, Cole headed down the hall and quietly entered the back room where a giant black Newfoundland was sprawled on the cool linoleum floor.

Cole crouched down beside the dog, smoothing a palm over her once thick black fur. It should have been long and silky but was matted in stringy clumps. Beneath his hand, in spite of round-the-clock care, Cole still felt the erratic beat of the dog's heart, its labored breathing, and its skeletal frame.

Three days ago the Newf had been brought into the clinic, its nearly lifeless body dehydrated, malnourished, and completely neglected by a drugged-up malcontent the police had arrested for vagrancy and theft.

Inside, Cole seethed with anger over the abuse. If he could get his hands on the dog's *former* owner, he'd string him up by his balls and let him go without food and water for a few days to see how it felt.

He'd wanted to do something equally as degrading and painful to the foster mother who'd, quote-unquote, cared for Holly for three months before Claire adopted her. She'd smacked the two-year-old if she cried. Smacked her for taking off her diaper when it became too soiled to wear. Smacked her for any infraction, big or small.

Before Claire died she had worked wonders with Holly; and since then, Cole had done his best to make the little girl believe she'd never be hurt again. But Nanny #13 could have easily driven the child back into her fear-filled cocoon when she talked about hitting her with a switch from a tree.

Damn, but he'd made a mistake when he'd hired that woman. He plowed his fingers through his hair. God help him if he'd made another mistake hiring Autumn Leeves.

A kindergarten teacher? Cole chuckled and the Newf opened her sad black eyes, peering cautiously up at him. "It's okay, girl. Go back to sleep."

She closed her eyes again and Cole stroked the top of her head, his mind wandering again to the bubble blower with the killer body who'd be spending tonight, and a lot of other nights, under his roof. As hard as he tried, he couldn't picture her sitting in a room full of five-year-olds singing "Itsy Bitsy Spider." He could, however, picture her doing a slow, mind-boggling and heart-thumping striptease.

The closest he'd ever come to having a teacher who looked like Autumn Leeves was Mrs. Brach, his seventh-grade swim coach. Mrs. Brach had had a face like a mule, right down to her protruding front teeth, but she'd had a body every twelve-year-old boy in school fantasized about when he went to bed. Long legs, nice ass, big breasts, and hard nipples that nearly poked right through the yellow one-piece tank suit she always wore.

Autumn Leeves had breasts he itched to touch and a sweet derrière. She had far nicer and far more enticing curves than anything Mrs. Brach had had.

No man in his right mind could have a woman like that in his house day in and day out and not want to strip her naked and crawl between her thighs. But, hell, he'd hired her to take care of the girls, not to take care of him.

Or had he? He knew literally nothing about her. Hadn't bothered with getting references and took her on in spite of her punctuality and dependability problems.

Hell, she'd mesmerized him.

He'd never been so gullible in his life.

If he didn't watch his step, he could end up in trouble.

When the Newf was breathing easier, Cole checked the IV taped to her leg, pushed himself up off the floor, and went out the back door into the cool night air.

It was quarter till three when he strolled

up the drive. The three-legged bull elk he'd been taking care of since it tried to outrun a semi stood in the moonlight and glared at him. They had a love-hate relationship like a lot of the animals he treated, and he had the scars to prove it.

But being a vet was the only job he'd ever really wanted.

Becoming a dad had never been a priority for him. It was only something he had on his list of things to do by the time he turned forty-two. But now, when he turned forty-two, he'd have a daughter in high school.

Amazing how things changed.

Gravel crunched beneath his feet as he strolled along. The night was fairly quiet — and dark . . . except for the light in the living room. He remembered turning off all but the low-wattage light outside the nanny's room. That way Autumn could come in through the side door when she got home from work and not disturb anyone inside.

His breath caught in his lungs when the kitchen light flashed on. Was Autumn back already, or had his parents arrived weeks earlier than scheduled? Would the custody fight begin tomorrow?

Through the pine and aspen that

blocked most of the house from view, he looked for the ancient gray Volvo his parents had driven since the early seventies, but it was nowhere in sight.

His white Suburban was, which meant Raven had returned early with the girls. But why?

He jogged to the house and bolted through the kitchen door. Raven had the refrigerator open wide. She turned at the thud of his boots on the oak-plank floor. A carton of milk was tilted up to her mouth and she took a long swig.

"Everything okay?" he asked, shutting the screen quietly behind him and letting the outside breeze cool the room.

"The girls are sound asleep in bed and everything's fine — for now."

"Did something go wrong?"

Raven licked milk from her upper lip, shoved the carton back into the fridge, and closed the door. "Everyone was sleeping on my mom's living room floor until Holly threw up her pizza, her ice cream, *and* the bright orange gummy worms the guy at Duffy's put on top of her sundae. I've never seen such a mess." Raven's overly annoyed eyes narrowed. "You owe me for that, Doc. Took me a good fifteen minutes to clean it up, and then I had to use almost half a can of Lysol to hide the stink."

"All right, another five cents an hour."

"Twenty."

"Ten."

Raven smiled triumphantly and plucked an apple from the bowl on the kitchen table. "After that, Holly started to cry and I had to rock her and then she wailed about wanting to go home and all the other girls woke up and before you know it —"

"They were all wailing?"

"You've got it. And if Holly throws up again, she's your responsibility."

"She's not running a fever, is she?"

"She just overate. I knew your pizza and ice cream idea sucked." Raven bit into the apple and chewed thoughtfully. "My mom said you should never feed little girls that much crap. She also said she'd send you the bill for the carpet cleaning."

"Did your always-outspoken mom have any other words to send my way?"

"She mentioned something about me deserving an even bigger bonus at the end of the year, and she'd prefer a honey-baked ham for Christmas rather than a turkey. She also said something about a *two*-pound box of Godivas, preferably dark chocolate truffles — no nuts or chews."

"I'll add it to my rapidly growing list of stuff you're trying to extort from me."

"Thanks." Raven leaned against the kitchen counter, ankles crossed. "So, how'd things go with Autumn Leeves? Did she accept your ridiculous housekeeper job?"

"She figured out the truth and, in spite of it, told me she was going to take care of the girls whether I wanted her to or not."

"The lady has balls, huh?"

Cole shrugged, wanting to avoid any discussion of Autumn's anatomy, particularly with his nineteen-year-old receptionist, who'd find some way to blackmail him with his words.

"Okay, so don't comment on the subject, but Joe from Joe's Gas and Bait was getting ice cream at Duffy's when we were there, and he was mouthing off to everyone about Autumn Leeves."

"Anything interesting?"

"He never once mentioned balls, but he did mention knockers." Raven took another bite out of her apple and aimed narrowed eyes at Cole. "Please tell me you didn't let her have the job just because she's got a pair of hooters that could knock your eyes out?"

"I hired her because she wanted the job,

because she's a kindergarten teacher, and loves children."

Raven grinned. "I get the picture, Doc. You hired her 'cause she's got a hot body and now you think you made a mistake."

"I hired her for the girls, not for me, and the only thing you need to concern yourself with is the fact that you no longer have to baby-sit."

"Good, because I've got better things to do than clean up vomit at midnight."

Raven tossed the apple core in the trash, threw open the kitchen door and trounced outside to the Honda Civic parked next to Cole's Suburban. She climbed into her car, slammed the door, and rolled down the window. "You know, Doc, if this new nanny doesn't work out, maybe you should give serious consideration to getting married."

Cole's brow rose. "You proposing?"

Raven's eyes widened. "I'm nineteen. You're thirty-four. God, Doc, that's disgusting."

"And it's not in my game plan, either."

"Yeah, yeah, I know. Age forty. It's on your to-do list."

"Yep, and that's one thing I'm not about to change."

Raven twisted the key in the ignition and

the engine sputtered to a start. "See you in the morning, Doc."

Tucking his hands in his pockets, Cole watched the Honda wind its way up the long gravel drive, one headlight lighting the sky, the other shining down on the ground. He made a mental note to remind Raven to take the car into Joe's Gas and Bait and get it fixed.

Heading back into the house, he flipped off the lights in the kitchen and living room just as he did every night before going to bed and went down the hall to check on the girls.

Karloff was sprawled on the floor between the twin beds where Holly and Jade slept. His ears perked when Cole slipped into the room, and his head jerked to attention, leveling wary eyes on Cole until realizing all was safe. Karloff yawned, tongue curled back in his massive mouth, then tucked his nose back between his front paws and rested with a watchful ear tuned to the girls he protected.

Cole yawned, too. It had been a long day and he had far too much on his mind, like making sure the girls weren't taken from him, like making sure Autumn Leeves did a damn good job taking care of them.

He stood at the end of Jade's bed. In the

dim light from the bedside lamp, he could see the little girls sleeping. Holly was curled into a ball with the covers pulled tight under her neck; Jade sprawled, her comforter pushed to the floor, the top sheet a tangle at the bottom of the bed.

Taking hold of the sheet, Cole pulled it up and laid it lightly over Jade's shoulders. If he hung around for another five minutes, he'd see her kick it once again to the end of the bed. He didn't know why he bothered; it just seemed the right thing to do.

He stepped over Karloff and gently swept a skinny black braid away from Holly's eyes and curled his palm over her brow. It was cool and dry, not a hint of a fever. His foolish plan to get the girls out of the house while he interviewed the prospective "housekeeper" was to blame for Holly being sick.

What on earth had he been thinking?

Holly rolled over in the bed, her fingers clutching the satin edge of her blanket. Her deep brown eyes opened sleepily, and Cole sat on the edge of the bed. "Feeling better?" he asked softly.

"I threw up on Mrs. W's floor and all over me and Jade, and Raven had to give us a bath and the house didn't smell too good and I wanted to come home."

Cole cupped Holly's cheek. "I'm glad. Not that you got sick" — he winked in the dim light, and watched her smile back — "but that you came home. I kind of like having the five of you jump on my bed in the morning to wake me up."

"That nanny who said we should be whipped didn't like us jumping on her bed. She said only bad little girls jump on beds." Holly frowned thoughtfully. "You don't think we're bad little girls, do you?"

"Only when you sneak Squeeze out of her enclosure and scare the nannies. And it's probably not all that nice to put rabbit turd in their food or iced tea, either."

"But you wouldn't hit us for doing that, would you?"

"No, Holly." He slipped his hand around hers and squeezed lightly. "I'd never hit you. But that doesn't mean you can continue doing cruel things to the nannies."

Holly sighed heavily. "Does that mean you're going to get *another* nanny to take care of us?"

"I already have."

"Do I have to like her?"

"You should try."

"I'll think about it."

Cole drew the covers under Holly's chin

and tucked her in good and tight. "Why don't you go back to sleep and dream pleasant dreams."

Again Holly yawned, her little eyes closing at last, a gentle smile touching her mouth. She tucked her hands beneath her cheek, and in only seconds, she was breathing deeply, sound asleep once more.

Cole crept out of the room, leaving Karloff behind to guard the girls through the night, and went to the bedroom where the toddlers slept. Just as Karloff had done, Lugosi and Rathbone raised their heads when he walked in.

Scratching the fur between the dogs' ears, he took a quick peek at the triplets slumbering peacefully in their pint-sized beds, then stole out of the room as quietly as he'd come in.

A sliver of light flashed through the partially opened doorway at the end of the hall, calling to him like a homing signal. Go to your room, Cole told himself, then disregarded his order, preferring to look at the stunning woman he could just barely see on the other side of the door.

Her poofy black hair wasn't as poofy tonight. It was sleek and sexy. Thick tresses brushed over the narrow straps of her tank top and the creamy skin of picture-perfect shoulders. She drew an ankle over her knee and slipped off a pink stiletto, her soft lush breasts nearly tumbling out of the lacy pink bra as she leaned forward.

God, she was beautiful. Close to perfection, as if she'd been airbrushed, or had spent endless amounts of money keeping herself gorgeous.

He took slow, deep breaths as he watched her curl long, slender fingers around the arch of her foot and leisurely rub the bottom, all of her movements sensual, designed by nature to please a man.

Walk away, he told himself. Go to bed, you fool.

But she was a magnet; and he couldn't leave.

He wandered toward the door, his footsteps silent on the thick carpeting, and knocked lightly. "Feet hurt?"

Autumn looked up slowly, her eyes shimmering in the light of the bedside lamp. "I should have ignored glamour for the sake of comfort. But I'm a sucker for pink stilettos."

He was a sucker, too. For her sky-high heels. For her longer than long legs. For a great derrière and fabulous breasts and a face that could have launched a thousand ships.

He proved just what a sucker he was when he slipped into her room without asking permission and pulled the easy chair sitting in the corner up close to her bed. Violet eyes followed his movements as he sat down. Sweet breasts rose and fell as he wrapped his fingers lightly around her calf.

"Your muscles are tight."

"They're rebelling over tonight's workout."

"Maybe I can help."

Through the stretchy black fabric of her capris, he could feel her tense beneath the press of his fingers, but felt himself relax as he hadn't relaxed in months. She was like a soothing balm. He hadn't realized how much he'd needed a woman, craved a woman, until his hands slid down the length of her leg and smoothed over her warm bare skin.

He curled his fingers around her ankle, just above the pink beaded anklet she wore, and drew her foot into his lap, resting it precariously close to a part of his anatomy he fought to keep under control.

Bright eyes flashed up at him through thick dark lashes. "I don't think this is such a good idea."

"Hiring you probably wasn't a good

idea, either, but it's done, your feet hurt, and I'm a doctor. I know how to make things better."

An I-don't-want-to-look-sexy-but-I-can't-help-it smile touched her lips. "In case you haven't noticed, I'm not the kind of patient you usually take care of."

He'd noticed all right. And that was all the more reason for doing what he was doing.

"Same treatment principles apply," he said. "Gentleness. Comfort. A desire to heal."

Her foot was warm beneath his hands. Her eyes were soft. Dreamy. His whole body was crying out to kiss her again, to press her back into the small twin bed and claim every inch of her flesh.

He should have gone to bed, but it was too late now.

Juliet's heart skipped a beat as Cole's blue eyes darkened, as his thumbs swirled over the arch of her foot, burrowed into the taut muscles and soothed the ache she'd known for hours.

It had been a mistake to open her door, a wanton thing to allow even a sliver of light to shine into the hallway when she knew Cole was just inside the girls' rooms, when she knew he'd see it and maybe, just maybe, come into her room to at least say good night.

But she'd wanted someone to talk to after that call from Garrett. She hadn't wanted to be alone.

She'd wanted someone to comfort her.

She'd wanted Cole, as strange as that seemed when they'd met just that morning. And now she had him close, and he was touching her, and taking her mind off of her troubles.

It was a mistake, but a mistake had never felt so damn good.

"Are the girls home?" she asked, knowing they were, but needing to strike up a sensible conversation when what was going on between them was anything but sensible.

His intense gaze burned over her eyes, her nose, her lips, while strong fingers sought out every speck of distressed muscle in her feet and slowly, sensually, kneaded it away.

"Holly's stomach couldn't handle pizza, ice cream, and gummy worms," he said, his voice like warm honey even though his words sounded like something scribbled in a pediatrician's notes.

"Not the best choice of meals for little girls."

171

"Beats the peanut butter and jelly sandwiches I usually feed them."

She might have laughed at their less than sensual discussion if it weren't for the fact that his palms were gliding up her leg and the ball of her foot now rested lightly on the buttons on his jeans.

"What did they eat when your sister was alive?" It was an inane question, words eked out of a mouth that wanted desperately to be kissed, words barely strung together by a brain that could think of nothing but what pulsed behind those buttons.

"Brown rice and tofu."

What was he talking about? *Brown rice and tofu?* Oh, yes. Food his sister had prepared for the girls.

There was a spark of laughter in his eyes, plus deep, dark, I-want-you-now desire when his thumbs wandered to the back of her knees and along the inside of her thigh.

Juliet sucked in a deep breath and fought for intelligent or at least seemingly coherent words. "It sounds like you don't like health food."

"Hate it. Rice cakes. Soy milk."

She hated rice cakes and soy milk, too, but she didn't hate the way his fingers made their unhurried descent back to the ball of her foot.

"How about you?"

"Excuse me?"

A soft grin touched his face. "What do you like to eat?"

"Hot dogs. Big, juicy hot dogs."

Beneath her heel she felt a twitch behind the buttons on his jeans. If she were smart, she'd pull her foot away, but no one had ever massaged her feet this way.

No one had ever made her this needy.

Cole drew her other foot into his lap, scraped the tender flesh over his belt buckle and clasped both feet within the palms of his hands, trapping her against him in a hold she could easily break, if she wanted to.

She didn't.

She leaned back on her elbows and let him perform his magic, forcing herself not to sigh when the arches of her feet pressed against the heavenly bulge between his legs, when his fingers captured her toes and skillfully massaged each one in slow, tantalizing strokes.

"Were you and your sister close?" she asked, watching his Adam's apple rise and fall as he worked.

"As close as two kids could be when one

wanted to save the world and one wanted to own it." He laughed, and she heard the brotherly love and affection deep inside him. Suddenly the enticing strokes of his fingers were those of a caregiver instead of a lover, and she found herself craving both.

"Claire got a kick out of living in a commune," he said, "sleeping in a room with a dozen other kids whose parents were in other rooms sleeping with who-knows-who. I gave myself haircuts, spent my allowance on blue jeans and button-down shirts, and sat on the floor in my little corner of our mattress-on-the-floor room making lists of all the things I would do once I escaped my parents' nonconformist lifestyle."

"Have you accomplished all the things you wanted back then?"

"I wanted to be a vet. I also wanted to be president." He winked. "I've had a change of heart about my second goal."

It was such a treat to hear a man talk about something other than his latest get-rich scheme or the size of the yacht he rarely ever sailed on. When they'd first met she wanted to give Cole a piece of her mind. Now she could spend hours listening to him talk.

"Did you put yourself through school?" she asked.

He shook his head. "My folks did. They might be quirky, they didn't like it when I rebelled, but when all is said and done, they wanted me to be happy."

"Let me guess, your dad's a three-piece-suit banker now and your mom is mayor of some conservative city in west Texas."

Cole's fingers stilled on her feet. "They create bohemian jewelry that's ugly to look at and only the filthy rich can afford. My mom still goes by the name Joplin and practices the Auntie Mame mindset of live life to the fullest — preferably naked. My dad, Jimi — after Hendrix, of course — shaves his head and wears flowing robes, and if you stick around a week or two, you'll get to meet them when they return from their spiritual sojourn in Tibet."

Did she detect bitterness in his voice? "You don't sound too happy about the visit."

"They're coming to take the girls."

Juliet sat up, pulling her feet from his hands and resting them once again on the floor. "Why?"

"They may love their son, but in my mother's words, 'I'm an unenlightened pagan who feasts on blood and wears the

175

hides of poor, defenseless animals.' And God forbid that her grandchildren should be raised by such a heathen."

"Are you going to let them go?"

"When hell freezes over."

Cole shoved out of the chair and crossed to the window. He rested his hands on either side of the jamb and stared out into the dark.

"Holly and Jade were both abandoned as babies, and both of them went through the foster-care system before they were adopted." He turned, leaned against the wall and settled his clouded, nearly discouraged gaze on Juliet. "They've been uprooted more than enough, and I'll be damned if I'll let my folks do it again."

"Don't you have some kind of legal rights since you've cared for them since your sister's death?"

"My sister didn't bother to leave a will, which means my rights are pretty much the same as my parents'."

"You don't think the courts would let your folks take them away from you, do you?"

"If we had a courtroom slug fest, I could argue that I've been taking care of the girls since my sister's death. I could argue that I've grown to love them. On the other hand, my folks could argue that they're wealthy, retired, and don't need to hire a string of housekeepers and nannies to watch the girls."

He crossed the room, standing now in her doorway, big and strong and hurting in a way she'd never seen a man hurt before. "Things could get dirty," he said, and she heard the pain in his voice. "I could bring up their long-ago drug abuse; they could bring up the fact that thirteen nannies have quit on me in the past six months. But if I can" — he drew in a deep breath — "I'm going to keep this out of the courts."

"Is there anything I can do to help?"

He smiled that same kind of smile he'd used on her when he'd not-so-accidentally pressed the bottom of her foot against the buttons on his jeans. "Yeah, but we just met this morning and you might slap me if I told you what."

Little did he know, he could probably ask for anything at this moment, and more than likely she'd give him whatever he wanted . . . and probably more.

"Cole?" she called out, when he took a step out of the room.

He turned slowly, worry taking all of the sparkle out of his eyes. "Don't tell me," he said, with only a hint of laughter, "I forgot to say good night."

Juliet shook her head. "It's not that at all, although I totally detest hasty good-byes." She smiled warmly, hoping he'd see the sincerity in her eyes. "I just wanted you to know that I'll do everything in my power to be a good nanny. I won't let you regret the fact that you hired me."

Ben stood in a cluster of aspen, his night-vision binoculars steadied on a low-hanging branch. A three-legged elk grazed in the moonlit pasture, keeping a wary eye on him from a distance, and a white swayback mare ambled in close and munched on tall grass and wildflowers, her occasional whinny mixing gently with the faint hoot of an unseen owl and the trickle of water in a nearby stream.

No one but the animals knew he was here. No one knew he'd followed Juliet to Doc Sheridan's place. Both times she'd come here he'd been invisible.

No one would know anyone had been watching until . . . until Nicole got his pictures and her stories plastered on the front page of *Buzz*.

Beyond the pasture and across the drive, Ben had watched Cole leave Juliet's room, watched him open two other bedroom doors on that end of the house and peek in on the little girls again, letting the Great Danes out for a break.

His cell phone vibrated on the back of his hip, an unwanted nuisance he couldn't ignore. He grabbed the phone and rested his thumb over the talk button. Nic was at the other end. Beautiful Nic, who was probably lying in Juliet's bed right now planning her revenge.

As always, Nic was thousands of miles away, keeping him at arm's length while he did her dirty work.

His heart beat hard inside his chest. He knew he should push the damned button, but he couldn't. If he answered the phone Nic would want a complete rundown of what had happened since he'd called her earlier, right after he'd walked out of the saloon and told her that Juliet was all alone. She'd want to know how Juliet reacted to the call from Garrett. She'd want to know if there was hurt or fright or anger in Juliet's eyes when she left the saloon.

And then, because it was the middle of the night and because she was lonely, she'd want him to make love to her over the phone, giving her a blow-by-blow description of everything he'd do to her body, if they were together.

But they weren't together. They were never together anymore. He didn't want a long distance relationship. What he wanted was to be with Nic in *his* bed, sliding into her slick, moist heat, tasting her flesh, losing himself in her arms.

He wanted her to talk about *their* relationship.

Not about Juliet.

Not about Garrett, the one person he'd helped destroy without blinking an eye.

He shoved the phone back onto his belt. Tomorrow he'd listen to Nicole's rage, demanding to know why he hadn't answered her call. Tonight, he just wanted to remember what it felt like to fall in love.

When he heard the click of the front door's lock, he swiveled the binoculars from the windows, toward the unfinished brick walk and the man stepping outside, followed by three lumbering Great Danes.

As Cole strolled toward the pasture, Ben zoomed in on his eyes, catching the worry that lurked inside the man . . . and the lust.

The dogs danced around Cole, slowing his movements. He swept a twig up from the drive and tossed it far. The Danes ran fast to retrieve it, brought it back and played tug-of-war with Cole until he skillfully twisted it from the mouth of the white and black giant.

Cole tossed the twig again, but an unseen cat meowed in the dark, and with no more thought given to Cole, the Danes raced toward the creek.

Cole watched them run, their massive paws stirring up dust in the gravel drive. When they disappeared from sight, Cole resumed his walk toward the pasture and stopped at the white wooden fence. He leaned against the top rail, put his fingers to his lips, and whistled just once, and the mare standing not more than ten feet from Ben jerked to attention. Her ears perked. She whinnied, and her warm breath turned to a thin mist in the cool night air.

Sweet grass forgotten, the horse wandered toward Cole's upturned palm and stole a fat red apple.

Cole stroked the beast's mane, her withers, and when the first apple was gone, he produced another from inside the lightweight jacket he wore. The horse wolfed it down while Cole smoothed his fingers over her jaw; and when she'd swallowed the last of it, she nudged his jacket looking for more.

"Sorry, girl, that's all there is tonight."

Climbing the fence, Cole sat on the top rail and looked toward the house, at the light coming through Juliet's bedroom window, at the occasional sight of Juliet pulling clothes from her suitcase to hang in the closet. The mare sidled up close to Cole, her neck brushing his side until Cole rested his arm on the top of her mane and scratched the spot between her ears.

"So, what do you think, Suz? Is Autumn Leeves just about the prettiest thing you've ever seen?"

The horse shook her head, smacking Cole in the side.

"No need to be jealous. She's here to watch the girls and" — Cole shoved his fingers through his hair — "hell, I'm going to keep my hands off of her or she'll be sleeping in my bed instead of the nanny's."

Ben laughed inside. Even if Cole's hands were shackled behind his back, he'd figure out a way to touch Juliet again.

Out of the corner of his eye, Ben spotted Juliet pulling together the white curtains to cut off the view inside her room. He pivoted the binoculars toward the window.

It was impossible to miss Juliet's body silhouetted between the bathroom light and the curtained window. She stretched leisurely, then peeled the lacy top over her head, doing a dangerously slow striptease for two men who watched in the silence of the night. She tossed the shirt somewhere across the room and then her shadowy fingers slipped behind her back. Ben knew, just as Cole knew, that she'd popped the catch on her bra.

She slid one strap from her shoulder and then the other. But it wasn't Juliet's actions Ben wanted to watch, it was Cole's.

Ben shifted his binoculars again and watched the rise and fall of Cole's chest. He could almost hear the heavy beat of the doctor's heart as he watched Juliet's tempting moves. God but he wished it was daytime so he could catch Cole's reaction on film, not for Nicole's use, but for his own collection, picture after picture of various people and their unguarded emotions.

Someday he'd spend all his time taking the photos he wanted. Someday he'd no longer have to spend his time spying on others.

Someday Nicole might even love him again . . . but he knew that was wishful thinking.

He could capture love on camera. He could watch it unfold through a high-powered lens.

But God knows when he'd ever again experience it up close and personal.

Chapter 10

If she wasn't mistaken, someone — or something — licked her toes. It was the oddest sensation, not exactly unpleasant, yet far from sensual. Caught halfway between dreamland and barely conscious, Juliet tucked her feet beneath the fluffy comforter and tried to drift back into blissful sleep.

Somewhere, maybe off to her right, she could hear the tick of a clock. Somewhere else Roy Orbison sang "In Dreams." The sounds soothed her, helped her rest, and adding a simple relaxation technique a psychologist had taught her when insomnia had become a big part of her life, she repeated over and over again to herself, *Sleep, Juliet. Just sleep.*

Tucking her hands beneath her pillow, she cradled her cheek in its downy softness and breathed deeply, concentrating only on tranquil nothingness and the lovely memory of Cole's fingers soothing away the ache in her feet, his deep, mesmerizing voice driving away the unease she'd been left with after Garrett's call.

Cole had left her with a sense of total relaxation and an urge to jump his bones.

Even in sleep, she felt herself smile.

Again she felt something wet lap at her toes and then slowly, ever so slowly, her soft, warm comforter slipped from under her chin. It skimmed over the top of her pink silk pajamas, taking a trip past her breasts, her stomach, her hips, to the end of the bed.

Sleep, Juliet. Just sleep.

A chorus of faint, childish giggles wrapped around her. Nothing but a dream; pleasant thoughts of the day ahead, when she'd meet Cole's so-called little devils. If he only knew the kind of fractious malcontents she'd worked with and partied with for years — heck, if he'd known Garrett Pierce or Frederick Dannen, her first director — he'd have no reason to doubt her ability to handle, or at least get along with, any and all people.

"Are you *ever* going to wake up?" The exasperated voice was close. Very close and very real.

Juliet cracked open one eye and saw only ceiling. Lifting her head just the slightest, she spotted Rathbone — at least she was pretty sure the white-and-black Dane had been called Rathbone — standing at the end of the bed, his nose and tongue inching ever closer to the sole of her foot, as if he could sneak another lick without her knowing or nibble on a toe or two for breakfast.

And then — *oh, God* — Juliet's stomach clenched as something big and slithery slid under her PJs and over her belly. It was long and round and firm and even though that could be a good thing, given the right set of circumstances, she had no doubt at all that this was the wrong set of circumstances.

The big, round, long and slithery thing slid between her breasts — and stopped. It was cold and dry. It nudged her right breast. It nudged her left breast. Fear paralyzed her. Her heart skipped a beat and for one very long, very uneasy moment, she ceased to breathe.

It moved again.

Slowly. Very slowly.

The top button on her pajamas popped open and a nightmarish head burst out from its hiding place like an alien invader and wiggled a forked tongue in her face.

Juliet screamed. The blood-curdling

shriek ripped through the bedroom. The window rattled. Three dogs howled, and the five little girls Cole had shown her pictures of before she'd headed off to work last night, huddled around the bed and giggled as the snake slithered over her neck, her right cheek, and around the top of her head.

Juliet's shoulders tightened. Fear swelled in her throat. She shouldn't be frightened. God knows she'd been forced to handle snakes day in and day out on the set of "Amazonia 2807," but forced was the key word.

Snakes terrified her.

Another spine-tingling shriek hurled from the very pit of her stomach.

"What the —" Cole tromped into the room and, in one fell swoop, swept the snake from her body.

"Are you all right?"

Juliet only stared at him in absolute horror. Speaking at that very moment was an impossibility.

Holly and Jade turned artfully bright and shining smiles on Cole, trying to charm the man coiling the massive peach and black serpent around his arm as if it were no more than a lightweight length of rope.

"Didn't I tell you to leave Squeeze alone?" Cole's heated eyes and palpable annoyance bore down on the girls. "And come to think of it, where on earth did you find the key to her aquarium?"

Jade, her cheeks pink, her blue-black hair shiny and straight, plunked her fists on her hips. "It was in Frankenstein's mouth. I saw you hide it there the other day, right after you gave Squeeze that big fat mouse to eat."

"Frankenstein's seven feet tall. How'd you get the key out of his mouth?"

"Excuse me." Finding her voice at last, and with her heart beating somewhat normally again, Juliet gently applied the ball of her foot to Rathbone's nose to push his tongue away from her toes, then waved her hands over her head to catch everyone's attention. "Am I dreaming, or is that a boa constrictor you're cuddling?"

"It's a red-tail boa," Holly corrected. "She's six feet long and weighs thirty pounds, but if she was bigger . . . she could eat you alive and take weeks and weeks to completely digest you."

"That wouldn't be all that pleasant, would it?" Juliet smiled sweetly.

"Not for you," Holly added. "But" — she smiled just as sweetly as Juliet had —

"Squeeze would like it."

And from all outward appearances, Holly would like it, too.

Aiming her eyes at Cole and trying to remain calm, she asked, "What about this seven-foot-tall creature named Frankenstein hidden somewhere in the house." Juliet gulped, swallowing an ounce of uncontrolled angst. "Is that a snake, too?"

"He's not a snake," Jade stated. "He's a monster and he lives in Uncle Cole's den."

Holly, her pretty face nearly as black as the hair flying around her head in a mass of braids and multicolored barrettes, poked Jade in the arm. "It's a robot, not a monster."

"Okay, so he's a robot, but he looks like a monster," Jade added. "And he's got ugly orange eyes that light up in the middle of the night."

"He's not a robot," Cole blurted out, obviously hotter than hell, and not just about the Squeeze incident. "Frankenstein's my one and only attempt at sculpture, and" — the hands that had masterfully massaged her feet last night gently stroked the constrictor — "if I catch any of you going near him or Squeeze or that den ever again, I'll —"

Lugosi bared his teeth and growled at

Cole's threatening but totally without malice words.

Had she somehow ended up in a mad-house? Obviously she had, because the forest green comforter she'd recently been snuggling under sailed out of the bedroom, gripped between Karloff's and Lugosi's jaws.

If that wasn't enough, Rathbone crawled up on the bed beside her and dropped his heavy head on her chest, popping open another pajama button, three curly-headed blondes with peanut butter and jelly smudging their faces scrambled onto the mattress and jumped up and down, and Cole *and* the fork-tongued snake glared down at her.

"*So,* did you sleep well?" Cole sounded just as annoyed with her as he had with the girls, although for the life of her she had no idea what she'd done wrong.

She hit Cole with the same kind of charming smile the girls had used on him. "I slept better than I have in years, thank you."

Cole seethed. "Were you planning to sleep all day?"

Juliet frowned at his unconcealed irritation. "Of course not."

"Only half the day, right?"

Her frown deepened. She'd set the alarm for six so she could get up and make breakfast, but she hadn't heard a peep out of the clock radio. Tilting her head to the right, she stared at the big red numbers glaring at her from the clock sitting beside the photo of her dad on the nightstand. She rubbed her eyes again. Obviously she had to be dreaming. But the time was still the same when she refocused on the clock.

"Please tell me it's not really noon."

"I would," Cole bit out, "but it is. Five after as a matter of fact."

"Uncle Cole fired the last nanny who overslept," Holly announced, "and I heard him call her a lazy, good-for-nothing —"

"That's enough, Holly." Cole rested a hand lightly on the little girl's shoulder, but the glance he hit Juliet with wasn't so light.

Juliet tried to push herself up onto her elbows but Rathbone's weighty head kept her from budging. "So . . ." she said, keeping her gaze off of Cole, looking instead at all the grubby faces around her, "I take it you've already had breakfast."

"We've had lunch, too, which was better than breakfast, 'cause Uncle Cole burned the pancakes." Jade plopped her elbows on the mattress next to Juliet's head. She

191

rested her chin on her knuckles. "He dropped the eggs on the floor this morning, too, and then he said a nasty word — a *really* nasty word."

"It's not all that nasty," Holly interrupted, nudging Jade over so she too could plop her elbows on the bed. "It's just another word for poop."

One of the triplets crawled up Juliet's body and peered at her over the top of Rathbone's head. "I gotta go poop."

Crap.

There was absolutely no way that Juliet was going to change a dirty diaper.

Grabbing the little girl under the arms, Juliet pushed aside everyone and everything else on the bed and made a mad dash for the bathroom. She ripped the tape strips from the diaper and plunked the toddler onto the toilet.

"You know, sweetie, this is where little girls should go poop. Little girls should *never* go poop in their diapers?"

"Why?"

"Because it's stinky and squishy and really quite disgusting. And it's much more fun to do it here, where you can swing your legs back and forth and sing."

Another toddler edged up to Juliet. "I want to go poop, too."

"One little girl at a time. That's the rule."

"Me go *now*."

Toddler #2 — Juliet really needed to figure out a way to tell them apart — flopped down on the floor, her blond curls bobbing up and down as fat tears squeezed out of her eyes.

"I want to poop, too," cried the third triplet.

Through the wailing, Juliet managed to pull toddler #3 into her lap. "I know you'd love to go poop right now, but, unfortunately, the toilet isn't big enough for all of you."

#3 bawled.

#2 whimpered.

Chaos reigned supreme.

Juliet stared through the door and through the window beyond, completely befuddled. What had she gotten herself into now?

Holly peeked around the bathroom door. "The nanny we had before the last nanny tried to potty train them and couldn't. What makes you think you can do it?"

"Because I've got magical powers."

"Uncle Cole doesn't like liars," Holly said. "He fired a nanny because she lied."

"You don't believe I have magical powers?"

"No. You're just a nanny, and I don't like nannies." Holly turned as if to run, but threw her arms around Cole's legs, instead, when he appeared just outside the bathroom door, the boa constrictor still coiled around his arm.

Cole's steely blue-eyed stare hit Juliet smack in the face. "Please tell me I didn't make a mistake hiring you."

"It may look like I have a major disaster on my hands. I may have looked defeated an instant ago, but I'm perfectly capable of working through this." At least she hoped that was true.

"Then I can head back to the clinic?"

"*Now?*"

"That was my plan."

"You don't want to stick around and make sure I do everything right?"

"Rathbone, Karloff, and Lugosi will be around. Trust me, if you do something wrong, they'll let you know."

Cole reached into the back pocket of his jeans and pulled out a folded piece of paper. "To make things a little easier, considering this is your first day on the job, I put together a to-do list, just so you'll know what I expect."

She wasn't quite sure she wanted to accept his list, but he was the boss and she was the nanny, and she really didn't know what kind of activities to plan for the girls, other than the trip they had to make to Joe's Gas and Bait by one o'clock, so she held her hand out and let him slip the paper into her palm.

"Think you can control the diaper and bathroom situation?" Cole asked, stroking the viper that continued to wiggle its forked tongue in her direction.

"Of course, I can."

"Good, because I need to get back to work."

Juliet watched Cole's back as he strolled from the room. It really was quite magnificent, all six-feet-four inches of it, if she'd correctly guessed his height. But he certainly had a severe mood-swing problem — one minute hot, one minute cold, one minute extremely sexy. She only wished she knew which mood was going to raise its head most often.

Leaning back against the cabinet beneath the sink, she avoided Toddler #1's kicking as she sat on the toilet and sang an unintelligible song, ignored Toddler #3's wails, Toddler #2's gentle breathing as she slept soundly on the floor, and Holly and

Jade staring at her as if she had two heads.

Relaxed in spite of the chaos, Juliet unfolded the piece of paper Cole had given her and focused on the words typed in big, bold letters.

TO DO

(Times are flexible — by 5 to 10 minutes only!)
(Punctuality, Ms. Leeves, is a must.)

7:00 A.M.	Serve breakfast
7:30 A.M.	Wash faces, hands; brush teeth and hair
7:45 A.M.	Make beds and clean bedrooms
8:00 A.M. till 9:00 A.M.	Nature walk *Bla, bla, bla*

There wasn't one thing on the whole entire list that she couldn't have figured out for herself.

Juliet shoved up from the floor. "Would you girls excuse me a moment?" She seriously doubted that the caterwauling triplets or Holly and Jade, who were jumping up and down on her bed, heard a word she said and also doubted that they cared if she stayed or went. Personally, she hated to leave them alone in her room for more than a moment, because calamity could rule while she was gone, but she had a few words to share with their micromanaging uncle.

Dashing out of the bedroom, Juliet threw open doors to every room and checked inside each one as she zipped down the hallway, not knowing if Cole had already left the house or was still inside. She flew through the living room, passed the kitchen, shoved open the door to a man-sized bedroom with a rustic, king-sized four-poster bed, and at last reached a room with OUTER LIMITS posted on the door.

That was probably code for KEEP OUT. Juliet threw open the door anyway, and was greeted by — *oh, God!* — seven-foot-tall Frankenstein, arms extended, eyes flashing neon orange, and big old hunky teeth gaping out of a wide-open mouth looking like he was going to chomp her head off.

Juliet screamed.

Something heavy clamped down on her shoulder and she spun around.

Cole glared at her. The snake's beady eyes stared at her.

And she screamed again.

She might have collapsed in Cole's arms if he hadn't been holding the ghastly snake.

Taking a deep breath, Juliet tried to regain an ounce of poise, but what little composure she had fizzled when Cole's fingers loosened on her shoulder, trailed deliciously across her collar bone, and whispered over the sensitive skin between her breasts and continued all the way down to her belly.

"Nice pajamas," he taunted, "but not all that appropriate for a nanny."

Cole walked past her, leaving her to hastily rebutton every popped button on her pajama top while focusing on the mass of horror-movie memorabilia plastered over walls and overflowing from bookcases.

"This isn't some kind of dungeon where you torture innocent nannies, is it?"

"It's my den," he said far too coolly, as he opened the lid on an immense aquarium.

"Obviously you're fascinated by creepy things."

"I spent a few years living over an old movie theater when I was little and sneaked downstairs a lot to watch all the old classics. I still watch them when I want to relax and get away from things."

"I see."

He thrust his arm into the aquarium and the constrictor slipped from Cole's body and slithered into a hollow log.

"And the snake. You relax with her, too?"

"I rescued her from a well-meaning citizen of our community who thought she'd be fun to own — until he had to come up with frozen mice to feed her once in a blue moon."

"Sounds yummy."

He looked up slowly, his gaze skimming over her bare toes, the entire length of her pink silk pajamas, and settling on her eyes. "Shouldn't you be with the girls?"

"I should, and I will be back with them in just a moment, but now that I'm calm and fully rational, not to mention wide awake and completely buttoned, you and I have some talking to do."

The lid squeaked eerily on the aquarium when Cole closed it and secured the lock. "I don't remember chitchatting being on my to-do list."

"It's not." Juliet stared at the list, stared at the cantankerous man, then held the contemptible piece of paper between them and ripped it in half. "Now" — she smiled widely — "there is no to-do list."

Cole's brow rose. "You have a problem with structure?"

"I have a problem with you planning

every speck of the girls' day, not to mention every speck of my day. It may be fine and dandy for you to have your entire life planned out, you know, marriage at forty, children at forty-two, but those girls are too damn young for you to be mapping out every minute of what they should do while they're growing up."

He folded his arms over the pale blue polo shirt covering his brawny chest. "The list was intended for you, not the girls."

He was becoming more and more annoying by the minute. "What on earth makes you think *I* need a schedule?"

"First" — his index finger popped up — "you were late for our interview. Second" — another finger popped up — "you overslept."

Juliet crossed her arms over her chest, too. "First" — she popped up an index finger — "I ran out of gas. Second"— she popped up a second finger — "I set the alarm but for some unknown reason it didn't go off. Third" — she stalked across the room, stood within inches of his chest, and stared him almost eye to eye — "you seem to forget that you've had thirteen nannies quit or get fired in the past six months, you're in desperate need of someone to watch your girls until you can find

200

another nanny, and if you don't get rid of the bee that seems to have flown up your butt this morning, you might not even have schedule-hating me to watch them."

A slow grin touched his mouth. "Do you talk back to everyone you work for?"

Cole was the first. Except for running away from college, she'd always done what she'd been told, but not anymore. "I told you last night that I'd do everything in my power to be a good nanny — *until* you can find a *real* nanny. If that means doing things my way instead of your way because I think my way is better for the girls, I'll do it. If that means arguing with you to make you see things my way, I'll do that, too."

"If you decide to do something your way instead of my way, are you going to consult me first?"

"I wouldn't think of doing something without your permission."

"Why do I find that hard to believe?"

"Because you don't trust me."

"Should I?"

"You've entrusted your girls to me for safekeeping. You've given me a room in your home. And" — she circled her fingers around Cole's wrist and drew it toward her so she could see his watch — "in fifteen minutes or so, I'll be packing your little girls into the car and taking them into town with me." She shrugged lightly. "So, maybe you *should* trust me."

His jaw tightened. "I've got a refrigerator and a pantry full of food. The girls have clothes and anything else they could possibly want. I don't see any need for you to go into town."

"But I do." She smiled sweetly. "In case you've forgotten, I have to beautify Joe's Gas and Bait and the girls are going to help me."

"Your first day on the job and you think I'm going to let you drive off with my kids?"

Juliet ran pink fingernails gently down his chest. "You're going to do even more than that."

"What?" he asked gruffly.

Juliet turned the palm of her hand face up in front of him. "You're going to loan me the money to buy flowers."

Chapter 11

"Look, Doc, before you start lecturing, I built the kind of kennel you told me to, and I got a stronger leash, but Hector got loose anyway."

Cole stared at the Akita through the wire-mesh cage in the back of Floyd Morgan's pickup. Dried blood stuck to the gashes across the dog's muzzle and right eye. Fur and flesh had been ripped from his hip, and there were countless bite marks about his neck. "Who'd he pick a fight with this time?" Cole asked. "Les Bailey's Rottweiler?"

"A coyote. You shoulda seen the fur flyin', not to mention the dirt. When it was over, the coyote was a goner and Hector, well, he mighta won, but he sure looks like hell."

The dog was lucky to be alive considering the number of fights he'd gotten into in the last couple of years.

Cole leaned close to the cage and whispered, "Y'know, Hector, you wouldn't have to come here so often if you'd realize that you're not the only animal with the right to live and breathe."

Hector bared his teeth and growled, but Cole knew he was in for far worse when he and the animal were pitted against each other in the examining room.

"Why don't we get Hector inside so I can take a look at those cuts," Cole said, latching on to the handle on one side of the cage.

"Getting him inside's one thing, but you takin' a look at him might be easier said than done. Hector doesn't like you on a good day. And I hate to tell you this, Doc, but right now he ain't in the best frame of mind."

"I ain't either," Cole said, slapping Floyd on the back. How could he be when Jim Foley's friggin' lawyer had stopped by early this morning to get free shots for his dog and to dish out the news that he was going to sue Cole's ass off since he'd killed — *killed!* — Jim Foley's horses.

On top of that, he'd spent most of the night and most all of today wondering if he'd made the mistake of a lifetime hiring Autumn Leeves to watch his girls.

He'd hired her without asking for references. He'd hired her because she was pretty. He'd hired her because he liked the idea of her sleeping right down the hall, liked the idea of touching her and kissing her again. Hell, he'd hired her because he was horny and desperate.

Damn poor reasons to hire a nanny!

She'd proven to him just how bad a mistake he'd made when she overslept this morning, which meant he'd had to deal with the girls until noon, and the little devils had run around the clinic like bats out of hell, disturbing anyone and anything that got in their way.

She'd torn up his carefully constructed to-do list, the one he'd slaved over while she slept.

She'd proceeded to tell him off — and he'd let her.

She'd conned him out of money and driven off in his Suburban with his girls.

But, damn! She looked mighty fine in unbuttoned pink silk pajamas.

He ought to rot in hell for hiring her because she was gorgeous and not firing her because she was sexy.

And then there was that friggin' lawsuit.

"Someone or somethin' giving you trouble?" Floyd asked, huffing and puffing as they lugged the kennel toward the door.

"He's had a bad day," Raven quipped as she came out of the clinic to help. "It was free-rabies-and-distemper-shot morning and the place was swarming with people, dogs, and cats, and" — she aimed angry eyes at Cole — "five little girls that *I* had to baby-sit from eight till noon."

Raven opened the door for Cole and Floyd to squeeze through with the Akita's kennel. "As if that wasn't bad enough, Paul Phillips, that scuz-bucket of a lawyer was the first in line for free shots," she rattled on. "I like his dog Gus, but Mr. Phillips is a nasty son of a gun who should take a flying leap off the edge of the earth."

"Funny you should mention him," Floyd said between huffs and puffs. "I was having breakfast at the Elk Horn this morning, and Joe from Joe's Gas and Bait came in and told everyone within hearing distance that Paul's gonna be rakin' in the dough on some malpractice suit he's handlin' for Jim Foley."

"Yeah," Cole bit out. "Against me."

Floyd's eyes narrowed. "You serious?"

"Dead serious." Cole could see his chances for ever having a big clinic with additional vets and a string of emergency hospitals going right down the drain.

"The way I see it," Raven said, letting the door bang shut as she followed Cole, Floyd, and Hector to one of the examining rooms, "someone ought to shove a cattle prod up Jim Foley's —"

"Get me a few doggy treats, will you, Rave," Cole interrupted, hitting Raven with a frown, even though he'd had thoughts of doing something equally painful to the good-for-nothing bastard. "And make sure the Danes don't get anywhere near this room while Hector's here, or we're in for some major trouble."

"Sure. Whatever you say." Raven stalked out of the examining room, slamming the door behind her.

"Y'know, Doc," Floyd said, panting for air after they set the heavy kennel down near the examining table, "I never much liked Jim Foley, so if you want, me and Hector could go after the guy. I been reading those Juliet Bridger mysteries you told me about the last time I was here, and I know lots of ways to get rid of someone, or to make them think twice about causing someone trouble."

Cole unlocked a cabinet and took out a bottle of morphine. "I don't want you or Hector doing anything at all to Mr. Foley, especially something that could wind up getting you in trouble."

"Well, if you change your mind, you just tell me. Hector and I can be real sneaky."

"Yeah, but Jim Foley can be pretty sneaky, too."

"I heard he's got a girlfriend up in Jackson. You know, Doc, if you had evidence about that, you could blackmail the guy, tell him you've got pictures of his little indiscretion — that you'll show his wife if he don't call off the suit."

"I'm a vet, not a blackmailer."

"I realize that, Doc. In fact, that's the reason I think you should try this blackmail thing. There was a doctor in one of them Juliet Bridger books, I think it was the fifth one, you know, *Five Ways to Kill Your Lover*. Anyway, this doctor blackmailed his own blackmailer and then when the blackmailer turned up dead, the doctor was arrested for committing murder, even though he didn't actually do the killing."

Had Floyd lost his mind? "And how's this supposed to help me?"

"I don't rightly know if it would help you or not, I just figured the whole thing was pretty clever. If you haven't read that one yet, you should. Great story, and that Jayne Mansfield-Smythe — you know, the forensic pathologist who solves all the cases — well, she's one heck of a broad, if you know what I mean. And there's some hot sex —"

The door burst open. "Jeez, Doc, I leave for a couple of minutes and you're already talking nasty."

"We were talking mystery novels."

"Yeah, right." Raven slapped the dog biscuits into Cole's outstretched hand. "By the way, your mom called. She was in a rush and I figured you wouldn't want to talk anyway, so I took a message."

The fact that his mom had called was the last thing he'd needed to hear this morning. "Do me a favor and tell me they've extended their stay in Tibet."

"I would if I could, but" — Raven shrugged — "there's no easy way of breaking this to you, Doc. Your mom and your dad are in L.A."

Cole's gut clenched. "Did she say anything about coming for a visit?"

"Yeah. If all goes well — your mom's words, not mine — they'll be here tomorrow or the next day. Oh," Raven added, heading out the door again, "she wanted me to tell you that they're bringing friends along. I think she said their names are Butterfly and Slick."

All of a sudden, Jim Foley's lawsuit didn't look so bad. Having a string of emergency hospitals up and down the state and a dozen vets working in his clinics would mean nothing if he ended up losing the little girls who'd become the most important part of his life.

"You didn't by any chance lose a little girl, did you?"

Juliet glanced up from the pile of dirt she and nearly a dozen little-girl hands had been digging in. Through her Kate Spade sunglasses she spotted Joe with a struggling Holly slung halfway over his shoulder, her untied red Keds kicking his hulking belly.

Juliet tried not to sigh. Tried not to look like she was making a mess of this nanny business, but she was. How could Holly have run off without her even noticing, when she'd also run off at the nursery and the hardware store?

She had to do better or Cole was going to fire her sorry butt.

Wiping her hands on the back of a pair of candy cane–striped capris that were already heavily speckled with dark brown mud, that she seriously doubted would come out in the wash, Juliet stood and pulled Holly from Joe's arms. "Where'd you find her?"

"In the driver's seat of Opal Vander-hooven's silver Mercedes." Joe scratched the stubble on his chin. "Used to have pale gray leather upholstery, but it's kinda smeared with dirt now. Steering wheel don't look too good, either."

Juliet looked into Holly's unrepentant brown eyes, but the little girl didn't look back. Instead she stared somewhere over Juliet's shoulder, probably willing a gigantic serpent to come slithering down from the sky to swallow Juliet up in one fell swoop.

It was sheer instinct that told Juliet not to scold Holly for running off and making a mess of Opal Vanderhooven's silver Mercedes. She wasn't too sure what she should do about this latest troubling incident, but the thought of disciplining Holly had NO-NO stamped all over it.

They needed a bond. Something to cement their relationship in a good kind of way. But what that was, Juliet didn't have a clue.

Yet.

"Sorry, Joe." Juliet boosted the now limp little girl in her arms. "We'll get it cleaned up."

Joe shrugged. "Nah, don't bother. I gotta get it detailed anyway. Opal likes her car spotless after I do the quarterly tune-up, and when the second richest lady in town wants something spotless, you'd better make sure it's spotless."

Joe pulled off his greasy baseball cap and wiped his brow. "I'm heading over to the Elk Horn for a Mountain Dew break. You want anything?"

"No, but thanks. We've got the kick-the-Coke-machine-out-back-for-a-free-drink technique down pat."

"All right, then. I'll see ya later."

Joe tugged his cap back on his head and sauntered off toward town, accompanied by his Andy Griffith whistle. Only then did Holly struggle out of Juliet's arms, drop down on her knees, and dig in the dirt beside her sisters.

Taking care of five little girls wasn't exactly a piece of cake. But there was something immensely satisfying about the job. She'd enjoyed the laughing, the singing, the hop-skip-and-jumping while they shopped for flowers and hand trowels, and pretty gardening gloves, and made a trip to a souvenir shop and had personalized T-shirts, caps, and beaded necklaces and bracelets made so Juliet could tell one triplet from another.

The only holdback from the laughing, the singing, and the hop-skip-and-jumping was Holly.

That had to be remedied, and soon.

Getting back on her knees, not the most comfortable thing to do on asphalt, Juliet blew a big pink bubble while scooting close to Cole's oldest niece. Holly moved farther away, and Juliet let her go, figuring the best way to deal with this right now was to not do anything. After all, there were four other children who also needed her attention.

"You know," Juliet said, digging her fingers into the cool, moist earth, "I think we've added enough mulch to the soil for now."

"Does that mean we get to plant the flowers?" Jade asked, her pretty face and new pink T-shirt a nightmarish mishmash of dirt and weed stains.

"Sure does."

"I want to plant the petunias first," Jade announced, grabbing one of the small plastic pots.

"Me too!" "Me too!" "Me too!" Carly, Caitlin, and Chloe warbled.

"I want to dig the holes," Holly stated, speaking at last, even though her words were forced. "My mommy showed me how to plant flowers and she did it better than anyone — even you."

"Want to show us how she planted flowers?" Juliet handed a trowel to Holly. "I wouldn't mind learning some new techniques."

Holly snapped the trowel out of Juliet's hand and moved to the far side of the brick planter. She stared at the ground, as if deeply contemplating what to do next, then dug the trowel into the dirt and flicked the scoop full of soil at Juliet. It caught in her hair, tumbled down her nose, under the neckline of her once white tank top, and slid between her breasts, settling in her bra.

Juliet drummed her fingers against her thigh, keeping her temper, sensing that Holly was doing everything possible to make Juliet explode.

She refused to blow her top.

Jade poked Juliet in the arm. "Aren't you going to get mad?"

"About what?" Juliet asked innocently.

"Holly threw dirt at you."

"Did she?" Juliet pulled her tank top away from her skin and inspected the mess. "I'm so dirty I couldn't possibly notice anything else splattered on me."

"Uncle Cole would send Holly to her room if she threw dirt at him."

"But she didn't throw dirt at Uncle Cole, did she?"

"As far as I can remember, no one's ever thrown dirt at me."

Juliet spun around. Cole stood behind her, his unreadable glare moving over the colorful plants, the pile of brand-new tools purchased, courtesy of his good credit, five grubby little girls, and the blob of dirt Juliet assumed must be speckling her face.

She blew a big pink bubble and fluffed her unfluffed hair as Holly ran to Cole and flung her arms around his legs. "Are you going to plant flowers with us?" Holly asked. "They're pretty and they smell nice and —"

"I wish I could, Holly," Cole said all too quickly, lifting her into his arms in spite of the dirt smearing over his dark blue shirt and faded jeans, "but Mrs. O'Neil's ferret has a runny nose and she wants me to make sure it doesn't have pneumonia and —"

"Could I help you take care of Mrs. O'Neil's ferret?" Holly asked, her grimy hands planted firmly on her uncle's cheeks.

"Why would you want to take care of a

ferret when you've got all these pretty flowers to plant?"

Holly shrugged her little shoulders. "I don't like planting flowers."

"I do." Jade popped up from her place by the planter, a petunia strangled in her grasp. "Nanny let me pick everything out because I told her how good I am at planting petunias."

"Me too!" "Me too!" "Me too!" the triplets sang in unison, tossing more mulch out of the planter than they'd helped put in.

Holly heaved a gigantic sigh, gripped Cole's cheeks, and forced him to look at her again. "Tomorrow we're going to paint flowers and stuff on the building, but —"

"But we didn't tell Joe that," Jade interrupted, then haphazardly shoved a wilting petunia into the ground. "He might not approve."

"Does Ms. Leeves approve?" Cole asked, his questioning eyes lighting on Juliet in all of her dirt-dappled glory.

"It was her idea," Jade said, scooping another petunia out of its pot. "She's got lots of good ideas — for a nanny."

"But she's not good at watching kids," Holly added, getting Cole's attention at last. He frowned slightly as he looked at his niece, and Juliet sensed what he was about to hear wasn't going to win her the Meritorious Achievement Award for Extraordinary Nannies.

"I got lost at the nursery," Holly said, "and I got lost at the hardware store and I skipped away from Nanny a little while ago and played in Mrs. Vanderhooven's car and she didn't . . . even . . . miss . . . me."

Cole's angry eyes flashed at Juliet. Even from where she sat in the dirt she could feel the steam brewing. He sucked in a deep breath and let it out slowly — counting to ten, no doubt — then, when the heat in his glare had tempered somewhat, warmer eyes sought out his dearest darling little girls. "Mind if I steal Ms. Leeves away from you for a minute or two?" he asked softly, but Juliet could still hear the almost teeth-gritting fury behind every word. "We need to talk."

"It's okay with me," Jade said, stabbing her trowel into the dirt. "I've got petunias to plant."

Cole pushed a little black braid away from Holly's eyes. "How about you? Do you mind?"

Holly's lips puckered. She shrugged her little shoulders. "Guess not."

Cole planted a kiss on Holly's cheek, but

she latched on to his shirt when he started to set her down on the pavement. "Are you going to have dinner with us tonight?"

"I'll try."

"Try harder, Uncle Cole." She pulled out of his arms and joined her sisters around the flower bed.

"So . . . what do you think of our garden?" Juliet asked, hoping to cool Cole's anger as she stood and, once again, brushed her hands on the back of her cotton capris.

"The flower garden's fine. The fact that you —"

"Maybe we should discuss this over by your truck." Juliet nodded toward little girls with big ears who really didn't need to hear the vile things their uncle was on the verge of uttering. "You know, where we can have a little more privacy."

"Fine."

Cole latched on to her arm and half dragged her toward the pickup, her Jimmy Choos — which weren't all that good for gardening but were better than her Ferragamos — almost sticking in great gobs of grease as she traipsed at his side.

Spinning her around, Cole trapped her against the driver's door of his truck, one hand on the window at either side of her shoulders. "So . . . is it true? Did you let Holly just skip off and not even notice she was gone?"

Juliet avoided the fire leaping in his eyes, and focused on the little girls off in the distance. "I could easily tell you no, but that would be a lie."

"I don't like lying."

She could throw back at him the fact that he'd led her to believe she was interviewing for a housekeeper rather than a nanny position, but since she herself had told him and the people in town a bucketful of fibs, she decided to keep the spiteful retort to herself.

"I'm not going to make excuses for what happened," Juliet said. "I'm not even going to tell you I'm doing my best because obviously I screwed up."

"Big time."

Juliet took her eyes off the girls and looked into Cole's worry-filled eyes. "I am sorry."

"Sorry doesn't cut it. Holly could have run into the street. She could have gotten hurt, and you wouldn't have known."

"You're right." Juliet turned her gaze back to the brick planter and five little girls having a dirt fight. "It's just that I haven't had so much fun in a long time, and I suppose I was enjoying myself when I should have kept a closer watch on Holly and everyone else."

Cole's finger slid under her chin. He tugged her face toward him. "Could you look at me when we're talking?"

"I could" — she removed his finger and twisted her head to visually supervise the dirt fight again — "but since you're paying me to watch your girls, and since I've failed miserably at that a few times today, I figure I shouldn't flub up again. So . . . I'd rather watch them than you, if you don't mind."

Out of the corner of her eye she saw his jaw clench. "I should fire you."

"I'd probably fire me, too, if I were you. After all, I showed up late for our interview, and I overslept, and I've demanded money from you."

"I can sum it up in just a few words. You've been one big pain in the butt."

Her eyes flicked toward him for an instant. "Is that what you thought when you kissed me?"

"Damn right."

A smug smile touched her lips, but still she averted her gaze. "You kiss every pain in the butt you meet?"

"Only the beautiful ones."

"Have you known a lot of beautiful pains in the butt?"

"Only you."

"So" — she took a deep breath, and because he'd had the audacity to pin her body against his truck, her breasts flattened against his chest — "are you going to fire me?"

"I should and I would," he said, his brawny body getting up close and personal with hers, "but it just so happens I need someone to watch the girls, and right now it's either you or me, and you'll just have to do."

"Wait a minute." She shoved him a good two feet away, then poked him in the chest with a dirty fingernail. "Are you telling me that a lousy nanny is better than no nanny at all?"

"I never said you were a lousy nanny, you're just . . ." He scratched the back of his neck and leaned against the truck.

Juliet spun around and pinned him to the side of the vehicle. "I'm just what?"

"Irresponsible."

"Wait a minute —"

He grabbed her finger before she could poke him in the chest again. "I already waited a minute."

Juliet glared. "If you hired me thinking

I'm irresponsible, that makes you pretty irresponsible, too."

"I don't have an irresponsible bone in my body."

"Then why did you hire me?"

"I don't recall hiring you." Cole looked past her to the girls. "The way I remember it, you told me you were taking the job whether I wanted you or not."

Her shoulders stiffened. "You didn't want me?"

"Oh, I want you all right." His eyes flitted toward her for only a moment. "Wasn't that pretty damn evident last night?"

"More than evident."

"Which means I should fire you because I hired you for all the wrong reasons."

"Fine. Fire me."

"I can't."

"Why not?"

"Because, damn it, I may have hired you for the wrong reasons, but obviously you're the right person for the job. Hell, I watched Holly flick dirt at you and then I watched you pretend nothing had happened." Cole reached out and softly brushed traces of dirt from her cheek. "Nannies one through thirteen would have yelled at her, or sent her to a corner, or told her she was a rotten kid who should be spanked."

"Yeah, but I didn't do anything because I had absolutely no idea what to do."

His blue eyes, which were deep and penetrating and mesmerizing, narrowed. "You mean you didn't have some carefully orchestrated plan in mind?"

"You're the one with all the carefully orchestrated plans. I have a tendency to act by the seat of my pants —"

"It's a rather nice seat."

"Thank you, but we're talking about your nieces at the moment, not my derrière, and to be perfectly honest with you, I must have been absent from school the day they dished out instructions on how to care for six-year-olds who want to be taken care of by their uncle rather than by a nanny."

His fingers found their way to her face again, smoothing away another hunk of earth. "You might have missed that class, but obviously you've got good instinct when it comes to troubled little girls."

"I think the only thing troubling Holly is that she wants to be with you — not me."

Cole again turned his gaze to the planter. "I can't be there for Holly or any of the other girls every second of the day."

223

"I realize that; but Holly doesn't, and she's having trouble accepting it."

"Any suggestions?"

"Maybe you should talk to her, find out what she wants."

"You make it sound awfully simple."

"Children usually don't want all that much, but sometimes their simple wishes go completely unheard, because their parents think they know what's best."

"Did you learn that in kindergarten teacher school?"

"I learned it at the foot of a doting father who loved me completely but never had any idea what made me tick."

Juliet brushed a bit of dirt off of Cole's polo shirt, feeling the incredible muscles under the fabric. "And now that we've gotten this argument out of the way, and I've revealed a bit of my past, which is something I don't do as a rule, we should get back to the girls before they think they've been abandoned."

"Actually, I need to get going."

Those words did not set well. Juliet blew a big bubble and sucked it back into her mouth. "Then I take it you didn't come into town just to see the girls or to check up on me?"

"I wish that was the case, but I'm getting

hit with a malpractice suit and have to see my attorney and, then, like I mentioned before, I've got to get back to the clinic to check out Mrs. O'Neil's ferret, and after that I need to figure out how to keep my head above water if I lose the suit."

All right, maybe he did have some worthwhile excuses.

"You don't think there's a chance of you losing, do you?"

He shrugged. "I don't know. But I've got to come up with a contingency plan in case the worst happens."

"Could you work on it after dinner?"

"You're determined to tamper with my carefully scheduled list of things to do, aren't you?"

"I wouldn't think of it. But . . ." Juliet strolled toward her Suburban, pulled a pen and piece of paper out of her flamingo bedecked tote, and scrawled a few words. "Just in case you find a hole or two in your schedule, why don't you slip this in."

Cole stared at the paper she placed in his hand. "6:30 — dinner with the girls. No excuses accepted."

"That's just a couple of hours from now, so you can't possibly forget," Juliet said. "And you'll make a lot of little girls very happy simply by joining them at the table."

"Will you be happy, too?"

"All I'm concerned with right now is the girls, but . . . yeah, I'll be happy, too."

Cole thought about it far longer than Juliet expected. She knew he was a busy man. Knew he'd hired a nanny so he could have the flexibility of spending whatever time he needed at his clinic. But she was also pretty darn sure that he loved the girls, and she'd hoped he'd jump at the chance to have dinner with them.

"So," Juliet said, when his answer didn't come, "are you going to have dinner with us or not?"

He rubbed the back of his neck. "I've got a lot to do, but I'll try —"

"Try really hard." Juliet put on her most charming smile, not knowing if that would have any affect at all, but she had to give it all she could. "Please," she added for good measure.

Cole looked at the girls and she couldn't miss the spark of love in his eyes. Then he looked back at her. His fingers curled beneath her chin and he slid his thumb gently over her lower lip. "All right, I'll be there."

"Is that a promise?"

"Yeah, and I never go back on my word."

Chapter 12

He was dead meat.

It was after eight when Cole plowed through the kitchen door, knowing he was late but hoping against hope that he hadn't screwed up completely by getting totally absorbed in medical texts and profit and loss statements.

But the house was still and quiet.

Damn.

He shoved his fingers through his hair when he spotted a vase of yellow and red roses sitting in the middle of the kitchen table. Autumn and the girls must have picked them from the overgrown bushes he'd meant to prune eons ago. They'd even found a tablecloth one of the Sleuths had given him as a housewarming present five years before, telling him that a bachelor should always set a nice table if he wanted to attract a bride.

Even if he'd wanted to catch a bride, the

only thing he could attract right now were steel-tipped darts fired from Autumn's angry eyes.

Hell, maybe things weren't all that bad. The girls — and he included Autumn in their number — had been nice enough to leave him a dinner plate filled with food. It was covered with a white linen napkin that matched the tablecloth. He leaned close and inhaled, hoping for the scent of pot roast. Instead, he caught the all too familiar aroma of peanut butter and jelly.

Lifting the napkin, ready to eat just about anything, he found what he'd expected, his favorite meal — PB&J — just about the only thing he could concoct without setting the room on fire. But Autumn's concoction was cut in the shape of flowers, as if an attractive presentation could enhance the flavor.

It meant nothing to him other than making him wonder where the crust and outer edges of the sandwich had gone. To the girls, cutting those fancy shapes had probably been the crowning event of their day.

He might have hired Autumn for every selfish reason in the books, but she sure as hell knew how to take care of little girls.

Grabbing a daisy-shaped wedge, he

headed down the hall and took a quick peek into the girls' rooms, just to make sure they hadn't abandoned him, run off to who knows where with the nanny who'd dropped out of heaven. But the dogs stood watch, each little girl slept soundly, covers tucked in tightly, covers tossed aside, on stomachs, on sides, sprawled partially on the bed and partially off.

They were safe and, for the most part, happy, except for wanting him to be around a little more. He'd made a promise, and then he'd forgotten.

He should be shot, and probably would be if Autumn had her way.

Outside in the hallway, he heard the water running in the shower, and hell if his mind didn't conjure up the image of Autumn's body underneath the spray, all slick and wet and smooth, hands rubbing slippery soap over every curve.

Her door was open halfway and he leaned against the wall, watching for any movement inside her room, hoping to catch even one minute glimpse of her coming out of the bath, one speck of skin not usually visible to a casual observer.

Taking the last bite of his sandwich, he gazed at the black capris and pink T-shirt laying out on the bed. A lacy pink bra sprawled across the mattress and matching panties, nothing more than a skimpy pink thong, rested right beside it.

He could picture Autumn in that thong and bra, her body long and luscious and perfect, all but a few inches of flesh bare, the scant specks of silk and lace hiding the intimate details, and making him want her that much more. Damn, but he wanted to slide his fingers over and under the fragile fabric, wanted to feel the warm velvety softness of her skin, wanted to peel each piece away slowly and savor Autumn's body as it was revealed to him bit by bit.

Why the hell hadn't he come home on time? If he had, the girls would have been happy, Autumn would have been happy, and maybe, just maybe, she would have turned that happiness on him, expressing it in ways he'd now have to dream about.

But he'd blown it, and no doubt he couldn't possibly salvage what might have been. Not when his transgression involved the girls. Not when he'd broken a promise.

The bathroom door opened and the light from inside flashed across the bed. He thought for half a heartbeat about leaving, about getting away before Autumn saw him standing there, waiting, but only a fool would walk away now. He stood in silence outside the triplets' room and watched Autumn wander to the bed wearing nothing more than a fluffy white towel.

He held his breath as she combed slender fingers through wet black hair, slicking the thick locks away from a perfectly beautiful face, a familiar face, one that he'd seen somewhere, maybe sculpted by Michelangelo.

As if she sensed his presence, she looked up from the far side of the bed and stared at him through the partially opened door. "You missed dinner." She tugged the towel a little higher over her breasts, but didn't run and hide. "It wasn't anything fancy, just peanut butter and jelly since I ran out of time to prepare anything else, but the girls set the table for seven people, hoping you'd be there."

He walked toward her bedroom and leaned against the doorjamb. "I got wrapped up in paperwork."

"So I gathered."

She sat on the edge of the bed, lifted a tube of lotion from the nightstand, and squeezed creamy white liquid into her hand. "Holly drew a picture of a runny-nosed ferret for you, and when you didn't show up for dinner, she hid in the closet and cried."

Not bothering to look at him, she rubbed her hands together, spreading the lotion between her fingers and up and over her arms. "I joined her in the closet and we had a lovely little chat."

"About why I didn't show up for dinner?"

"No, about why she hates nannies."

"That's an easy one. Because they're mean and old and ugly. At least that's what she told me last night."

"She doesn't like me, either and, call me vain, but I really don't think I'm mean or old or ugly."

"No," he admitted, as he watched her rub lotion into her skin. "You're just the opposite."

"But . . . I'm also the person who keeps her out of your hair."

"Not out of my hair, just entertained, doing things that little girls should be doing."

"Oh, I see." She squirted a glob of lotion onto her right leg. "You think little girls should do nothing but color and play with dolls and plant petunias?"

"I never said that."

"Well, in case you're interested, Holly hates dolls and coloring, and she's not all that crazy about planting flowers, either."

232

"So what does she like?"

"You'd know if you'd listened to her a little better in the past six months."

He gritted his teeth. "You could make things much easier if you'd just give me the answers instead of chastising me for my errant behavior."

"All right, here's the scoop. Holly doesn't like having a nanny because nannies keep her away not only from you but from the clinic. And when she's not at the clinic, she doesn't get to spend time with sick animals. And" — Autumn was seething now; he'd hate it if she wasn't so damn pretty — "she likes taking care of sick animals because she wants to be a vet."

"She's six years old. She'll change her mind."

Autumn's head jerked around. "I knew what I wanted to be at six, and by the time I was eighteen and heading off to college I no longer had any dreams of my own. You know why? Because my father felt his dreams were more important than mine, and I tried so hard to please him that I let him tell me what to do and how to do it. That's what you're trying to do to Holly, and I don't like it."

"And I suppose you think I'm too stubborn to take those words to heart?"

"Probably." Her breasts rose and fell beneath the towel as she took a deep, obviously calming breath. "But . . . I'll give you the benefit of the doubt."

"Have any suggestions on what I should do?"

"Plenty. Add one hour every morning to your schedule as Holly-time, because she's the one who really, really needs your undivided attention. Take her to the clinic with you first thing every morning and tell her about IVs and neutering. Let her wear a little uniform if she wants."

"That's it?"

"I'm sure you can think of other veterinarian-type things, but that should do for starters."

"And what about the others girls?"

"You could show up at dinner when you're supposed to. God, Cole, those little girls picked a bouquet of flowers for the table. They wanted this to be a special evening . . . just for you."

Autumn looked at him with violet eyes that radiated with disappointment. "You can't believe how quiet it was at dinner. The girls sat around the table in their prettiest dresses, swinging their legs back and forth, keeping their eyes glued on the door, saying nothing, just waiting anxiously for you to walk in."

"Are you going to give me a play by play of what I missed and make me feel even guiltier than I already feel?"

"What do you think?"

"That you're anxious to torture me."

"Right now, I'm so angry I could spit nails, but I have another job to go to in half an hour and I need to save my energy."

Cole strolled into the room, closing the door behind him. He went to the window and leaned a shoulder against the sill. "If you think I make a habit out of ignoring the girls, you're wrong."

"What I think doesn't matter. What the girls think is all that's important."

"They know how much I care."

"They're children. They're not thinking about all the things you did for them yesterday or the day before, they're thinking about what you promised them you'd do today."

He turned away from the window and looked at Autumn again. "I promised you, not the girls."

"You don't owe me anything; you owe Holly and Jade and Carly and Caitlin and Chloe."

Cole drew in a deep breath and let it out slowly. "Do you really want to know why I didn't show up for dinner tonight?"

She smoothed lotion over one right leg, looking completely disinterested in him, still giving him hell for screwing up. "I'm listening."

"Because I want Holly and Jade and Chloe and Caitlin and Carly to have all the things I didn't have when I was growing up. Things like roots and stability and a room of their own if and when they want one. And they're not going to have that if I sit back on my laurels and let some prick take everything away from me."

Her hand stilled on her leg. He watched a slow smile touch her lips as she looked up. "That's a much better excuse than the one I expected to hear."

"What did you expect?"

"That you forgot."

"I did forget."

Autumn's eyes narrowed.

"Don't look at me like that. I forgot because I was trying to figure out what I could have done differently to save those two horses yesterday morning. Not just because I want to keep from losing my ass in a lawsuit, but because I don't want to lose any more animals than I have to." He plowed his fingers through his hair. "Damn it, that mare shouldn't have died. Her foal shouldn't have died, either."

Autumn stood, clutching the towel about her breasts as she walked toward him. Her body was so close he could feel her warmth. Could smell the clean scent of soap and the fragrance of strawberry lotion on her skin.

He swallowed hard, trying to keep his senses when the terry cloth brushed across his arm as it fluttered to the floor and her soft hands cradled his cheeks. "Was there anything you could have done differently?"

"I don't think there was a chance in hell of saving either one." Cole slipped his hands around Autumn's sweet, hot body, and gathered her against him. "But that doesn't make it any easier for me to swallow," he whispered against her hair, "and it sure as hell isn't going to keep Jim Foley from getting every last penny my insurance company will fork out, from draining my bank account, and maybe from closing down my clinic."

Long, slender fingers wove about his neck and tangled in his hair. "Is he really that vindictive?"

Cole pressed his lips against her brow. "I could tick off half a dozen stories about the people who've ended up bankrupt because of Jim Foley."

"Does your attorney know he's sue-happy?" she asked, her balmy lips whispering against his neck, moving ever closer to his mouth. "Does he think you've got a fighting chance?"

He kissed her lightly, drinking in her sweetness, trying to lose himself in the softness of her arms, yet somehow he told her the truth that had haunted him since late afternoon. "He thinks I'm screwed. He thinks Jim Foley's attorney will tell the court that I'm inept, that it was the middle of the night and I was tired, that my mind's been preoccupied by my sister's death and taking care of her five children and the possibility of losing them, which is the truth, every last word of it."

"You're not inept."

"No. I love what I do too much to be a bad vet."

"You can fight this," Autumn said, her breasts crushing against his chest as they clung to each other.

"I did everything in my power to save those horses. Everything, damn it, but I don't know if I can save my clinic and everything else I've worked for, not now, not when I've got so many other things hanging over my head."

"You're not going to lose anything." Autumn breathed against his mouth, kissing him, making him believe what she said was possible.

Her lips were like velvet. Her skin like silk. He held her tight, his fingers skimming over the slender curve of her waist and the soft, gentle swell of her bottom. Her lips parted with a sigh and he sought her tongue with his, tasting her sweetness as they mingled and danced.

God, how he wanted her.

But all too soon she pulled away, smiling the sexiest most seductive smile he'd ever seen as she stood before him, naked and beautiful and more beguiling than he ever could have imagined.

"I have to go to work now, but trust me, Cole" — she shooed him out the door with a wave of her hand, and like a mesmerized idiot he backed out of the room, catching one more glimpse of her body and hearing her parting remark as she closed the door — "one way or another, Jim Foley is the one who's going to lose."

Chapter 13

Hotter than hell and hornier than she thought was humanly possible, Juliet shoved through the doors of the Misty Moon Saloon, repeating to herself the same mantra that had gone through her head since she'd stood stark naked in Cole Sheridan's arms: Jim Foley was a bastard and Juliet Bridger aka Autumn Leeves wasn't about to let him screw with the people who, in just two days, had made her life a living dream.

"Bad night?" Molly asked, when Juliet ducked behind the bar, ready to work another five hours to pay off her debt.

"Best night I've ever had in my life," Juliet admitted. But of course it would have been better if she hadn't had to rush off to work and had locked Cole in her room instead of shoving him out.

Then again, maybe that had been for the best.

Molly scrubbed a water spot off of the

copper bar with her ever-present towel. "Is that why your shirt's on backward?"

Juliet looked down at her tank top. In most cases it might have been hard to tell a tank top was on backward, but this tanktop was pretty much backless, which pretty much left Juliet with only her lacy pink bra on for cover.

"Obviously I was a little out of it when I was getting dressed." Juliet slid the spaghetti straps off her arms, tugged the skintight top around, and in a matter of seconds, she looked like a new woman. Still, she was afraid to ask Molly if any other article of her clothing was askew, or just plain missing.

Truth be told, Cole had turned her whole existence inside out, made her do things that were totally out of character, without asking her to do anything at all.

God knows she wasn't in the habit of dropping her bath towel in front of the men she knew. Hell, she'd never been with anyone other than Garrett, yet she'd chucked the towel without any compunction at all, and stood in front of Cole with nothing on but the skin she was born in as if it was the most natural thing in the world to do.

Even now she shook her head in absolute shock.

"You know," Molly said, her words shaking Juliet back to the here and now, "if working here and for the Doc *and* for Joe is too much for you, you can call it quits right this very minute and head on home."

Juliet's eyes widened. "*What?* You don't want me to work tonight?"

"It's not that I don't want you to work. My word, people have been talking about your Rattlesnakes and Purple Geckos all day, and I expect this place to be popping tonight with regulars and people I haven't seen in years, everyone wanting to have one of your drinks. Heck, I was thinking about asking you to stay on, maybe just cut your hours back a bit, say from nine until midnight."

"It's a deal."

Molly's eyes narrowed into a frown. "You don't want to think about it?"

"No. I make my best decisions on the spur of the moment."

Molly popped the top on a Moose Jaw and took a sip. "What about your teaching job?"

"I don't have to be back at work until the middle of August." Again the lies slipped easily over her tongue.

"You gonna want to go home when the time comes?"

Juliet shrugged as she dumped dirty glasses into hot soapy water. She'd told a pack of fibs. She'd deceived a lot of people, and in the end, she wasn't going to have any choice, unless she wanted to hurt her newfound friends. "I may not want to go home, but I'm going to have to . . . eventually."

"Well, that's too bad," Molly said, heading for her office. "I kind of like having you around."

An hour went by and, ever so discreetly, Juliet had asked this person and that about Jim Foley, but everyone clammed up at the mention of his name.

"He's an asshole," Molly had said, not one to beat around the bush. "A man you and everyone else on the face of the earth should stay away from."

Unfortunately, Cole hadn't stayed away. He'd gotten up in the middle of the night to help the bastard, and now he was sweating bullets over the fact that he might lose everything he'd worked so darn hard to build.

But there was only so much prying a bartender could do for the sake of someone else, especially when the real gossips — the Sleuths — hadn't graced the saloon with an appearance.

Of course the sentiment about butting out of other people's business flew right out the swinging doors when Ben, the photographer for *National Geographic*, bellied up to the bar, ordered a whiskey, then tugged a pack of Marlboros out of his pocket, tapped out a cigarette, and lit it up.

Not prying could only go just so far.

It was a crazy thing to do, but Juliet strolled to the end of the bar, plucked the just lit cigarette out of Ben's mouth, and smashed it in an ashtray. "You told me last night those things are bad for you and you're right. On top of that, I don't like inhaling your secondhand smoke, so I'm going to help you break the habit right here and now."

Ben flipped his silver lighter over and over in his fingers. "Going cold turkey might kill me."

"Drinking whiskey might kill you, too," she said, filling his glass again, "but we'll work on one bad habit at a time."

Taking a couple of beers to the back of the bar for Larry and Steve, the creeps who monopolized the dart board night after night, Juliet almost missed the arrival of Scarlett Wolfe, the very pregnant owner of the town's mystery bookshop. They'd met last night, shared a lot of laughs and a few plotting details about the Jayne Mansfield-Smythe books written by Scarlett's favorite author, none other than Juliet Bridger.

Scarlett was followed through the swinging doors by the Sleuths, and Juliet knew her moment had come to dig for dirt on Jim Foley, bastard extraordinaire.

"What'll you have, ladies?" Juliet asked, slapping napkins down in front of each woman when they scooted into their regular booth.

Mildred dumped her white patent purse on the table. "A Waikiki Woo-Woo, please."

"And I'll have one of those Fuzzy Nipples." Lillian giggled.

"That's a Fuzzy Navel, not Nipple." Ida Mae tsked, shaking her head. "As for me, I guess I'm designated driver again so make my Waikiki Woo-Woo a virgin."

Scarlett rested her hands on her very pregnant belly. "I'll have something sweet and virginal, too."

"Be back in a jiff." Juliet hustled behind the bar to fix the drinks, anxious to get back to the table and talk trash.

"Think I could get a few more peanuts?" Ben asked, nudging an empty bowl toward the edge of the bar.

"Of course you can. In fact, you can have just about anything — but not a cigarette," Juliet said, hastily refilling the peanut bowl before working on Fuzzy Navels and Waikiki Woo-Woos.

"Hope you don't mind," Ben said, "but I took some pictures of you and a bunch of little girls today. Thought they might be good for that article of mine."

Juliet forced herself to take that statement nonchalantly, even though her insides clenched and she gripped the chilled glass she was holding so tightly it could have shattered in her hand. She hated having her photo taken, especially behind her back. God knows her picture had been snapped again and again without her being aware, and all too often, the photographs had been used in the worst of ways.

But *Buzz* and the other tabloids had never asked permission. Ben had, which put him a zillion levels above those sleazy bottom feeders who exploited her for fun and profit.

"Any chance I could see them before they're printed?" she asked, scooping up the peanut shells littering the bar in front of Ben. "You know, just to make sure I don't have some crazy expression on my face."

"There's a good chance they won't be printed. Like I told you last night, my editor wants hard-edged."

"I'm not at all hard-edged."

"No," he said thoughtfully, "you're not. More than likely I won't even send her the film I took today."

What a relief. "If you do decide not to use the pictures, could I buy them from you?"

"I doubt there's anything you'd want." Ben shrugged. "But tell you what, if I don't get around to using your photos, I'll give them to you."

"That's awfully nice, considering we just met."

He plucked a peanut from the bowl and cracked the shell. "Yeah, well, maybe I owe it to you."

"For what?"

He flipped his lighter again and again between his fingers. "For helping me try and break a bad habit."

Juliet scooped up his empty ashtray and shoved it under the bar. "The pleasure's all mine."

Putting the finishing touches on the Waikiki Woo-Woos and Fuzzy Navel, Juliet headed to the booth and slid drinks in front of her friends.

"It's kind of quiet in here right now," Juliet said. "Mind if I join you for a bit?"

Mildred scooted over in the booth and patted the now empty seat beside her. "We'd love it."

"So," Scarlett said, long before Juliet had her tush affixed to red Naugahyde, "is there any truth to the rumor that Cole is being sued by Jim Foley?"

Lillian clapped a hand over her chest. "No! That's absolutely awful."

"But it's true." Juliet folded her arms on the tabletop. "I don't know the first thing about this Jim Foley, but —"

"He's an ugly, cud-chewing bucket of pond scum." Ida Mae latched onto the virgin Waikiki Woo-Woo Juliet had slipped in front of her. "The vermin should be drawn and quartered and hung up by his balls to rot."

"Obviously you're talking about Jim Foley," Molly said, sliding into the booth next to Ida Mae. "I told you, Autumn, the man's no good."

"The bastard, excuse my French," Mildred gasped, "screwed poor Mr. Duffy at the ice cream parlor. He even did a number on Art Steinman, the barber, that was before he went to prison, of course."

Molly shook her head in disgust. "He's

screwed a lot of people."

"You don't know the half of who he's screwed." Ida Mae took a sip of her drink, as if she needed to wash away her distaste for the subject at hand. "I've seen that good-for-nothing checking into the Teton Lodge with some little honey who does nails at the Cut and Curl Salon up in Jackson. The way I see it, someone should hack off his privates for fooling around on his wife."

"I'd do it if I wasn't worried about germs," Lillian said.

"Well, I don't like him screwing around with Cole," Molly said. "That poor man has had enough crap dumped on him lately."

"I wish there was something we could do to help him." Scarlett stirred her very healthy mango, banana, and strawberry slushy. "Something that wouldn't get us into trouble, of course, because Logan would have a fit if he caught wind of me even thinking about snooping around."

Juliet leaned close so only the ladies surrounding her could hear. "You don't by any chance have any evidence of Jim Foley's little dalliance, do you?"

"Of course I do." Ida Mae plopped a peanut into her mouth. "Last year, when we were doing some serious undercover work —"

"Which case was that?" Lillian asked.

Ida Mae rolled her eyes. "All right, no one else was involved besides me, but if you must know, I was trailing that no-account ex-husband of mine who not only cheated on me but is now cheating on that hussy he married when he dumped me."

"No!" Mildred gasped again.

"Yes." Ida Mae tsked, her eyes narrowing as she shook her head. "Anyway, I picked up this nifty new high-powered lens for my Nikon, and I was snapping pictures of Hiram and his newest tramp checking into the lodge when who should pull into the parking lot? None other than Jim Foley and Cutie Pie from the Cut and Curl. Believe it or not, that's her real name; and I figured while I was snapping pictures of my no-account ex cheating on his new wife, I might as well snap pictures of Jim Foley cheating on his long-suffering wife."

"And you still have the pictures?" Juliet asked, thrilled and exceedingly pleased that everything was falling into place so easily.

"Of course I do. I keep everything."

Juliet flashed a sly smile at her companions. "Mind if I ask you all a personal question?"

"Go right ahead," Molly said.

"Anyone here have a problem with blackmail, if it's done for a good cause?"

Molly, Scarlett, and the Sleuths grinned. "If it has to do with getting Jim Foley off Cole Sheridan's back," Molly said, "I'm all for it."

Scarlett and the Sleuths nodded in unison.

"Good." Juliet bent over the table. Her friends did the same, and the conspiracy began. "It might take a day or two to arrange everything, but here's the plan."

Juliet's Jimmy Choos clacked on the peanut-strewn floor as she raced across the saloon to catch the ringing phone. She had a tray of dirty drink glasses in one hand, a towel slung over her shoulder, and looked as if she'd worked in the saloon forever, although she was still completing day number two.

She slid the tray into an empty gray wash bin and latched onto the phone. "Misty Moon."

"Juliet? Is that you?"

The familiar voice took her completely by surprise. Cupping the phone close to her ear, she leaned against the bar and stared into the mirror so she could see the people coming and going behind her. "Nic?" she whispered.

"I can't believe I've found you." It was definitely Nicole, her voice imperious yet sweet and concerned. "I've called every hotel and motel in Plentiful asking to speak to Juliet Bridger and the people acted as if I'd lost my mind. It's as if no one even knows you're in town."

"They don't. How did you find out?"

"I checked your bank account on-line and I saw where you'd last used your ATM card, then took a wild guess that you might still be in town."

"I told you I'd call in a few days."

"It's been five. I was worried, and when I couldn't get you on your cell phone —"

"My cell phone died between here and Idaho, and I haven't bothered to recharge the batteries. But everything's fine." Juliet felt herself relaxing, comforted somewhat that someone knew where she was — just in case an emergency arose. "I'm working as a bartender. Can you believe that?"

"You don't know the first thing about tending bar."

What a typical remark. It seemed as if her friends back home thought she was the epitome of a blond bimbo, never knowing enough to take care of herself. But she wouldn't let Nicole's comment get her down. "I've had a crash course in bartending and now I'm an expert."

Juliet switched the telephone to her other ear, and watched Scarlett, the Sleuths, and Molly yacking it up in their circular booth, with no idea at all that she was talking to Nicole Palisade, former co-star of "Amazonia 2807," now the personal assistant to Juliet Bridger.

"Has it been crazy there?" Juliet asked, not the least concerned about business, but it seemed appropriate to ask.

"A lot of calls. *People* wants to interview you for a feature they're doing about Garrett."

"No. And you can tell them that's my final answer."

"Frederick Dannen wants to make a *Slash McCall* reunion movie and bring you back from the dead."

"Have him" — Juliet lowered her voice to a whisper — "talk to my agent."

"I've got a stack of messages that don't require any immediate attention, but . . ."

"But what?"

"I've heard rumblings that *Buzz* is printing another story about you. Something not the least bit flattering."

"I've survived them before. I can survive them again."

"You sound terribly disinterested."

"I've just found something else" — a lot of something elses — "to take my mind off of everything."

"You sound happy."

"Happier than I've ever been."

The silence stretched between them, as if Nicole resented Juliet's contentment. But that was impossible. Nicole had always wanted the best for her.

"I take it you've pulled off the disguise you wanted?" Nicole said.

"It was the simplest thing in the world. Just a few little changes, but" — Juliet looked around to make sure no one was listening — "it seems to be working."

"You can't stay disguised forever, Juliet. And what's going to happen when you're forced to tell the people in Plentiful who you really are?"

Juliet thought about Plentiful's former chief of police who was despised after the people learned he'd pulled a fast one on them for years. She thought about Brace Harrington and the fact that the towns-people had wanted to tar and feather him when they learned he was really a shyster named Bill Deal.

She looked in the mirror at the Sleuths, at Scarlett and Molly, friends she did not want to hurt. She thought about the girls whose trust she wanted to earn, and Cole who'd fired a nanny because she'd lied.

"I don't know what will happen," Juliet said. "But that's not something I want to worry about now."

Out of the corner of her eye, Juliet saw Ben raise his glass, needing another drink. "I'll be with you in just a moment, Ben."

"Ben?" Nic asked, her voice tinged with utter disbelief. "Is that some new friend of yours?"

"A photographer I just met. Nice guy, but he smokes too much, drinks too much, and" — Juliet laughed lightly — "he has an editor who doesn't understand him."

"You'd be wise to stay away from him, Jules. You know how treacherous photographers can be, springing little surprises on you when you least expect it."

"Don't worry, Nic. For the first time in a long time, I know what I'm doing."

Ben craved another cigarette. If he'd kept count, he'd probably reached for his pack of Marlboros a hundred times in the last hour. God, how he wanted to inhale the smoke, wanted to feel the burn in his throat, taste the tobacco on his tongue. But Juliet was right — the cigarettes were going to kill him.

He washed away the remembered taste with the whiskey Juliet had just poured into his glass. Next time he'd order a cup of coffee, black and strong, and tell Juliet to keep an eye out on his drinking, too. Like too many things in his life, whiskey had become an addiction.

His cell phone vibrated at his hip and he thought about ignoring it. But he'd ignored Nicole last night and hadn't talked with her at all today. She wouldn't be happy; but he wasn't happy, either.

How could a man love a woman so damn much and one day wake up and wonder why?

Grabbing the phone, he stared at Juliet as she ducked back behind the bar, an empty tray in her hands and laughter in her voice.

When had he last seen Nicole laugh? Three years ago? Five?

When had they last been together? Really together, not merely conversations over the phone, or phone sex, or a hasty grope before Nicole pushed him off on a mission to get photos of Juliet?

God forbid, Nicole was ruining her life. And she was also ruining his.

But, damn it, he owed her something for all the time she'd stuck by him in the hospital and during recovery.

He'd stick by her now.

He hit the talk button. "Hey, babe."

"I miss you, Ben."

It had been a long time since he'd heard those words. "Everything okay?"

"It just seems like forever since we were together. Really together."

Had Nicole heard his thoughts? "Want me to come home? We could pack some things, you could quit your job and we could get the hell away. Go to Bermuda, maybe."

"In a few weeks."

"How about tomorrow?"

"I want to be with you, baby. I want it more than anything in the world. But it all depends on the photos you get for me, on *Buzz* printing the story I want printed. You did get some good photos since we last talked, didn't you?"

Yeah, photos of Juliet lying in bed with a snake slithering up to her neck. Photos of her in a bath towel. Some shots of her leaning through the window of a Cadillac, chatting with a cattle rancher when she helped him carry a large takeout order of fries and cheeseburgers for the men hanging out at the grange.

It just so happened the guy looked like an arms dealer. The right focus on the rancher, plus the right angle, had made the man's features indistinct in the fading light of day. With the right sexy pose on Juliet's part, and the money exchanging hands, the photo had been perfect. Exactly what Nicole was looking for.

But she'd never see the photos. Not a one.

"I put a few things in FedEx this afternoon. I think you'll like them." It was a lie. Tomorrow he'd make up another lie if necessary, but she'd never again receive pictures of Juliet — the woman who was intent on helping him break his bad habits.

"Is everything okay, babe? Are you bored there?"

"It's been a long day. That's all."

"Maybe you're staying up too late?"

"You know what this job is like. I don't get a lot of sleep when I'm trying to get good pictures."

Nicole laughed. It wasn't a having-fun, good-time laugh. It was cynical. Contemptuous. "You wouldn't by any chance be fooling around, would you? Staying up late with some cute cocktail waitress?"

Ben's gaze shot toward Juliet. Friendship, that's all he wanted from her and nothing more. Nicole didn't know he'd finally come out of hiding around Juliet. She never would. "There's only one woman I've ever wanted," he whispered to Nic. "You know that."

"I know, babe. And the next time we're together, I'll prove to you just how happy I am that you're mine. *All* mine."

It wasn't more than another minute before Ben shoved the phone back on his belt, then caught Juliet's attention. "Get me another whiskey, will you?"

Juliet grabbed the bottle of Jack Daniels from the back counter, and as she walked toward him, Ben tapped a cigarette out of the pack of Marlboros and stuck it between his lips.

Tomorrow he'd try to quit again.

Nicole trembled with rage. How could Ben do this to her? How could he play around with Juliet when he knew what a bitch she was?

Juliet would pay.

Sitting at Juliet's desk with the tape recorder in front of her, muscles tight, breathing rapid, Nicole picked up the phone. "Bitch," she whispered against the receiver. "How dare you try and steal Ben from me. He's mine; no one else can have him."

She punched in the number to the Misty Moon Saloon, readied the recorder as she had so many times before, and when she heard Juliet's terribly familiar voice, all sparkling and bubbly and full of life, as if she had something to celebrate, she pressed the play button.

Garrett's insidious breathing shot through the phone lines. His menacing words came next. "You've been a bad little girl. Very bad, as a matter of fact, and you must be punished."

"Don't do this to me, Garrett. Please."

Nicole heard the anguish in Juliet's voice and smiled. The recording she'd made of Garrett in bed with a soap opera diva had just the right effect.

"You're a bitch." Garrett's rage-filled words from the courtroom came next. "I'll get even, Jules. I'll get even."

Nicole hung up. She didn't care to hear any more of Juliet's whimpering pleas. She just wanted to hurt her.

Chapter 14

To hell with Garrett Pierce.

Her ex — the jerk of the century — was not going to ruin her life. She wouldn't let him.

Damn it all.

Juliet swung her legs out of the Mustang and trudged through the gravel toward the kitchen door, thinking every step of the way that she should leave Cole's place, leave Plentiful, and return to her Carmel cocoon where life had become plain, downright blah.

That menacing phone call from Garrett was proof that she needed to confront her demons, she couldn't run from them. That phone call had made her well aware that she had to make a trip to Garrett's rich-boy prison cell, confront her vicious ex face-to-face, and beg him to leave her the hell alone — because obviously her pleas over the phone had fallen on conveniently deaf ears.

It was crazy to stay in Plentiful when Nicole had found her, when Garrett had found her, when the paparazzi could easily find her, too, then ruin her masquerade and start a chain reaction that could turn her friends against her, which, when all was said and done, was a hell of a lot more frightening than getting another phone call from that stinking jailbird.

But she couldn't leave. Not yet.

The blackmail scheme was in place, and until Cole's worries about losing his clinic, his livelihood, and his girls were put to rest, she was going nowhere.

No way.

No how.

Besides, she couldn't possibly leave without kissing him again, without . . . without doing all of those insanely sinful things she'd thought about doing when she'd dropped her towel and stepped into his arms.

Juliet breathed deeply, trying to force the ache and stiffness out of her body. But she couldn't will it away. She needed to find that comfort in Cole's arms. In his kiss.

She slipped into the house through the kitchen door and wandered toward Cole's den and the OUTER LIMITS sign. Eerie sounds — like those in a dank, dark castle in the nether regions of Transylvania — slid from under the door.

The creepy creaks and groans made her smile. Cole told her that this place was his refuge, where he came when he needed to unwind. It was pure insanity, but maybe she needed that, too.

As long as Cole was there.

Because she firmly intended to jump his bones.

All right . . . her thoughts were premeditated. Maybe dropping that towel had been calculated too. Who cared? She needed Cole. She wanted him and she was going to have him — at least once, before the truth about her was uncovered.

Twisting the knob, Juliet opened the door an inch at a time and stepped into Cole's inner sanctum. The walls were covered with posters, everything from Boris Karloff's *The Mummy* and Bela Lugosi's *Dracula* to the seaweed-dripping monster in *Creature from the Black Lagoon* and Michael Rennie and the giant robot in *The Day the Earth Stood Still*.

Frankenstein's monster had been pushed to a far corner, and his neon orange eyes blinked in the dark. An old black-and-white movie flickered on the big screen TV and a woman's screams — *her* screams — echoed through a sophisticated sound system.

She should have known Cole would be a *Slash McCall* fan. What red-blooded all-American boy with raging hormones wasn't? After all, every movie started out with a similar scene — the blond bimbo doing something utterly ridiculous, like being terribly frightened by a noise in a creepy mansion, yet wandering aimlessly through the dark to find the source instead of turning on a roomful of lights to make sure nothing sinister and vile lurked around the corner.

Juliet had been the resident blond bimbo in all seven of the *Slash McCall* flicks. She never turned on the lights. She always walked around in virginal white bra and panties. And she was almost always primping in front of a mirror when Slash McCall leaped behind her, wielded his trusty saber, and began to slash her into bits and pieces, her breasts heaving and jiggling — that's what the red-blooded all-American boys really wanted to see — while she screamed bloody murder.

Personally, Juliet wished the first movie she'd appeared in and its six sequels would drop off the face of the earth.

"You're home early."

Juliet spun toward the sofa. Her heart thudded deep in her chest. Cole was stretched out on the plush black leather, his head propped up on pillows as he watched *Slash McCall* — as he watched her.

"Molly's put me on a new schedule. One with shorter hours," she said, resting her hands on the back of the sofa and looking down at the man she craved, but forced herself not to touch — for the moment.

Cole aimed the controller at the TV and turned down the sound. "I thought tonight was your last night."

"I like bartending too much to quit so I'm going to stick around a few extra days — maybe a couple more weeks." She couldn't miss the glint in Cole's eyes or the slight tilt of lips. "That means, unless you kick me out for oversleeping again, or for doing something that messes with one of your to-do lists, I'll have time to whip you into shape where the girls are concerned, and maybe learn a bit more about you in the process."

"I'm an open book." He folded his arms over the pillow behind his head. "What do you want to know?"

Everything, but she'd settle for learning

265

a few bits and pieces at a time. "I suppose I could start with a totally off-the-wall question like, do you wear pajamas to bed or sleep in the nude?"

Cole's grin widened. "That's not something I want to answer verbally. You'll have to find out first hand."

And she imagined she would before too long.

Wandering across the room, Juliet stopped in front of Frankenstein's monster. She reached out and touched the mishmash of steel and leather, electrical cord and light bulbs, not to mention blinking neon lights. "I like this, you know."

"He made you scream the last time you saw him."

"That was surprise. Nothing more." She smoothed her fingers over the monster's broad chest. "If you were serious when you said this is your first — and only — piece of sculpture, I really think you should do more."

"I'm a vet, not an artist. As for Frankenstein, he's not the product of some unfulfilled fantasy of being a sculptor."

"No?"

Cole shook his head. "He's the result of a killer snowstorm that trapped me in the house for a week with nothing better to do than tinker with a pile of junk I'd planned to throw out after I bought this place."

"Well," Juliet said, walking toward the back of the sofa again, "if you ever decide to sell him —"

"He's part of the family. Kind of attached at the hip, and I don't get rid of anything I've grown attached to. So if you want to gaze at my fabulous creation, you'll have to do it here."

Juliet gripped the back of the couch and looked down at Cole — another fabulous creation. He watched her, too, his gaze filled with unasked questions.

And then he pushed up from the couch and stood before her in faded blue jeans that rested low on his hips and a chambray shirt that hung loose and unbuttoned, baring hard abs and powerful pecs that were as bronze and smooth as she'd imagined they'd be.

"Were there any other questions you wanted to ask?" Cole said.

"Right now, asking questions is the last thing on my mind."

Juliet reached across the sofa, her fingertips just barely touching Cole's heated flesh. "A few hours ago I was standing in your arms," she said. "I wasn't wearing a thing and" — she drew a nervous breath — "I wanted you to be naked, too."

Flames blazed in Cole's eyes. "Is that so?"

"Oh, yeah. I want to see every inch of you." And to give him some incentive for stripping, she peeled her tank top over her head, then watched Cole's gaze settle on her lacy pink bra.

In turn, Cole drew off his shirt, taking his time, letting her observe the flex of muscle rippling in the lamplight.

"Are you always this brazen?" Cole asked, tossing his shirt on the couch.

"No." Juliet released the catch on her bra and let it slip to the floor. "You made me this way."

"Me?" Cole popped the top button on his jeans. "I haven't known you long enough to make you do anything."

"Maybe it was preconditioned." Juliet unzipped the side zipper on her capris. "Maybe this need in me has been in hiding for thirty-two years and decided to come out of the closet a few hours ago."

The second button popped on Cole's jeans. "Whatever you do, don't send it back into hiding."

"Why?" Juliet asked, shimmying out of her capris with Cole's eyes bearing down on her slow, meant-to-seduce movements.

"Because I like this side of you." Cole popped a third button. "Of course, I'll take you any way I can get you, but you should know right off the bat that I've always had a fondness for bad girls."

"You've known a lot of them?"

"Only you."

"Honey, you haven't seen bad. Not yet."

"What I see right now," Cole said, focusing on the scrap of hot pink thong that was the only barrier between naked and dressed, "is pretty damn good."

"I have the feeling, if you'd get the hell out of those pants of yours, I'd see something pretty damn good, too."

"I aim to please."

In less than a thudding heartbeat, Cole stood before her in all his brazen bronze glory.

Juliet whistled long and slow. "That's a really nice package you've got there."

Cole wiggled his brows. "I bet you say that to all the guys."

"There's been only one other guy. My ex — and I'd like to keep him out of all future discussions."

"Fine by me."

Cole strolled around the couch. He headed for the door, and twisted the lock.

"Might be best if we keep little ones out of here for a few hours."

"Try the rest of the night. I'm starved." Juliet walked toward him, feasting her eyes on the finest body God and heavy-duty weight-lifting had ever created. "And I don't want what's going on between us to stop until I'm fully satisfied."

She pushed Cole against the door and claimed his mouth. Her fingers snaked into his hair, tugging his face close, hard against hers, because the need in her was raging, burning stronger than anything she'd ever known.

Fear swelled in her that he might push her away, might tell her to slow down, to take things nice and easy, but she didn't want nice and easy. She wanted hot and fast and —

Cole lifted her, strong hands sweeping beneath her thighs, spreading her legs wide, spinning them both around until her back crashed against the wall, until her hands clung to his shoulders, his neck. His mouth tore away from hers as he thrust her higher and captured her breast in the heat of his mouth.

Her butt and her back slammed against the wall as he labored over each taut, dark pink nipple. Her body quivered beneath his touch. Goose bumps rose on her flesh.

His breathing was ragged; hers was labored — and she wanted, needed more.

"Hold me," he murmured through the deepness of each breath. "Hold me tight because we've got a little trip to make and I'll be damned if I'll put you down until I'm good and ready."

With her legs wrapped tightly around his waist, and his fingers moving treacherously close to the hot, wet center of her, Cole stalked across the room, tore open a drawer in the middle of Frankenstein's belly, and pulled out a condom.

"If I hold you good and tight" — he slapped the condom into Juliet's anxiously waiting hand and grasped her thigh again — "can you get this thing on me?"

"I'll do anything you want, as long as you tell me what's going to happen next."

"I'm going to feed that hunger of yours," he said, as they fell together against the far wall. "And not just any old snack. A ten-course meal with appetizers and desserts that are so damn rich, you'll swear you've died and gone to heaven."

"I like dark chocolate and rich creamy butter and lobster. And you. Definitely you." She dragged in a deep breath as his teeth settled around her hard, pebbled nipple and teased and licked. She thought she'd go out of her mind but she couldn't. Not quite yet.

They had so much more to do. So much more to enjoy.

She ripped the foil pouch open with her teeth, peeled out the slick little roll, and maneuvered her hands between their sweaty bodies. "Give me room, cause I'm a woman with work to do, and I'm anxious to get to it."

Cole held her bottom, his fingers digging into her cheeks as he leaned back. That fine, fine package he wore between his legs popped into view, mighty and magnificent and ready for action.

"You enjoying the scenery?" Cole asked, his eyes dark and fiery.

"Oh, yeah." He was long and thick and the darkest dusty pink — her favorite color — and she rolled the condom down, down, down, then wrapped her fingers around him tightly, giving him a little tug.

"Do that again," he ordered, and she obliged without another word, slipping her curled fingers around and around and up and down.

And then he touched her. "Oh, my God, Cole. Do that again."

Her head rested against the wall behind

her and his fingers, long and strong and infinitely gifted, slid between her legs, pulling apart her gentle folds of skin, and slipped inside her. Deep. Deeper.

"What else do you like to eat?" he asked. "Marshmallows? Raisin Bran?"

"Hot dogs. Big, juicy hot dogs."

"Veggie? Tofu?"

"All beef. And not those skimpy quarter-pounders."

"How's this one?" He lifted her again, muscles bulging in his arms as her butt slid up the wall, then came down slowly to meet solid steel. He settled her at the very brink. Teased her with a little twitch. A little thrust. And then he helped her fall, impaling her, and catching her scream in his mouth.

He kissed her. Heaven forbid, his mouth was on fire and his tongue tempted and teased and sought out everything inside.

He tasted like peppermint, all fresh and hot and tingly, and she would have been mindless to the action going on further south if it wasn't for the utterly fabulous way he was moving in and out of her and making her body tremble with need and desire and want.

"Too fast?" he whispered against her lips.

"Never."

"Not enough?"

She laughed. "My God, Cole, jumbo-sized would have been sufficient, but this —"

He thrust into her again. "I could give you time to get used to me —"

"I don't want to get used to you. I want every time to be like the first time."

One second they were against the wall, the next she was lying on the sofa and Cole had dragged her ankles around his neck. He was moving hard and fast and nonstop inside of her, driving her to the brink again and again, refusing to stop when she begged him to, because he knew just by looking at the sheer pleasure on her face that the last thing on earth she wanted was for him to call a halt to such bliss.

Shrouded tightly in her velvety softness, Cole plunged deeper, seeking out the darkness, the sweetness, dragging from her new purrs and moans and sighs. He slid one hand between them, touching the slick, moist heat between her legs, swirling his middle finger over the hot button that drove all her thoughts away except the pleasure of what she was feeling, made her body convulse and writhe and beg for more.

Again he captured her mouth. He

couldn't get enough, and when she whispered his name against his lips he felt as if she'd breathed hope into him. Made him feel he could conquer the world — and his parents — and lift the weight he'd been carrying around off of his shoulders.

He drove into her again and again. She clung to him, her fingers burying into the muscles in his back, holding him close, begging him to go on and on.

Pulling her up and into his arms, he rolled backward on the sofa, carrying her with him until she straddled his hips. A tangle of black hair fell over one of her eyes and she smiled down at him. Moving with the grace of a cat, Autumn rode him, rising slowly, her muscles clenching to hold him tight, then just as slowly she let him slide back inside her, deep, deeper.

A trickle of perspiration trailed between her breasts. Her eyes closed. Her mouth parted to allow a sigh to escape, and once again she called out his name.

Cole thrust upward and Autumn's eyes jerked open. A soft grin tilted her lips. "I thought for a minute there that I was in heaven."

"Any minute now," he growled, holding her tight, driving upward until her pants, her moans, became indistinguishable from his. One more thrust. One more.

Autumn could barely breathe. Each sensation was dizzying, almost heart stopping. The fire blazed inside her, Cole's fire, Cole's heat, hot and powerful, all consuming and highly combustible.

He pushed her higher. She felt his muscles tense. Her own clenched.

And the flame exploded inside them — and he kissed her, a touch so sweet, so fulfilling, that she couldn't possibly want for more.

Ever.

Then, again, the appetizer Cole had treated her to had been incredibly delicious.

When Cole opened his eyes, she couldn't help but smile and ask, "How soon will you feed me the second course?"

Chapter 15

Cole woke to the crunch of tires rolling through the gravel outside his den, and no amount of pretending the noise was all in his head would make it go away.

Autumn lay on top of him, their legs hopelessly entwined, her hair slung over his nose, his mouth. Her sweet, lush breasts pressed against his chest as she slept the sleep of the dead.

His right hand was asleep as well, numb and resting where he last remembered it being — between her legs. She was hot and wet and no doubt would be ready to take him on again for course number five or six — hell, he'd lost count! — if only those damn tires weren't crunching through the driveway.

He reluctantly pulled his fingers away, flexed both hands, and somehow twisted his head to see the clock protruding from Frankenstein's forehead. Four A.M.

Who the hell would show up at four in the morning?

"Wake up," he whispered against Autumn's ear.

"Are we going to make love again?"

"Not at the moment."

"Then let me sleep until you're ready."

"I'm ready," he said, kissing her brow, "unfortunately, I think we've got company outside."

Autumn's head jerked up. "You aren't serious, are you?"

"Dead serious."

She rolled off of his body and landed with a thud on the floor. She rubbed her sweet derrière. "I think I have rug burns on my butt."

He swung his legs over her head and searched the room for his jeans. "Sometime later today you can come by the clinic and I'll find just the right balm to soothe anything that might be burning your body."

Sweeping his jeans from the floor, he struggled into them. God knows where his shorts were, but he didn't have time to look for them now.

The crunching was getting closer.

He stumbled over a bra and made his way to the window. Poking his finger through the blinds, he made a small peep-hole and looked out into the darkness of early morning. The headlights looked too damn familiar. And then he saw the aged Volvo that had carted him, his sister, and his parents from peace rally to rock concert when he was small.

Shit.

"Something wrong?"

Cole slipped away from the window, took hold of Autumn's fingers, and pulled her into his embrace. "My parents are here."

Autumn stared at him in stunned disbelief. "It's the middle of the night."

"Time holds no meaning for Joplin and Jimi Sheridan."

He gathered up Autumn's bra and thong, wrinkled capris and tank top and thrust them into her hands. "Joplin's into nudity, but I don't want to share your body with anyone else, so you'd better get dressed fast."

"Please tell me they won't just barge in here without knocking first."

"They could."

"*Shit.*"

"Did you learn that word from me?" Cole asked, shrugging into his shirt.

"I learned a whole hell of a lot from you

in the past few hours, like the fact that I prefer being bad to being good. But right now, I need to find a hairbrush and a toothbrush —"

"You don't have time. You've gotta go outside and meet my folks."

Autumn stared at herself in the mirror protruding out of Frankenstein's chest. "I'm a mess. My God, my hair's flying every which way. I'll tell you what, you keep them outside and I'll run to my room and hide."

"I'd rather have you beside me for moral support." He tugged on her arm. "Come on, you're in for a treat."

Heading outside through the kitchen door, they stood under the porch light just as the Volvo lumbered to a stop. Cole would have advanced, but Joplin liked to make a grand appearance.

The car door suddenly flung open, and a vision in flowing white robe, waist-length gray hair, and a zillion jangling bracelets alighted from the car.

"Are you okay?" Autumn whispered, clutching Cole's arm.

"I've known this moment was coming but hoped it would never arrive, but, hell, they are my parents, and even though we haven't seen each other in two years and at least two million differences separate us, I suppose part of me is glad they're here."

"Cole. Darling." Joplin Sheridan — she'd adopted the name when her idol, Janice, OD'd — flew toward him. In a matter of seconds, his flamboyant, vegetarian-pacifist mother gathered him into her arms and planted kisses all over his face.

"Hello, Mom."

"Joplin. Please."

He should have remembered. Motherhood and Joplin didn't mesh.

Hands tightening on his shoulders, she pushed him back to arm's length. "You look terrible, darling. Aren't you sleeping?"

"On occasion."

"Nothing ever changes with you, does it. Too much work is making a mess of you, and you must remember, darling, sleep is vitally important. Sleep, meditation, and the right food."

She turned pale blue eyes on Autumn. "Is this lovely creature the reason you're not sleeping?"

"Joplin," Cole said, as an introduction, "this is Autumn Leeves — the girls' nanny."

"And from all appearances" — Joplin grinned — "a whole lot more."

Joplin kissed Autumn's right cheek and then her left.

"It's nice to meet you Mrs. Sheridan," Autumn said.

"I've never gone by that name. Please, call me Joplin after my late, great friend, bless her tortured soul." Joplin shook her head, lost as she so often got lost, back in the world of the 60s. "If I'd known thirty-odd years ago what I know now, I'm sure poor Janis would still be singing in the city instead of singing in heaven."

"Do you really think she would have enjoyed tofu and brown rice?" Cole asked, fighting to keep the sarcasm out of his voice.

"I'm sure she would have enjoyed all of my culinary creations." Joplin linked her arms through Cole's and Autumn's, her bracelets jangling. "The two of you will enjoy them, too. In fact, my mission here is to make sure you find complete health and well-being during our stay." Cole groaned inwardly, imagining he'd have to eat tofu for the next few days. "In fact, your father and I have sacks full of groceries in the trunk and some new recipes we're just dying to try out."

"You're planning to stay awhile?" Maybe he should have sounded more excited, but

Cole couldn't forget the real reason his folks had come to visit.

"Of course, darling. Two or three weeks, maybe, unless something unexpected spirits us away."

Hopefully the ghost of Janis Joplin would appear at the Fillmore. They'd definitely hightail it to California for such an occasion.

A tall, exceedingly thin man climbed out from behind the steering wheel. His head was shaved, he wore round rimless glasses and the same flowing robes as Joplin. But there was one big difference between the two. Joplin rarely stopped talking; Jimi — as in Hendrix, another idol who'd OD'd — believed that silence was a virtue. The last Cole heard, Jimi hadn't said a word in seventeen months.

"Hello, Dad." Cole stuck out his hand; Jimi bowed.

So much for playing baseball out in one of the pastures, tossing a football back and forth, or discussing sex.

Cole peeked around his dad, waiting for the back doors to open and for Butterfly and Slick to pile out. They were part of the old San Francisco commune, aging hippies who'd once gathered at the Fillmore, smoked pot, and talked about flower power.

They now existed in their own foggy little world.

Most everyone else in the hippie generation had grown up, grown wise, and gotten jobs. His parents and their set of friends had just grown a little more bizarre with every passing year.

"Looking for something, darling?"

"I thought Butterfly and —"

"They're on their way. Another half hour or so and they'll be pulling into the drive. They still have that old Volkswagen bus. You remember it, don't you? The place where you were conceived?"

"I don't remember the moment, but I do recall you pointing out the spot on numerous occasions."

"Don't be flippant, Cole."

"Sorry."

Joplin's little boy aimed to be polite, no matter what the cost to his sanity.

"By the way, darling, I hope you don't mind terribly, but Butterfly and Slick invited some of our old friends to join us here. You remember Woodstock, of course."

"Yeah. He's quite a character."

"Juniper's coming, too."

"Anyone else?"

"Donovan and Ravi, naturally. They

should be here about six or seven, and with any luck, Dylan and Guthrie will be with them."

"In other words, most everyone I had the pleasure of living with when I was a kid will be converging on my little corner of the world."

"Isn't it exciting?"

Cole shoved his fingers through his hair. "Yeah. Real exciting."

"So, can I see my grandbabies now?"

The dreaded moment had arrived. "It's four in the morning," Cole said. "I'm afraid you've arrived while they're sound asleep."

"Nonsense, Cole. Children should not be tied to those conventional perceptions of what's the right time or the wrong time to sleep. They should be given a choice to do what they want when they want."

"It's not so much a conventional thing, Mom —"

"Joplin. Please."

"Look, Joplin, they're little. Three of them are still in diapers. They're hyper during the day and they're tired at night, and right now they need their sleep."

"Yes, darling, I understand how you feel, but your father and I will be taking them with us when we leave, and we'd like to get to know them. They'll need to get accustomed to our ways, and the sooner the better, I always say."

"You know, Joplin," Autumn said, hopefully coming to Cole's aid since he was losing ground fast, "why don't Cole and Jimi bring your things in from the car. I'll show you into the kitchen, and we can make some tea."

She didn't acknowledge Autumn's words, but turned frowning eyes in Cole's direction. "You have tea, Cole? Something that doesn't come out of a can or a bottle and isn't loaded with sugar?"

"Not unless Autumn smuggled some into the house when I wasn't looking."

"Actually, I did. A little something that Scarlett Wolfe gave me from her shop. Jasmine Pearls."

"Oh, my dear" — Joplin slapped a beringed hand over her chest — "you have won my heart forever."

And forever, as Cole well knew, could be a good long time, especially when his parents were living under his roof.

"Grandma!"
"Grandpa!"
At seven A.M., after three hours of holding Joplin at bay, Juliet stood in the

286

kitchen doorway, a steaming cup of Jasmine Pearls close to her lips, and watched Jade and Holly race into the living room and launch themselves into Joplin and Jimi's outstretched arms.

Joplin, of course, did most of the hugging. Jimi was rather reserved, kissing each girl on the forehead, then standing back, looking totally befuddled by the two little girls.

A moment later Cole appeared out of the hallway's darkness, with Caitlin on his shoulders and Carly and Chloe in his arms. The triplets rubbed their just waking eyes, unsure what was going on around them.

Juliet could almost feel the ache in Cole's heart as he watched the two oldest girls being swallowed up in their grandmother's robe, smothered with kisses and lavished with love. She wished there was something she could do to take away his fear of losing them, but the only way she could do that would be to tell him the outcome. She'd been many things in her life, but, unfortunately, she couldn't predict the future.

Cole set the triplets on the floor, his movements reluctantly slow, not wanting to give them up for even a moment. He looked toward Juliet as if for guidance. His smile was so slight, she was probably the only one who could detect it; but knowing what he had to do, he patted the girls lightly on their diapered bottoms and watched them toddle toward their grandma and grandpa — complete strangers who'd invaded their little world.

Cole backed away slowly, giving Joplin and Jimi the chance to know the girls without his interference. He strolled toward the kitchen and gripped Juliet's arm. "I'm going to the clinic," he whispered, and with no other words, headed for the outside door.

Juliet's Jimmy Choos clicked on the tile floor as she traipsed after him. She grabbed his hand before it reached the knob. "You're not going anywhere."

Cole's brow rose. "Why not?"

"Because if you step out that door, I'll find it very hard to believe you deserve custody of those girls."

"You're siding with my parents?"

"I'm not taking sides."

He grasped her shoulders and pulled her close. "You slept with me last night. Seems to me you'd think I deserve custody of those girls."

"You want to know what I really think?"

"What?"

"That the girls should be the ones making the decision. Not you; not your parents."

"They're too young to make that kind of a decision."

"There you go again, thinking children don't have a brain in their head."

"I never said that."

"Okay, then maybe you think you're the only one with enough smarts to know what they should do."

The kitchen door opened and a short, decidedly skinny fellow who looked a lot like Jimi, only with darker skin, intruded on the discussion.

"Fighting is a rather dreary way to spend the day," Ravi said, pressing his hands together and bowing in front of Cole and Juliet.

"Make love; not war. Right?" Cole bit out.

"I see you remember the principles you were taught when you were young. Such a shame you do not practice those principles now."

Ravi passed through the room like an ethereal ball of light, sat down on the living room floor, and picked up his sitar. Naturally, he began to play, to the total dismay of Rathbone, Lugosi, and Karloff, who howled in the hall.

"You know, Cole" — Juliet swept gentle fingers over his cheek — "if you don't stop gritting your teeth your mother is going to pull some ancient Tibetan artifact out of her sleeve, wedge it inside your mouth, and tell you it's good for what ails you."

"Actually, Autumn" — oh, God, had Joplin heard what she'd just said? — "an Indian friend of ours, Charishma, gave me a fabulous recipe for tofu pancakes. I don't believe it will keep Cole from gritting his teeth, but hopefully the honey that goes into the mix will sweeten his disposition."

"There's nothing wrong with my disposition."

"Then please, darling, put a smile on your face as I most certainly know you can do, and go into the dining room and help Guthrie and Donovan with the table. I'd like it set extra nice, considering that this is the first breakfast we've shared in years."

"Why don't I go do that," Juliet said. "You and Cole haven't seen each other in ages. Maybe you should —"

"Actually, I'd like Cole out of the kitchen so the two of us can talk."

A lump of dread caught in Juliet's throat. "About what?"

"Sex and marriage and babies and my son, of course."

Suddenly Juliet was gritting her teeth, and Cole smiled smugly. If he hadn't disappeared so quickly, she might have murdered him.

"Cole tells us you're from San Francisco," Donovan said, delicately lifting a morsel of pancake toward his mouth with his chopsticks.

Even though she knew she was the one being addressed, Juliet kept her eyes focused on the tofu, low-fat yogurt, whole wheat pancakes she was busily drowning in honey.

Guthrie tapped his chopsticks on the edge of his plate and Juliet hesitantly looked up. "You've been to the Fillmore, of course?"

"Once or twice." Juliet reached under the dining room table and surreptitiously shoved the toe of Cole's boot away from her inner thigh. "I saw Eric Clapton perform there about ten years ago."

"Too bad you weren't around to see Eric in his younger days," Guthrie said, no doubt ready to wax poetic. "When was it he played there with Cream? Sixty-five, sixty-six?"

Donovan chewed thoughtfully on his pancake. "That would have been sixty-seven."

"Good times the sixties, and everything was happening at the Fillmore. We saw it all, of course." Butterfly sighed as the memories flitted around him. "Jefferson Airplane, the Byrds, the Who."

"Don't forget Janis and Jimi," Joplin said. "Remember when Janis sang . . ."

Cole's mom and dad and their friends drifted back to the sixties, reliving concert after concert, love-ins, sit-ins, pot smoking to "In-A-Ga-Da-Da-Vida," and endless nights of partying. It was hard not to like them; but impossible to see them as parents to the girls she was rapidly growing to love.

Juliet sat politely at the table, in spite of Cole's boot wandering up and down her leg, and watched Cole covertly drop bits of pancake between Rathbone's jaws, while Jade and Holly fed theirs to Karloff and Lugosi. Obviously Joplin had no idea — or didn't care — that her pancakes tasted like semi-dry paste.

"Cole, darling." Juliet's gaze shot toward Joplin, who waggled her chopsticks at her son, "Autumn tells me you and the girls have a big project ahead of you today. We'd be happy to help."

The toe of Cole's boot ceased to move up and down Juliet's thigh. But his irritated gaze hit her dead on.

It was his fault he didn't know about the project. If he hadn't found numerous ways and reasons to stay far away from his mother while Juliet was forced to make tofu pancakes at Joplin's side, he'd know all the down and dirty details about the project. Now he'd just have to go along with the program.

"We'd love extra help," Juliet said, anxious to get son and parents together. "All we need to do is get extra paint brushes at the hardware store —"

"Are you going to paint with us, Uncle Cole?" Holly asked, her eyes wide with excitement.

"I —"

"Of course he is, Holly." Juliet would be damned if she'd give Cole a chance to back out of this. "He told me so just last night."

"What is it you're going to be painting?" Ravi asked. "A landscape, perhaps?"

"Joe's Gas and Bait." Cole didn't look 100 percent happy with this change in his plan, but at least his boot was again caressing her thigh.

"We're beautifyin' it," Jade said, eyes

bright with excitement. "Yesterday we planted petunias."

Holly added her two cents. "We're going to paint Joe's office pink."

"*Pink?*" Cole sounded a wee bit stunned.

"It's not really pink," Juliet added, coming to her defense long before necessary. "Actually, the white paint seemed a little too stark, so I purchased some hot pink that had been sitting around the hardware store for far too long, and I mixed a bit into each can of white. It's the loveliest color."

"It sounds quite soothing, Autumn." Ravi pressed his hands together and bobbed his head like a wise old sage. "Personally, of course, I would rather we eradicate all gas stations and ride bicycles —"

"You drive a Volkswagen," Woodstock chided. "How do you propose to get around if you don't have gasoline?"

"Now, now, no fighting." Joplin rose from the table, looking very much like the queen of the universe, and looked at Cole. "I'd love to help you paint Joe's Gas and Bait, if it weren't for the fish angle. My sensibilities cannot accept the idea of catching defenseless fish, frying them in lard, and ingesting them. And, really, darling, it's been a long night and I'm rather tired, so if you don't mind, I'll curl up on your sofa and call it quits until dinner-time."

"You're sure you don't want to join us?" Juliet asked, to which she received a nudge from Cole's boot.

"Not this time." Joplin patted her mouth as she yawned. "I need to be fresh and wide awake by nightfall, as I have some lovely recipes for this evening's dinner."

"Barbecued steak?" Cole asked.

Joplin hit her son with the evil eye. "Actually, lovely lentil loaf, which I'll serve with —"

"Brown rice?" Cole interrupted.

"Of course, darling. But I'll also be serving sambal oelek, which is a hot and fiery chili sauce, and paneer pudding."

"Which is?" Cole asked, the toe of his boot resting just inches from Juliet's panties. She could smack him, for being so forward and flip with his mom, but Joplin seemed to take it in stride.

"Paneer pudding, darling, is a combination of Indian cottage cheese and ground pistachios. Naturally, I sweeten mine with honey and I use coconut milk rather than that which comes from a cow."

"Naturally."

Juliet kicked Cole, which seemed to knock some niceness into him.

"Why don't I bring your things in," he said. "And why don't you and dad take my bedroom while you're here."

"Thank you darling, but the sofa is fine. And the boys can bring in the rest of our belongings. Of course, if you don't mind terribly" — she rested her eyes on Cole — "your father would like to set his Play-Station up in your den. The noise from those Amazonia 2807 games he likes to play gives me a violent headache."

Oh, dear. Good old Jimi, who hadn't said a word in over a year, had a penchant for Amazonia 2807, while his son was into *Slash McCall*. Couldn't Juliet have found a more sane family to get involved with?

The girls ran off to help their grandmother, the rest of the aging hippies seemed to vanish into thin air, and Juliet stacked a zillion dishes to take to the kitchen.

Cole followed her with his own stack and cornered her next to the sink. "Have you forgotten that I've got a schedule full of patients today?"

Juliet knew this was coming.

"I haven't forgotten a thing."

"Then how do you think I can be in two

places at the same time?"

"I don't believe you can."

"Then you lied to my mom, and Holly and the other girls, when you told them I'm going to help paint Joe's Gas and Bait when I'm really going to be in my clinic neutering cats and dogs?"

"No, I didn't lie. You're not going to be in your clinic, you're going to be with your girls, pretending to be a good dad."

"I *am* a good dad."

"Only when it fits into your schedule. And speaking of schedules," she ducked under Cole's arm, anxious to get away before anger struck. "I've got to go to the clinic and make sure Raven cancels everything for the day."

Before her fingers touched the door knob, Cole latched on to her arm and spun her around. His eyes had narrowed. "Are you trying to ruin my business?"

Juliet sighed heavily, then planted a big kiss on his terribly unenlightened kisser. "No, Cole, I'm trying to help you keep your children."

Chapter 16

"*Pink?* You're painting my gas station pink?"

"Calm down, Joe." Juliet watched Joe's cheeks turn red as she stirred the thick paint. "As I've explained to a lot of other people numerous times today, the paint is more white than pink."

"What you're stirring might be, but there's half a dozen other cans sittin' in front of the bait box, and not a one of them is white."

"Of course they're not white, Joe." Really, did she have to continually explain the details of her creative endeavors? "If we painted white fish on the side of the building, no one would be able to see them."

A decided frown washed across Joe's mug. "Wait a minute. Are you telling me you're gonna paint fish on my building?"

"This is a bait shop, isn't it? Don't you want people to associate your gas station with the best in fishing?"

"I don't sell fishing gear. I don't sell tackle or poles or hooks. I sell worms."

"Good point, Joe. We'll paint big hooks with grape-colored worms hanging from them. And then, now this is the really good part, we'll paint big old fish swimming toward the *best bait this side of heaven* — and we'll spell those words out on the wall. You'll have people coming from miles around to buy your worms."

Once again Joe frowned, ripping off his baseball cap to wipe perspiration from his brow. "Grape-colored worms, huh?"

"The last time I looked at a worm, which, I should tell you, was quite some time ago, it looked rather grapish in color."

He tugged his hat back on his head. "And what color are these fish you're gonna paint?"

"Pumpkin, kiwi green, and princely blue, which is a deep, electric color" — Juliet hit Joe with her most charming smile — "kind of the color your eyes are right this very second."

"The only reason they're electric blue is cause they're in shock."

Juliet checked the color of the paint she'd been stirring and added a dab more hot pink. "Trust me, Joe, you'll feel much better after you see the final results."

"Just one more question." There was that frown again. "Who's going to paint these fish?"

"Holly and Jade."

Joe slapped his forehead with the butt of his hand. "That does it. I'm goin' over to the Elk Horn and drown myself in Mountain Dew."

For a change, Joe stalked away from the station without whistling like Andy Griffith.

"That went well."

Juliet looked up to see Cole half frowning, half grinning at her. It was an odd expression, but it looked rather good on his gorgeous face.

"I told Joe I was going to beautify this place and I aim to please."

Juliet grabbed the bucket of paint she'd been stirring and headed toward the front wall of the station, where she felt the pinkest of the pinkish white paint should be applied — she just wouldn't tell Joe.

Cole followed along at a leisurely pace. She had the distinct feeling he was watching her butt wiggle as she walked. "Do you have plans for beautifying my place, too?"

"Now that you mention it," she said,

pouring a healthy amount of paint into a rolling pan, "the pale blue trim would look better if it were forest green. The doors need to be stripped down to the natural wood and stained, and don't let me even get started on the inside."

"Are you sure you're a kindergarten teacher and not a designer?"

"I've never designed a thing in my life." Other people had always done it for her. Told her what colors and styles were "in." That an Aztec design would be the best in Carmel, when she would have dearly loved to decorate the inside of her home in gingham and chintz.

"You know," Cole said, backing her against the speck of wall she'd just painted pinkish white, "you're not at all what I wanted in a nanny, but —"

"God, Doc, couldn't you do that some-place private?"

Juliet peered around Cole to see Raven, hands on hips, the toe of her combat boot tapping on the greasy asphalt.

"It's about time you showed up." Cole shoved away from Juliet and grabbed a can of paint. "Scarlett's long past due for a break, so I'm gonna let you take her place watching the girls while they decorate the building."

Raven's eyes narrowed. "Let me guess. I have to supervise the painting of fish all around the bathroom door."

"You've got it."

"As long as I don't have to paint the inside of the head." Raven wrinkled her nose in disgust. "Last time I used that thing I puked my brains out after a party, and I don't think it's been cleaned since."

"You know," Juliet said, rolling her paintbrush over the speck of wall bearing her derrière print, "we're never going to get this place beautified if everyone stands around lollygagging. And when we're done, Cole's buying pizza for everyone."

"Only because I can't handle the thought of lentil loaf."

Cole ushered Raven around the far side of the building, and Juliet could hear the Doc giving his receptionist detailed instructions on what was expected of her. Raven, of course, told him he was all wet if he thought she was going to follow his instructions when she was volunteering for this duty and not getting paid.

Juliet rolled her brush over a massive section of wall, staring at the bait box, trying to figure out how to beautify that despicable mess, when out of the corner of her eye she spotted Ida Mae and Molly scurrying toward the station, looking as if something dreadfully important were on their minds.

Hopefully it had something to do with that bastard Jim Foley.

Juliet dropped her roller just as Scarlett rounded the station, and together they headed for the Mustang to rendezvous with their friends. "Did you bring me the pictures?" Juliet asked.

"Half a dozen really good ones." Ida Mae looked right, then left, and when she was certain no one was looking, slid the white business-size envelope into Juliet's hands. "Everything you need is in there. Just make sure the wrong person doesn't get hold of it."

Ida Mae looked right, then left again. "Perhaps," she whispered, "you should keep it where I keep anything I want to keep out of harm's way."

This ought to be good, Juliet thought. "Where's that?"

Ida Mae leaned forward. Molly and Scarlett did, too, wanting to hear the full and complete details. "Deep down inside my bra. Trust me, anyone gets close, I knee 'em in the groin."

"Well, if things go according to plan," Juliet said, looking at Scarlett, who'd been pegged to serve as her #1 accomplice, "no one will have to be kneed in the groin."

"I can't see why everything shouldn't go according to plan." Molly leaned her kilt-covered tush on the hood of Juliet's Mustang. "We've worked things out to the very last detail, and before this evening's over, Jim Foley's going to wish he'd never been born."

Juliet still had a few questions. "You're sure you can get him to the Misty Moon?" she asked Molly.

"Oh, he'll be there, all right. Jim Foley was all ears when Floyd Morgan told him —"

"Who's Floyd Morgan? I thought we were going to keep this to ourselves," Juliet said, keeping a watchful eye out for Cole as she reached through the Mustang's window and stashed the envelope full of incriminating evidence against Jim Foley under the front seat. She didn't dare put it in *her* bra.

"Don't worry, hon. Floyd's an old friend — a special friend — who hangs out at my place a few nights a week." Molly grinned, and, if Juliet wasn't mistaken, a bit of a blush touched her cheeks. "Floyd, bless his heart, despises Jim Foley as much as the rest of us do, and he's got a soft spot for

Cole, too, so he was perfect for the job. Better still, he won't tell a soul what he did."

"So what did he do?" Ida Mae was obviously just as confused as Juliet.

"Well, Floyd just sort of *accidentally* ran into Jim at the feedstore this morning and told him about the hot number tending bar at the Misty Moon."

Juliet nearly choked on her gum.

"You all right, hon?"

"Fine. Just fine, but who's this so-called hot number."

"You, of course." Molly grinned. "Now don't go getting all flustered. I'm sure you don't like being called a hot number, but we have to pull out all the stops to make this little *blackmail* plot work, and that means calling you a hot number."

"Obviously there's more to this story," Juliet said. "I can't believe Jim Foley decided to come by tonight just to look at the *hot number*."

"Not exactly. Floyd told Jim that a bunch of the guys were getting together at ten o'clock tonight, and they were taking bets on who could get you in bed first. Jim said he could, and put ten bucks in the pot."

"Wait a minute," Juliet sputtered. "I'm

not going to bed with anyone — especially Jim Foley."

"Don't go jumping to conclusions," Molly said. "There's no bet, except for Jim's, and even though I'm positive 99 percent of the guys around here *would* like to get you in bed, they know you're already spoken for."

"I am?"

"Of course you are." Molly was very adamant about this unknown fact. "If you weren't in love with Cole, you wouldn't have any reason to put the screws to Jim Foley."

"But I'm not in love with Cole."

"I said the exact same thing about Logan." Scarlett shook her head. "Never in my wildest dreams did I think I could get stuck on a cop, but I did."

"You know" — all heads spun around at the sound of Cole's voice as he rounded the station, paintbrush in hand — "if you ladies don't have anything else to do but gossip, I've got more paintbrushes."

"I'd love to stay and help," Molly said, pushing away from the Mustang, "but I'd best get back to the Misty Moon."

"You can't go yet." Mildred gasped for air as she bustled toward the Mustang, Lillian at her side, waving a paper over her head. "I've got Juliet Bridger news that's going to set tongues a waggin' from now till doomsday." Mildred slapped the dog-eared copy of *Buzz* on the hood of Juliet's Mustang. "And since we're all Juliet Bridger fans —"

"Speak for yourself." Ida Mae tsked. "She's a blond bimbo who can't write herself out of a box of soda crackers."

"Yes, yes, we know how you feel," Mildred said, "but the rest of you are going to be *shocked* when you hear this."

Juliet wanted to snatch the paper away, but she had to play it cool. She had to look disinterested, when she was anything but.

Cole crossed his arms over his chest. "You can't believe the garbage published in that rag. It's all fabricated, total and complete lies."

"Maybe so, but this is very, very interesting." Mildred shook out the paper and began to read.

BLOND BIMBO
OR
BABE BEHIND THE BOMB?

Juliet Bridger, *New York Times* best-selling novelist, creator of blond bombshell forensic pathologist and super-sleuth Jayne Mansfield-Smythe, ran from her Carmel mansion on the Fourth of July and hasn't been seen or heard from since.

Critics around the world can attest to the fact that Ms. Bridger is no Agatha Christie, but her disappearance smacks of the stunt the late, great author pulled off in the 1930s, when she holed up at an exclusive hotel for several days, telling no one where she'd gone . . . not even her husband or children.

"Ms. Bridger is vacationing," was the official statement from her publicist, her editor, and long-time assistant and former co-star, Nicole Palisade. Police say they have not been consulted and see no need to investigate.

Vacationing or not, rumor has it that the jet-setting socialite, author, star of the *Slash McCall* horror classics and *Amazonia 2807* TV series, not to mention ex-wife of billionaire video game and software developer Garrett Pierce, now serving a seven-year prison sentence for corporate corruption, is the mastermind behind the fraud that put her husband behind bars. Sources confirm sightings of Ms. Bridger luxuriating on a yacht in the Mediterranean, blowing the hard-earned cash rightfully belonging to thousands of her former employees, working-class men and women who not only lost their jobs in the scam she perpetrated, but their life savings.

And who is the man she's so chummy with in the photos captured by Buzz photographers? Although his face is obscured, sources identify him as Armand Bruno, an arms dealer who will sell to anyone — good or evil — if the price is right.

For more on Juliet Bridger's diabolical deeds, check back next week for more of the *Buzzzzzzzz*.

Juliet's heart sank. Hadn't *Buzz* plagued her enough over the years? The rumors about her being involved with Garrett's scam were nothing new. But linking her with an arms dealer, and printing a blurry photograph of a woman standing stark naked on the deck of a fabulous yacht, her breasts being fondled by a man who allegedly supported terrorists, and then claiming that that woman was Juliet Bridger, was going too far.

Mildred tapped her finger on the article

and shook her head in dismay. "This is dreadful."

"Scandalous," Ida Mae added. "I thought Juliet Bridger was a bimbo. But this . . . this is beyond outrageous."

Cole slung his arm over Juliet's shoulder. "It's a pack of lies."

"It's fiction at its worst." Ben, the photographer from *National Geographic*, had come from out of nowhere and was now peering over Juliet's shoulder.

"You're a Juliet Bridger fan, too?" Juliet asked, glad to have at least one other person besides Cole on *her* side.

"Yeah. I've read all her stuff. Not bad. But this is a load of crap."

With shaking hands, Juliet lifted the paper and examined the photo. "This has got to be someone other than Juliet Bridger. Her hair's all wrong. Her profile's off and . . ." She looked up, and everyone gathered around the Mustang was staring at her.

Cole cupped his hands over her shoulders. "Are you all right?"

Juliet leaned into the comfort of his chest. "This just took me by surprise, that's all."

"*Buzz* is a gossip rag," Cole went on. "Normal people don't believe what they print."

"But this isn't your normal kind of gossip," Juliet said. "This is the kind of stuff that ruins a person."

"Which means they couldn't possibly print it if it weren't the truth," Scarlett added. "It's libelous. *Buzz* could be sued for something like this."

"The trouble is," Ben stated, "something like this has shock value. One article of this type can pull in millions of dollars and make a lawsuit seem insignificant. Obviously they thought this story was worth every penny they paid for it."

Mildred shook her head in utter dismay. "Poor Juliet Bridger. I wonder what she'll think when she sees the article?"

"I doubt she'll even care," Ida Mae said slowly. "More than likely she's on a yacht in the Mediterranean, laughing at all the people she screwed."

Or, Juliet thought, crying on the inside, because so many people, even her die-hard fans like Scarlett and Mildred, could believe the worst about their favorite author.

Juliet buckled Caitlin into her car seat and smoothed a curl away from the purple and green streaks of paint on her cheek. Exhaustion had set in hours ago, but just like her sisters, Caitlin had gone strong until the very last second, then fell asleep the instant Cole and Juliet put her into the Suburban.

Closing the door almost soundlessly, Juliet leaned her arms on the open driver's window and looked at the man she was rapidly falling in love with. "Promise me you'll be on your best behavior when you get home? And no wisecracks about your mom's cooking?"

Cole curled a lock of black hair around Juliet's ear. "You could always go home and keep an eye on me."

"And then I'd have to turn around and come straight back." She smiled softly. "That's why I brought a change of clothes and asked Molly if I could shower at her place."

"You sure you want to keep working at the Misty Moon? I mean, Joe's torn up the bill for your car repairs, in spite of the pink paint, and Molly told you last night that the two of you were even."

"If I stopped working for Molly" — she sighed, knowing Cole would hate her next words — "I'd have no real reason to hang around Plentiful."

"*Excuse me?* What about the girls? What about me?"

She was going to miss them terribly

when she left. Hell, leaving them might kill her, but she had another life too, one that was in jeopardy.

Somehow she managed to laugh. "I'm a pain in the butt who's messed up your perfectly orderly life, and as soon as you find a new nanny, I'm out of here. I told you that at the beginning."

"I haven't bothered to look for a new nanny."

"But you know I can't stay all that long. This is just a vacation. I go back to work in a few weeks and" — she lied — "I really should leave in a couple of days."

Cole's brow furrowed. "What about last night?"

"This really isn't the place to be talking about last night."

"Then we'll talk about it tonight."

He wouldn't give up. But she couldn't give in.

"I'm already dead on my feet. As soon as I get off work, I'm heading to bed . . . alone."

His strong hand curled over her cheek. "Is something troubling you?"

"No."

"You can tell me, you know."

And if she did, she'd lose him.

Juliet drew in a deep breath and let it out

slowly. "Everything's fine. I'm tired, that's all." Tired of running. Tired of lying. Tired of trying to fight what she felt for Cole. And as soon as the Jim Foley blackmail was over, she was going home to try and salvage what was left of her former life. Until she did that, she couldn't move on.

Ben ground the cigarette butt beneath his boot, swearing he'd never touch another one again. They were vile and sick, and they'd kill him if he didn't stop.

Damn it all. The same was true of Nicole.

She'd pushed the limit this time. That goddamned arms dealer shit might have come about because of something he'd said, but it had been a joke, words spoken in frustration and anger. God forbid, he'd never expected her to go so far.

At his hip, he felt the vibration of his phone, the beckoning call of the woman he'd thought he loved. He took a long, deep breath, and striking out across Plentiful's lush green park, he looked for a quiet place to end it all.

He grabbed the phone from his belt, pressed Talk, and at the other end of the line heard Nic's soft, gentle voice.

"Hey, baby."

Ben slammed his back against a tree, willing himself not to give in to her, but her voice, her goddamned voice, and memories of what they'd had, made him weak.

"Hey, Nic."

"Did you see it?" Ben heard Nic giggle on the other end of the line. "I didn't think they'd print it. Not that story, not the best piece I've ever done. But they did, and everyone in town's talking about it."

"I saw it, Nic. And guess what? You got what you wanted."

Silence. Deep breathing, as if she were trying to understand what he meant. But she knew. Hell, Nic wanted one thing and one thing only — the destruction of Juliet Bridger.

"Did I really get what I wanted?" she asked all too innocently.

"I was there when Juliet saw your piece in *Buzz*."

"You were? Oh, God, Ben. Tell me what happened."

His fingers tightened around the phone. "I saw the disbelief in Juliet's eyes, the shock, and then the horror that comes when someone realizes their entire life has just crumbled around them."

"Did you get pictures?"

"No, damn it. Don't you realize what you did?"

Nicole laughed. "You sound as if you feel sympathy for the bitch."

"She didn't deserve this."

"You're siding with her?" Nicole's anger seethed through the phone lines.

"Someone has to."

"Not you, baby. Not you. Please. You're on my side, remember?"

"I remember too damn much, Nic. That's the problem. I remember what we used to have until your obsession became the only focus in your life."

"Ah, baby, don't talk like that." She laughed softly. "Come home, Ben," she cooed. "Crawl into bed with me and let me remind you what a good thing we have together."

"I'm not ready to come home. Not yet."

"You're going to get more photos for me?" Her voice rose in anticipation. "Something more I can —"

"Stop it, Nic. I'm not taking any more photos of Juliet. I'm not snapping anything else for you or for *Buzz*. It's my turn to do something for me. Do you hear me, Nic? This time I'm taking pictures for me."

Nicole whispered into the phone, which was almost as good as her whispering against his ear. "And then you'll come home. Right baby?"

Ben wiped the anguish from his eyes, knowing that if anyone shed a tear for what they'd had, it would be him. Only him.

"I don't know, Nic." He rubbed at the pain in the back of his neck. "This time, I just don't know."

Chapter 17

Jim Foley swaggered into the Misty Moon at five minutes past ten. Juliet could have picked him out from Ida Mae's description of an ugly cud-chewing bucket of pond scum, but the fact that Molly nudged her in the arm as she was shaking a martini was an even better clue.

"That's him, hon. Dry your hands, put on some lipstick, and do your thing."

Juliet knew perfectly well how to create the perfect femme fatale within the pages of a book. Playing one, however, was a completely different story. Could she really pull this off? Could she seduce a complete stranger. A cud-chewing bucket of pond scum?

Well, she didn't have any choice. She had to make Jim Foley squirm. It was the only way to keep him from hurting Cole. And once that was done, she could go home.

And going home would be easy now —

after all, she had her wallet back, and not a thing was missing. Standing behind the bar, she looked at her pink flamingo tote tucked alongside a few unopened cases of Moose Jaw, and wondered who'd found the wallet, who'd stuck it inside her tote. She wondered, too, if someone in town now held the key to her identity, and if that someone would blackmail her, just as she was going to blackmail Jim Foley.

But she couldn't think about any of that now.

Jim Foley stopped to say hello to Floyd Morgan, who'd taken a table seat where he could get an unobstructed view of the action. And while Jim chewed the fat, Juliet slid the sleeves of her skimpy pink spandex T-shirt way down low on her arms, boosted her very best Victoria Secret push-up bra so her boobs spilled halfway out of her low-cut top, spritzed a bit of cheap eau de cologne on every little pulse point, painted her lips a deep dark grape, and sauntered out from behind the bar to give Jim Foley the works.

"Hey, sugar." Juliet rested five fingers on Jim's shoulder and blew a big pink Dubble Bubble bubble. It got bigger and bigger, and she hoped Jim Foley took it as some lascivious sexual connotation, when it was anything but. When it reached its max and exploded all over Juliet's lips, she slowly sucked it back into her mouth, nice and slow and easy. And Jim Foley was all eyes. "What'll you have, honey?"

There was no mistaking what Jim Foley wanted. He glared at Juliet's breasts. He licked his lips.

Juliet came darn close to punching his lights out.

The creep leaned close and whispered in her ear. "I know what I'd *like* to have."

"Something cold?" Juliet asked coyly. "Or something very, very *hotttt?*"

"I'll take it any way I can get it."

Juliet kept her breasts thrust forward while twisting her head to take a peek at Molly, who, just as planned, was keeping herself extra busy pouring one drink after another for each one of the Sleuths bellied up at the bar.

"Well, aren't we in luck." Juliet batted her eyelashes at Jim. "Since the boss is busy, we could sneak into her office for a moment or two and who knows" — Juliet giggled — "we just might be able to find something nice and *hotttt* to quench the appetite of a nice, big strong fellow like you."

Juliet gave it her best Jayne Mansfield-

Smythe-slash-Marilyn Monroe impression as she sashayed toward Molly's office. Her behind wiggled inside her skin-tight capris, her Jimmy Choos clicked on the hardwood floor, and everybody in the place except for Molly and the Sleuths turned goo-goo eyes on the "hot number" and the creep who could barely keep control of the thing between his legs.

Pushing into Molly's office where paper-thin walls and a hidden and very pregnant "observer" would protect Juliet if something went wrong, she closed the door behind Jim, sauntered across the room, and leaned provocatively against a file cabinet. "Well, here we are."

Jim strutted after her. He reached out to pinch her breast, and after Juliet caught the first faint camera click, she slapped Jim's hand away.

"Naughty boy. You mustn't be in such a hurry." She wagged a finger at him. "There's plenty of good stuff, so let's make sure you get what you really want."

"Yeah, baby, something *hotttt.*"

Juliet wiggled across the room with Jim following. She bent over Molly's desk and wiggled her derrière a little more. "Oh, my, look what I've found."

She plucked a hot barbecued rib from a

plate and took a bite, letting the dark red sauce stain her lips. Slowly, ever so slowly, she licked the sauce away while Jim watched, and drooled.

"Molly has a bad habit of keeping the really *hottt* stuff in here so she can have it all for herself. I don't think that's very nice, do you?"

Jim kept right on drooling as he watched Juliet bite into the rib. "That's not exactly the kind of *hottt* stuff I was thinking we were gonna have."

Juliet frowned. "It's not?"

Jim moved in close. "No, baby, it's not."

Click.

Click.

Click.

"Were you hoping for spicy chicken wings?" Juliet asked sweetly. "Maybe some jalapeño peppers?"

"It's you I want, baby."

Juliet ran with a decided wiggle when Jim chased her around Molly's desk.

Click.

Click.

"Come on, baby, stop your running. You know what I want."

Juliet's eyes widened in feigned innocence as she struggled to keep her distance. "I do?"

"Of course you do. What's a guy gotta do? Pay for your favors?"

Juliet's eyes widened even more. "I don't know what you're talking about? Honest, I don't. I just came in here for some hot and spicy barbecued ribs."

"And I came in here for you. You can be as coy as you want, sugar doll, but I intend to have you no matter what it costs."

He reached into his pocket and pulled out a five. Now Juliet really did want to punch him out. Only a five!

"Here you go, sugar baby. Take it and let's get the deed done."

Click.

Click.

Click.

"What deed are you talking about?"

"Sex, baby. Any way I want it. You got the goods and I'm paying you to deliver."

Click.

Click.

A very pregnant and very petite redhead stepped out from behind Molly's curtains. "Jim Foley," Scarlett announced, "you have got to be the stupidest man on the face of this earth."

"Get out of here, Scarlett. I've got business to take care of."

Scarlett grinned as she held up her right

hand. "Let's see, here we have a camera that caught you offering Autumn Leeves money." She held up her left hand. "And here we have a tape recorder that caught you saying you had every intention of paying her to have sex with you. The way I see it — and the way my husband, you know him, the chief of police, will see it — is you just solicited what you hoped was a prostitute. And you know what, buster, that's illegal in Plentiful."

"I was framed."

Scarlett's eyes narrowed. "Were you?"

"You know damn good and well I was."

"Well, I'll just hang on to these little goodies here" — Scarlett wagged the camera in front of his face — "and if I ever hear about you being a bad boy, doing things like suing the best vet this town has ever had, I'll hand them over to Police Chief Wolfe. And trust me, Jim, that husband of mine will make your life a living hell."

"And," Juliet said, pulling one small photo out of her push-up bra, "if you don't call off your lawyer and drop your suit first thing tomorrow morning, I'll be marching up to your doorstep and presenting all the copies I have of this photo" — Juliet waved it in front of Jim — "and a whole lot more to your missus."

"But that man killed my horses."

"*You* killed your horses, Jim. You and you alone, because you were too cheap to pay a vet to take care of the mare the second she went into labor. You knew she was going to have a troublesome birth, but —" Juliet took a deep breath and smiled. "You know what, I've already wasted enough of my precious time on you."

Juliet slapped the barbecued rib against Jim Foley's too-tight white T-shirt and watched it roll over his beer belly and plop on the floor.

"Now, if you don't mind, please get your fat butt out of the Misty Moon and don't bother to come back — ever!"

Jim marched out of Molly's office to a chorus of hisses and boos. When Scarlett and Juliet walked out, the patrons gave them rousing applause.

Juliet smiled in spite of the tears hiding behind her eyes. She might go down in history as the woman who'd saved Cole Sheridan's hide — but once the people in town learned the truth about her, no doubt she'd also go down in history as the woman who broke his heart.

Chapter 18

Cole stared at the TV screen, his thumbs rapidly working the buttons on his dad's PlayStation controller, putting Amazonia through her paces as she fought off leopard soldiers and warrior snakes. There wasn't much chance to watch the clock because a glance away from the screen could mean sudden death.

Yet his gaze flicked to the clock anyway. Midnight. 12:15. 12:25. 12:42. Damn. Autumn had to get home soon, or he'd begin to worry about her safety. Hell, from what he'd heard from Floyd Morgan, Jim Foley was pretty damned pissed at Autumn right now. He might even be seeking revenge for . . . blackmail.

Blackmail? What the hell had Autumn been thinking? And why would she go to that much trouble for him — and then insist on leaving?

The woman made no sense at all.

Down the hall the girls slept peacefully, exhausted from their foray into the paint-a-run-down gas station business. And the Haight-Ashbury crowd, after finding his wild-in-the-country lifestyle far too boring for words, had driven up to Jackson to party all night long with a millionaire lawyer friend who'd once been arrested with them during a flag-burning at Berkeley.

Across the room, Rathbone's ears perked, a sure sign of someone coming. At last Cole heard the familiar crunch of car tires on gravel. Heard the engine go silent, the car door open and shut. His body ached, waiting for Autumn to come into his den.

He wanted to drown inside her. Wanted to rid himself of the worry that somehow or other he could screw up and lose his girls. Wanted to forget that Autumn could be leaving when, for the first time in his whole miserable life, he thought he might be falling in love.

He smacked the off button on the video game while Amazonia was in mid-hand-chopping stance, turned off the TV, and sat in silence, with Frankenstein's bright orange eyes blinking off and on.

Nearly five minutes went by. He hadn't

heard the squeak of the screen door in the kitchen. Hadn't heard the click of Autumn's heels on the tile in the front entry or the near silent way she opened and closed the girls' bedroom doors when she checked on them at night.

Cole pushed up from the sofa and left the den, walking toward the far end of the house. No light shone beneath the door to her bedroom, and then he heard the sound just outside the front door.

Turning the knob, he stepped outside onto the unfinished brick walk and saw Autumn slipping a petunia into the cool, damp earth. "Do you make a habit of gardening at midnight?"

She didn't look up, a sure sign that something was wrong. "If I don't do it now, I might not get another chance."

He leaned against the doorjamb. "You're not serious about leaving, are you?"

"In a day or two, as soon as everything's resolved with your folks, as soon as you can find someone else to watch the girls."

"I'm not going to look for someone else. I told you before that Holly and Jade had been shunted off on too many people in their lives. I'm not going to push them off on another temporary baby-sitter or nanny or anyone. They need some permanence.

That's what I'm looking for now."

She stared at her dirty hands, at the grime beneath her once pretty pink nails, refusing for some damned reason to look his way. "How do you go about finding someone permanent?" she asked softly.

"I don't know. I guess maybe you just hope and pray the right person falls down from the sky and lands in your lap."

She picked a sliver from the end of her left index finger, and flicked it into the dirt. "Sounds like a fairytale to me."

"You're sounding awfully cynical tonight."

"I'm just showing you my true colors."

She stood at last, wiped her grubby hands on the backs of her pants, and looked at him out of the corner of her eye. It wasn't much, but right now he'd take anything he could get.

"I noticed that your folks' Volvo is gone. They didn't leave for good, did they?"

Cole shook his head. "They've just gone out for the evening."

"Did you get a chance to talk with your mom about the girls?"

"She talked about the girls and all she plans to do for them, while I listened. I talked about *my* plans for the girls, and she turned a deaf ear." Cole managed an uncomfortable laugh. "She's determined to take them; I'm more determined than ever to keep them here."

"She'll change her mind."

"And what about you?"

Finally Autumn turned his way, and he saw the tears in her violet eyes. "In spite of last night, in spite of the good times I've had, I have to go home."

He caressed a tear from her cheek. "You don't act like a woman who wants to leave . . . so stay."

"I have a job to get back to."

"You can quit that job and work here in Plentiful."

"It's not that easy. I have another life there. Friends. A home." This time she wiped her own tears away. "As much as I want to stay here . . . I can't."

Something wasn't adding up. There was too damn much she wasn't telling him, and he couldn't help but ask, "Are you married?"

Anger flashed from her eyes. "I wouldn't have made love to you if I was."

"You mentioned a husband last night. I just thought —"

"I told you he's an ex-husband. *Very* ex."

"Are you going to tell me about him?"

"He isn't someone I like talking about."

"Are you still in love with him?"

"No." She shoved her fingers through her hair. "We had a messy divorce, but that was over and done with two years ago. The marriage" — she shrugged — "ended a long time before."

"Are you running away from someone?"

"Why all the questions?"

"Because I've dumped my whole life story on you but I know nothing, not a goddamned thing about yours."

"I teach kindergarten in San Francisco. What more do you need to know?"

"Everything. Your middle name. Where you were born. What size bra you wear, and the year you graduated from high school. Hell, Autumn, I want to know every goddamned thing there is to know about you because —" Cole reached out for her and dragged her against him. "I want you in my life," he whispered against her lips. "Can't you understand that?"

He lifted her in his arms, and as he carried her into the house, he captured her mouth with his, letting her know the depth of his need. She tasted like fruit and bubble gum and he lost himself in her.

"This is crazy," Autumn said, tearing her lips away. "I've just told you I've got to leave —"

"I don't want to hear any talk about leaving tonight. I want to make love. Nothing else."

He kicked the front door closed and took her into his bedroom. He let her feet slide to the floor, and without saying a word, peeled off her shirt and unsnapped the hook of her bra, pulling it away from her body, freeing her glorious breasts.

With the tips of his fingers, he circled her soft, velvety nipples and watched them pebble before him. "This is one very good reason why you can't leave."

"I thought we weren't going to talk about that."

"*You're* not going to talk about leaving. On the other hand, I can talk about why I don't want you to go until I'm blue in the face."

"So" — she threw back her shoulders — "why don't you want me to go?"

"Because you have got the finest pair of breasts man has ever set eyes on, and I'd probably die if I couldn't see them every so often."

Looking up, he caught the smile on her face.

"You've lost your mind."

"I know what I like." He slipped his fingers beneath her breasts and weighed them in his palms, cherished them, his thumbs circling, teasing, enjoying.

"Are you just going to stand there and stare at me?"

"That could be a rather nice pastime, but I want to tell you another reason why you can't leave."

"I'm listening."

"Because we don't have any other blackmailers in town." He offered her a knowing smile. "It's a special skill that might come in handy next time another citizen is being screwed by a jerk."

Juliet looked into his eyes, hoping he wasn't angry with what she'd done, but she saw nothing but desire. "That little escapade was supposed to be a secret. But obviously someone let the cat out of the bag."

"Word travels fast in Plentiful. Seems to me I got word of the deed while it was going on."

"The bastard had it coming," she said adamantly. "He's been screwing around on his wife, he screwed with you. Somebody had to stop him, and I'm sorry, I wasn't going to let him ruin everything you've worked so hard for."

He cupped her cheek and she nearly drowned in the heat of his eyes. "I owe you for that."

Her fingers trailed over his chest, latched on to his belt buckle, and tugged him close. "There's only one thing I want from you."

"What's that?"

"I want you to kiss me."

"All in good time."

"Now, please."

He smiled, teasing her, and she wanted to lash out at him and threaten him, and tell him how much she needed his kiss. But he drew her fingers into his hand and led her from the bedroom, into a dimly lit bathroom smelling of amber and cloves, the aftershave he splashed on every day.

In the privacy of the room, Cole's hands locked around her waist, taking possession of her body, which she was more than willing to give. He tucked her back into his chest, her curves melding with his heated body, as he turned tepid water on in the sink, and let it flow.

Ever so slowly his fingers slipped over her hands, drawing them into the heat, taking the soap and massaging it over her fingers, her wrists, while his lips sought the heat of her neck, and kissed her softly, tenderly.

Their hands tarried together in the water, until all of the soil from the earth had washed away and her fingers were slick and wet. He spun her around, claiming her mouth, her mind, her senses, while her fingers, so warm, so soft, slipped into his hair and held him close. Her lips parted on a sigh, and he took possession of even more.

She clung to him, relishing their closeness. There was no mistaking his need, his desire, as his fingers swept from her waist to her bottom, somehow pushing away her capris and then ridding himself of every barrier between them in their feverish swirl of passion.

He held her close, but not close enough. Her fingers swept over the bulging muscles in his arms and the tightness in his shoulders, and thrust into his shock of sandy blond hair. She pressed into him, wanting him to know that her need was as strong as his, if not stronger.

Their lips melded together. Their tongues danced, making beautiful music that told more than mere words.

With every fiber of her being she concentrated on the moment, pushing away her uncertain future — a future that couldn't include Cole unless she told the truth, and she couldn't. Running away from Cole when this was all over, leaving her newfound friends, would be a far sight easier than having them shun her, despise her, see her as a fake and a fraud.

A woman who'd deliberately deceived them.

She knew that hurt all too well, and she wouldn't hurt someone — anyone — in the same way she'd been hurt.

But that was the future, this was now.

Cole carried her to his bed and stretched out beside her. He caressed a lock of hair away from her face and kissed the skin he'd just uncovered. She kissed him too, relishing his heat, the spicy scent clinging to his skin in the same way she wanted to cling.

It was madness to want her so desperately, Cole thought, sheer, unadulterated madness, especially when she had a driving need to leave, an unexplained desire to run away from him after she'd saved him from near disaster. Didn't she know how much he needed her, when he'd never needed anyone ever before?

He couldn't stop her if she wanted to run — but he'd always need her.

He claimed her mouth again, captured her tongue, one shock after another slashing through him until he could wait no longer. Pulling away, he smiled down at the woman whose breasts heaved with each hard and needy breath she took. Her lips were swollen and red, and he wanted them again.

Desperately.

Cole cradled her face in his palms and kissed her softly, gently, until her fingers worked their way into his hair and a tender sigh escaped her lips and tickled his tongue. The kiss deepened, so hot, so mind-shattering, that her entire body quivered.

A warm, calloused palm splayed over one breast, teasing as their kiss deepened and fire spread through her chest and belly, and to a moist hidden place she wanted him to touch. Casually his fingers moved from one needy nipple to the other, trailed to her belly button and lingered, played, then dipped further still.

He took her quickly — long, strong fingers slid inside her, and she felt as if her entire body melted at the heat of his touch. He searched, he stroked, coaxing one moan after another from her throat.

She ached inside. She needed more, so much more. As if he'd heard her silent plea, he opened a small drawer in the nightstand, took out a condom, and rolled it on. And then he joined her again, lifting her legs to wrap around his waist.

He kissed her, stealing her breath, driving her passionately, deliriously mad as he stilled, poised and ready at the very center of her, as if he were waiting for a green light that said Go.

What magic flashed before him to spirit him into action she didn't know or care. Cole thrust into her, his own moan escaping his lips.

Eyes closed, he tucked his hands beneath her bottom and helped her meet his every move, a smooth, slick glide in and out of her tight, decidedly excited body. With each thrust, hot and bold and brazen, he took what he wanted and gave back even more — his power undeniable and unending, burying so deep inside her that she could swear he was touching her heart.

Juliet woke to the crunch of gravel outside Cole's bedroom window. "Shit."

Cole popped open one eye. "There you go, using that foul language again."

"I learned it from you." She pressed her hands against his chest and shoved, but he refused to budge, and three-quarters of his body was lying on top of her, pinning her to the mattress.

"Could you do me a huge favor, Cole,

and get off of me?"

"I take it that means you don't want to go another round. Have a little dessert, maybe."

"Oh, I'd love to have a little dessert, but if you'd stop thinking about sex and listen to the gravel crunching outside your window, you'd realize that your folks are on their way into the house, and I have to get back to my bedroom before anyone sees me here."

"They're not going to care."

"They may not but I do. Then, again, they *might* care and may decide to use 'sleeping around' as a good defense in a custody battle. So do me a favor, Cole, get off of me."

He sighed heavily and rolled away from her. "You gonna traipse back to your bedroom naked?"

"No, I'm going to *run* back there naked, because right this moment, I have no idea where my clothes are."

"Mind if I watch you run?"

"Damn you, Cole Sheridan. You are the most insufferable man —"

"You'd better run," he said, waving her off with a brush of his hand. "And come back soon. Okay?"

If she wasn't in such an all-fired hurry to

get back to her room, she'd give Cole Sheridan a piece of her mind.

And then, of course, she'd give him her body, too.

Chapter 19

"She's very pretty."

Cole excised the tenth porcupine quill from Cissy the Shih Tzu's furry face and looked up at his mom, who'd been hovering over him for the past ten minutes. "She looks a lot better when she's not sedated and her coat isn't mangled with blood and mud."

"I was talking about your absolutely delightful friend, Autumn."

"She's pretty, too." Being as noncommittal as possible, Cole's eyes shot back to the dog.

"Your father was telling me —"

"Has he started talking again?" Cole asked, catching his mother's eye for half a second as he worked on the ball of silky fur who, like Hector, challenged anyone and everything that got too close.

"No, no, darling. He writes everything he wants to say on his computer."

"Wouldn't it be easier to just spit it out?"

"He's made a solemn vow not to speak for five years. It would be a crushing blow to him if he gave in after just seventeen months. But as I was saying, darling, your father thinks Autumn looks terribly familiar. In fact, he's convinced she looks like Amazonia, the woman in his video game."

Cole laughed at the craziness of her comment. "Juliet Bridger posed for that character, not Autumn."

"Who?"

"Juliet Bridger. The mystery novelist."

"You know I'm not one for reading fiction."

"I assure you, Joplin, Autumn is flesh and blood, not some computer-generated woman, or a mystery novelist." Or, he thought, the blond bimbo in a bunch of *Slash McCall* movies.

The whole idea was crazy. Par for the course for his dad.

Joplin circled the examining table. "There's one other thing that has your father and I concerned."

"What's that?"

"Are you and Autumn sleeping together?"

Cole concentrated on his work and

didn't bother to answer.

"Obviously it's none of my business, but you're getting older day by day, and it's really best to have children when you're young enough to enjoy them. Your father and I were barely twenty-five when you were born. The late sixties and early seventies were some of the best years of our lives. You may not remember this, but your father and I took you to Woodstock with us."

"I was fresh out of the womb, Mom . . . Joplin. Needless to say, I don't remember all that much about those days."

"But I do, dear. I remember every minute of your life before you left us, especially when you were a baby, when you didn't have a care in the world."

"I didn't know a time like that ever existed."

"It did." Joplin smiled as she always did when she thought about the past. "You used to dance and sing —"

"Not me."

"As I said, you weren't much more than one, and at every party we went to, you entertained our friends, toddling around, naked as the day you were born."

"Me?"

"Yes, darling. You. In fact, that's one of

the things I want to talk with you about."

"I'm not about to run around naked to entertain your friends."

"It's not you I'm thinking about. I just want to know — You do let the girls run around in the nude, don't you?"

"Only the ones who are older than twenty-one, and only when we're alone."

"Oh, Cole, you're being flippant again."

"That's my natural state."

"Well, don't be that way with me. I'm talking about Holly and Jade and the triplets."

"I know who you're talking about."

"So . . . tell me, do you give them the freedom to express themselves, to commune with nature in their birthday suits, the way God intended them to?"

"Not as a rule."

"That will change, darling." Joplin parked herself in a chair where the owners of his patients usually sat. He wished she'd park herself outside, but he was stuck, and no one told Joplin what to do.

"There's this absolutely wonderful nudist resort in South Africa where your father and I've spent some time. Baboons roam free. Zebras. It's a veritable haven for all creatures great and small, and I want to take the girls there as soon as possible so they can become accustomed to our lifestyle."

That did it. She hadn't listened last night. He'd make her listen today.

"Have you stopped to even consider the fact that they might already be accustomed to my lifestyle? That they might already think of me as their dad?"

Joplin looked shocked by his statement, as if she'd never even considered the girls staying with him for good. "Claire had no intention of having them be raised in your lifestyle, Cole. That's the last thing on earth she ever would have wanted — except for dying young. I know you mean well, but your sister wanted her daughters raised in a free and natural way. She wanted them to be vegetarians and pacifists. She wanted them to be raised the same way we raised her."

Porcupine quills forgotten for the moment, Cole gripped the edge of the examining table. "The triplets were barely a year old when Claire died. They don't even remember her."

"Yes, and that's probably for the best."

"It has taken months for Jade and Holly to accept me, for them to understand that Claire isn't coming back."

"And they'll understand why they're

going to be living with grandma and grandpa, too. We'll tell them why, in our own time. It might take awhile for them to understand, but they will . . . eventually."

"Look, Mom, I'm the one who dealt with Claire's death, not you and dad. I'm the one who's held her daughters when they've cried. I'm the one who's changed diapers and sat with a kid who was throwing up half of the night. The way I see it, my lifestyle's been good enough for them for the past six months, it's good enough now."

Joplin's bracelets jangled on her forearms as she folded her hands in front of her as if in prayer. "I appreciate all you've done, Cole, but Claire specifically asked your father and I to take care of them."

Cole's jaw tightened as he fought to remain calm. "I know what she said, Mom. I was holding her hand when she was on the phone with you. I was holding her hand when she died. I'm the one who took her ashes to San Francisco and sprinkled them over the bay."

"That's what family members do for one another."

What have you done? Cole wanted to ask. Did you bother to come home when she died? Did you send flowers? Did you

346

stand at her side and coach her through labor — all things Cole had done for his sister, but he kept the words to himself.

Instead, he drew in a deep breath and changed the subject. "How's the Ripple hangover?"

"Far worse than the ones I remember from my teens."

Cole turned his focus back on his work. "Think we can talk about the girls later? I've got this dog to finish up. I've got surgery in an hour and other patients waiting outside."

"I know we've come at a bad time. Of course, you've always been one to work hard and rarely take time for yourself, so most any time is a bad time."

"I'm not trying to avoid you, but I live on a schedule and you don't. If I'd known when you were going to be here, I could have cleared my schedule, because I want to spend time with you and Dad. Hell, we hardly know each other anymore. And . . . we need to all be together when we talk about the girls' future."

Joplin got up from the chair and joined him at the examining table. "Is there really anything more to talk about, darling?"

"There's a hell of a lot more to talk about."

The soft knock at the door silenced Cole's words. He watched Autumn walk in. "Am I disturbing something?"

Joplin folded her arms over her chest. "Cole and I are having a small discussion about the girls."

Autumn crossed the room and leaned against the wall. "Let me guess, you're trying to decide who they should live with?"

"They're not leaving here." Cole was adamant. He refused to change his mind.

"You're wrong, darling." His mother was just as stubborn. "They're going with your father and me."

"You could divide them," Juliet said. "Or, as they did in biblical times —"

"Those aren't options," Cole bit out, wishing there were no other options and that this whole unfortunate incident could cease to be an issue.

Autumn stood at Cole's side and stroked a hand lightly over the Shih Tzu's head. "Anyone interested in hearing my solution?"

It was bound to be better than the girls going with his parents. "What would that be?"

"Ask the girls who they want to go with."

Cole shook his head. "They're too young

to make a decision like that."

"I agree with my son."

"You're wrong," Autumn tossed back. "They're old enough to make a choice, and the way I see it, they're the only ones who know what they want."

"Have you been telling them what they want?" Joplin asked, her eyes narrowing as she glared at Autumn. "Have you been telling them that Cole will —"

"I don't work that way." Frustration flared in Autumn's eyes. "But if I did, I'd tell them the same thing I'd tell you, that if they leave, Cole's heart will break."

"He's had them only six months —"

"And you haven't lived with them at all," Autumn fired back.

"He's got a practice to run," Joplin said. "He has to hire nannies."

"He wanted a string of clinics and gave up that dream to care for the girls. Darn it, Joplin, he didn't ask for fatherhood, it was thrust on him because you and Jimi wouldn't give up your retreat in Tibet to come back and help out when he needed you the most."

Joplin's eyes narrowed. "You don't know us well enough to judge our motivation."

"I don't want to judge you at all."

"No, you want the girls to judge us."

"The girls — Holly and Jade at least — love you. Didn't you see that when they ran into your arms yesterday morning?" Autumn took a deep breath. "They see you as exciting and vibrant and full of fun. They talk about the toys you send them from Africa and India, and Jade's dying for you to take her to the Himalayas someday and introduce her to the abominable snowman."

"Then, they should go with us."

"Not so fast. They run to Cole, too. When they're hurt. When they're scared. When they're sick. They know that they might be stuck with nannies they dislike, but they also know that Cole will fire them if they don't treat his little girls right, and that no matter what happens in their life, he'll be there for them."

"Jimi and I will be there for the girls, too. Our lives might be different from Cole's, but that doesn't mean we can't love the girls and give them everything they need."

"I know you can love them. But please" — Autumn swallowed back what appeared to be mounting tears — "let them make the decision themselves."

Joplin's lips pursed. Her eyes narrowed. Slowly she said, "This goes against my grain, but . . . maybe it is the right thing to do."

Autumn touched Cole's arm. "Cole? What do you think?"

Nothing in his life had ever frightened him so much. "I don't like it, but I'm sure you're right."

"Good. I'm making potato salad and Cole will grill hot dogs — half veggie, half beef — for dinner tonight. We'll picnic on the back patio, we'll laugh, we'll tell jokes, and at seven-thirty, I'll ask the girls to make their decision."

And Cole sincerely hoped it would be the right one.

Seven-twenty-seven.

How did the day slip by so fast? Juliet wondered, as she stuffed dirty dishes into the soapy water, wishing she hadn't come up with this ridiculous plan.

Didn't she have enough strikes against her without putting Cole's little girls on the line?

She heard Cole's boot steps long before he entered the kitchen. And then she felt him snake his arms around her waist. "You do realize that if this plan of yours fails," Cole said, nuzzling her neck, his thumbs reaching up and under the lace of her bra to caress the tender skin of her breasts, "that I won't need a nanny anymore."

"This plan won't fail. It's absolutely foolproof." Juliet turned in his arms, attempting to sound much more confident than she felt. "You're the one who should have the girls, Cole. Your parents are" — she shrugged slightly — "different. Not bad by any stretch of the imagination, and I seriously doubt they use drugs any longer, but they're not — Oh, hell, they couldn't possibly be as good for the girls as you."

"Wish I could give the girls a pep talk before the big face-off. You know, prep them on what decision to make."

"They don't need a pep talk, Cole. All you have to do is smile at them. They're smart. They'll make the right decision."

"And what about you? What decision are you going to make? Are you still going to leave us, or stay?"

"Don't you have enough to deal with now without thinking about me?"

"Yeah, I have a lot to think about. The girls. My practice. My home. But in just a few days you've become a part of most everything I think and care about." Cole's warm fingers slipped from under her shirt. Tenderly, they whispered over her cheeks, cradling her face. "I'm in love with you."

"That's impossible. We just barely know each other."

He kissed away her protest, his mouth warm and sweet and mesmerizing, yanking her from that world she'd known for so long and making her feel as if she belonged here in his arms.

"Last night," he said, his fingers threading through her hair and keeping her close, as his lips feathered over hers, "I knew I couldn't let you walk away from me. Knew I felt something I'd never felt before. But today, when you were going at it with my mom, I knew I'd found someone special. Knew that I'd fight for you, no matter what."

But how would he feel if she told him she was a first-class liar? That everything he knew about her was fabricated?

Then again, how would she feel if she left him? If she ran away from everything she'd grown to love in the past few days?

She'd crumble. And this time she might not be able to pick up the pieces.

Taking a deep breath, she held his face as he'd held hers, and tried not to think rationally. Instead, she thought with her heart. She'd deal with her lies later.

"No matter what happens with the girls," she whispered against his lips, "I'm going to stay."

Laughter sparkled in his eyes. "You didn't make me fight very hard."

"You've had enough fights on your hands lately. I figured the woman who loves you should give you a break."

"You love me, huh?"

Juliet nodded. "You're all my dreams rolled into one perfect package."

"Pretty fancy talk."

"Then let's forget about talking for now. Just kiss me."

Half a heartbeat later, she melted in his embrace, in the caress of his lips against hers, and all of her fears flittered away.

Not more than five minutes later, Juliet felt as if she were walking the plank as she and Cole made their way from the kitchen to the patio.

Joplin had a sketch pad in front of her, showing Jade and Holly how to draw peace signs and psychedelic paisleys. Jimi sat cross-legged on the grass reading the latest Amazonia 2807 comic book, looking at Juliet far too often for comfort, comparing her with the rainforest queen.

Someday soon she'd tell them the truth, but not today.

Juliet sipped her lemonade, then walked to the center of the patio. Like Jimi, she sat cross-legged on the brick surface. "Holly. Jade. Carly, Caitlin, and Chloe," she called out. Five small faces pivoted toward her. "Why don't you girls come over here and sit with me."

"Are you going to read us a story?" Jade asked.

"Not right this minute. There's something else we need to do right now."

Jade skipped toward Juliet and plopped down in her lap. The triplets toddled across the patio and sat in a semicircle facing her. Holly latched on to Cole's leg. "Do I have to go?"

Cole cradled her cheek in his hand. "Yeah, you have to go."

Slowly Holly made her way to Juliet's side, eyed her warily, then sat beside the triplets.

Jimi put down his comic book and joined his wife. Cole sat on the top of the picnic table, boots firmly planted on the bench. It was easy to see the tension in his face; the worry.

"It's time for you girls to make a big decision," Juliet said. "You know your grandma and grandpa love you very much, and Uncle Cole loves you very much, too. Right?"

All five little girls nodded.

Well, just spit it out, she told herself. "Your grandma and grandpa would like you to live with them."

"Here?" Jade asked, her eyes narrowed in confusion.

"Not here, honey, but in those faraway places they've written to you about. You know, Africa and India and Tibet."

"Would we get to see the abominable snowman?"

"He's a pretty elusive fellow who doesn't like to be seen. So your chances of running into him are pretty slim. But . . . nothing's impossible."

"Would we get to see lions and tigers and zebras?" Holly asked. "Could we go on safari?"

"You'll probably see a lot of lions and tigers and zebras — when you're in Africa. And I'm sure your grandma and grandpa would love to take you on safari. But they live other places too. India. Tibet."

"Uncle Cole will be going too, won't he?" Holly asked.

"No, honey. Uncle Cole needs to stay here and take care of all the sick horses and cats and dogs, but if you go to live with your grandma and grandpa, you can come and visit him once or twice a year."

Holly frowned. "He won't be there to tuck us in at night?"

"Your grandma and grandpa will do that. They'll read you stories, too."

"We'll make jewelry together," Joplin added, her voice cracking, "just like you did with your mother."

"Doesn't Uncle Cole want us anymore?" Holly asked, a fat tear rolling down her cheek.

"He loves you more than anyone on earth and he doesn't want to lose you, but, like your grandma and grandpa, he wants you to live wherever you want, with whomever you want — because he wants you to be happy."

Holly's head spun around and she looked at Cole. His eyes were red. He was biting his lip. "I don't want to go on safari if Uncle Cole doesn't go, too."

"Me neither," Jade said. "And Carly, Caitlin, and Chloe will do whatever I tell them to do."

"Then it's settled," Joplin said, walking across the patio, bracelets dangling, robes aflutter, her fight for the girls over in a flash. "The five of you girls — *and* your

Uncle Cole, of course — will visit us twice a year, at our expense." Joplin glared at her son. "You will take time off of work to bring them wherever we're staying, won't you?"

"I'm sure that can be arranged."

"Good." She patted Cole on the cheek. "And now that that's settled, your father and I will be on our way."

"But you just got here." Cole's eyes narrowed, and Juliet could see that deep down inside he wanted to know his mother and father better, wanted to spend time with them, now that his fear of losing the girls to them was over.

"We'd love to stay, darling, but Jimi has already packed our things and there are so many places to go and so many things to see, that we must be going. But not to worry, we'll write and send presents and before you know it, you'll all come to visit us."

It wasn't but a moment later when Joplin was dispensing kisses to everyone and Jimi was reluctantly giving hugs. When he got to Juliet, he looked deep in her eyes and smiled. Then he wagged a knowing finger at her, as if he knew her deep, dark secrets. At last, he turned on his heels, his robes all aflutter, and with little girls trailing after him, beat a hasty retreat to the Volvo.

Joplin studied Juliet, too. Her hug was hesitant at first, then tightened. "Take good care of my son. He's too rigid and needs someone like you."

And then she turned to her son, and gathered him into her arms. "We'll never see eye to eye, but I love you all the same."

"I love you, too." Cole squeezed her tightly. "And thanks — about the girls. I really couldn't have lived without them."

"You could have, darling. But life wouldn't be nearly as sweet."

Juliet slipped her arm through Cole's as the Volvo sputtered up the gravel drive. "Life's looking pretty good today, isn't it?"

She couldn't miss the smile on Cole's face as his gaze turned toward the corral where five little girls were already at play, tormenting pygmy goats. And then he turned to her and pulled her into his embrace. "Yeah, life doesn't get much sweeter than this."

Chapter 20

"Marry me."

The word seemed to come out of nowhere, buzzing around Juliet's subconscious, something she wanted to swat away — yet didn't.

A cool nose nuzzled her ear, and she might have thought that Rathbone, or Lugosi, or Karloff had plopped down beside her, but they didn't whisper sweet nothings. They merely licked.

Cole did that quite often, too. In fact, he'd done it an awful lot in the week since his parents had left. He'd done a lot of other sinfully delicious things, too. But he'd never asked her to marry him.

Until now.

"Marry me."

Juliet slowly let her eyes drift open. Above her she saw aspen leaves and blue sky and puffy white clouds. A bee was actually buzzing around, and five little girls played with three massive dogs in the corral just beyond where she lay on a blanket in the grass.

And Cole lay beside her, his head propped up on his hand.

"Marry me."

Juliet stretched. She yawned, hating to wake from her afternoon nap, but maybe waking wasn't so bad after all, considering that Cole was beside her, an awfully nice treat when he was usually busy during the day.

"Are you ever going to answer me?" He had a terrible frown on his face as he stared down at her.

"Before I answer, let me ask you a question. Are you fully awake," she whispered, "or talking in your sleep?"

"Marriage is the last thing I dream about, so I must be awake."

She scratched the mosquito bite on the middle knuckle of her right hand. "Then obviously you're out of your mind."

"Something tells me you'd prefer being proposed to with roses and violins and caviar."

Juliet folded her arms behind her head and stared up at the aspen leaves. "I hate caviar, and there was nothing at all wrong with your proposal." Except for the fact that accepting his proposal meant that she should finally get around to telling him the truth. And she *so* hated the thought of ruining their bliss.

"All right, if there was nothing wrong with the proposal, why aren't you saying yes?"

"It seems too soon."

"Maybe, but I want to adopt the girls, and it'll all be easier if we're married."

"Wait a minute." Juliet shoved up from the blanket and paced two feet until she stood next to a massive elm. She spun around and glared at Cole. "You're telling me you want to marry me for the girls' sake?"

"I'm telling you I want to marry you because I want to be married when we start the adoption proceedings."

"That's all fine and dandy, but we've known each other less than two weeks. In my mind, that means marriage is out of the question."

"What if I told you the last two weeks have felt like a million years?"

"I'd tell you to enroll in how-to-impress-a-woman school, because that line is a definite relationship killer."

Cole stood. Keeping his cool, he marched to the elm tree and faced Autumn eye to eye. "I love you. I want to marry you."

She blew a big pink Dubble Bubble bubble and thought about his proposal for a good two seconds. "No."

"And your reason is?"

"I like long engagements. And if I remember correctly, you're not scheduled to get married until you're forty, and heaven forbid that I should mess up one of the goals on one of your precious lists."

"The hell with lists."

Cole grabbed her hand and tugged her through the grass, across the gravel, slowing so her blasted stilettos could get through the bits of stone. He yanked open the kitchen door and dragged her inside.

Pulling his framed to-do list off of the wall, Cole slipped off the cardboard backing, peeled out the list, and holding it in front of Autumn's face, ripped it in half.

"There" — Cole dropped the list in the trash — "so much for my to-do list."

"You've had that list for years. It's got to mean more to you than that."

Cole gripped her arms and pulled her against his chest. "It's a blasted piece of paper, Autumn, and God knows I've learned in the last six months that things change too easily to always be confined to paper." His lips feathered over her mouth. "And sometimes, like in my case, you end up with more in your life than you ever dreamed possible. And I *want* you in my life — as my wife."

She was scared. So damn scared. "I don't know, Cole. I was married before —"

"I don't care about your past. I care about now. So I'm going to ask one more time. Marry me."

This could be the biggest mistake of a lifetime, but it was hard to ignore Cole's deep blue eyes, that looked at her with so much love. She had so many lies behind her, so much deceit, and so many things she was hiding from him, but still she said, "All right."

That, of course, sounded terribly hesitant. "Scratch that and let's start again."

Capturing Cole's gorgeous face in the palms of her hands, Juliet moved up close and very personal. "Marrying you would make me the happiest woman on earth."

She could almost hear the wedding march filtering through the screen door, but it was only a cool wind and the sound of rustling leaves.

Cole kissed her. What was it about his lips? They mesmerized her, transformed her, made her do silly things, and marrying him had to be the silliest, because now she had to tell the truth.

Oh, joy.

"You know, Cole, there are some things we should probably talk about."

"I know. Do we want to have children when we'll already have five?"

"I don't know. What do you think?"

"I think we should just have a lot of sex and see what happens."

"Having a lot of sex sounds like a good idea." This marriage idea was sounding better and better all the time.

"And I suppose I should tell you that I'm already planning a party at the Misty Moon."

Juliet frowned. "Wait a minute. You planned a party without even knowing if I'd say yes or —"

Her disgruntled complaint came to a sudden halt when the kitchen phone rang. "I'll get it."

Juliet grabbed the phone. "Hello."

The old and far too familiar laughter sent a painful chill up Juliet's spine. She gripped the phone and listened to Garrett's insidious words.

"You haven't forgotten me, have you, Juliet? You may think you're going to be happy, but I'll be there every day, making your life a living hell."

Juliet slammed the phone down.

Cole frowned, looking deeply worried as he gripped her arms. "What's wrong?"

She just stared at him, and once again realized that she couldn't move forward until Garrett was out of her life completely.

"I have to go home." She took a deep breath, keeping her eyes focused on Cole, who suddenly seemed like the only hold she had on reality.

"You are home," Cole said. "From now on, this is where you live."

"But I can't stay here. Not yet. I've got to go back to California."

In a near daze, she yanked out of Cole's arms and walked to her bedroom, wishing she'd taken care of this weeks or months ago. Wishing yet again that she'd never told a lie.

Cole's boots thudded hard behind her. "Would you tell me what the hell happened? Who called?"

"I don't want to talk about it now." Ripping open her closet and chest of drawers, she haphazardly threw clothes and purses and shoes into a suitcase.

"When *will* you talk about it?" Fear and frustration and a bit of anger tinted Cole's words. "In a phone call from San Francisco when I'm in the middle of surgery?"

"When I have my life straightened out."

"If I'm not mistaken, you agreed to marry me just a few minutes ago. The way I see it, your life *is* my life, and if it's going to be straightened out, we should do it together."

"This is something I have to do on my own."

"Does it involve your ex-husband?"

"No. Yes." Tears rushed from her eyes. "Please don't ask me about this, Cole. It's a long story and I can't tell you everything now."

Cole gripped her shoulders. "Tell me. Now."

"If I do — Oh, hell, Cole, I never should have agreed to marry you. It won't work. It can't possibly work."

"Why?"

"Because you know absolutely nothing about me, and if you did" — she sighed heavily — "I'm sure you'd despise me."

His eyes narrowed. "So I'm supposed to be kept in the dark? How do you think that makes me feel?"

Juliet touched his cheek. "I don't want to hurt you."

"You hurt me every time you lie. Every

time you hide something from me. So tell me what's going on."

The time for confessing had come.

"I'm not a kindergarten teacher."

Cole's jaw tightened. "Is that it?"

"I don't live in San Francisco."

"And let me guess, your name isn't Autumn Leeves."

Juliet shook her head slowly.

"You gonna tell me who you are, or do I have to guess at that, too?"

"Your father knew."

Cole's shoulders stiffened. "So, you really are Juliet Bridger, huh?"

"I wanted to tell you, but I didn't know how."

Cole laughed. "Hell, never in my wildest dreams did I think I'd propose to a multimillionaire."

"You didn't. You proposed to me."

"The bored little rich girl who was looking for fun times, right?"

"You think you've got this whole thing figured out already, don't you?"

"Yeah. You were out for a little excitement, or needed to do a little research, and the people of Plentiful were the perfect fodder."

"You can believe that if you want, or you can believe the truth."

"Could I believe you if you told me the truth?"

His words hurt terribly, but she knew she deserved them. "If you don't think so, I'm not going to spend my time trying to make you believe me."

"Then we're pretty much screwed, right?"

Juliet nodded. "Yeah, pretty much."

She didn't see any reason to try and talk sense into him. He'd made up his mind already, like so many other people, and no matter what he believed, in the end she had to leave.

She latched on to her suitcase and the old backpack her dad had given her fourteen years ago, and, with tears streaming down her face, walked out of Cole's life.

Chapter 21

Juliet crossed her legs and like every other woman sitting in the prison's visiting room, quietly and patiently waited for her man to walk through the door. Unlike some of the women, she had no intention of sitting quietly once he arrived. Garrett Pierce — the bastard — was going to get an earful, and she didn't give a damn what *Buzz* had to say about it.

The man had done his best to ruin her life, and now that she'd had a grand total of twenty-one-and-a-half hours to think about all that had been good in her new life and all that Garrett had helped turn upside-down, she was ready to shoot him.

Juliet's head jerked around when the heavy metal door clanked open. A tall bald-headed black guy was met with hugs and kisses. A bald-headed white guy was met with tears. And then Garrett Pierce walked in — tall, salt-and-pepper hair turned a lot whiter at the temples since she'd seen him six months ago. Even in prison garb he looked too damn good. He might not be drinking champagne or chowing down on caviar, but he was healthy and vigorous and obviously shocked to see her.

"Hello, Juliet."

Her bravado failed her when she needed it the most. God, she'd been married to this man for eight years, and now she just wanted to get far away from him. Still, she forced herself to say, "Hello."

His gaze trailed over her hot pink Jimmy Choos, the black capris she'd had on when she'd left Cole's yesterday afternoon, and the pink stretchy lace top that still held Cole's scent. He curled a finger around a lock of black hair. "Your new look is . . . different." He chuckled. "Did you just crawl out of someone's bed?"

She glared at him, refusing to dignify his question with an answer.

"Perhaps that was a crude question. Let me try again." He smiled his Cary Grant smile. "Have you been in hiding? Only the people closest to you would ever recognize you in this getup."

"You know damn good and well where I've been."

"I do?" His gray eyes sparkled. "You don't think I care enough to keep tabs on you, do you?"

"If memory serves me right, you stopped caring about six months after we were married —"

"Three. Pamela Donaldson entered my life right about that time. I passed her off as one of my programmers, and you were so involved in your career that you never even realized that she crawled into our bed only hours after you crawled out."

How many more wounds could he possibly inflict?

"Why are you doing this to me?"

"You're the one who came for a visit, Juliet. I didn't send an engraved invitation."

She would have slapped him, but he would have relished the moment. Made her do something she didn't want to do. Controlled her, as he'd always done. Instead, she took a deep breath.

"I want the phone calls to stop."

"Phone calls?"

"The ones you've been making at all times of the day and night. The ones where you simply breathe in my ear. The ones where you laugh or say nothing at all. The ones where you say you'll get even."

"I have no idea what you're talking about."

"The phone call you made to me in Wyoming at two o'clock yesterday afternoon."

"What in God's name would you be doing in Wyoming?"

"Trying to start a new life."

"With black hair? Looking like you should be standing on a street corner in downtown L.A. picking up five dollars from any pervert willing to fork out for your brand of sex?"

Juliet gritted her teeth. "I rather like this look," she said, rebounding at last. "I like your new look, too. How do you like prison food, Garrett?"

"I've had better."

"If you'd been a halfway decent human being during the last few years of our marriage, if you'd been remotely polite during the divorce, and if you hadn't resorted to making those vicious phone calls to me at all hours, I might have sent you care packages, but right now, I don't care if you rot in this place."

"There you go mentioning phone calls again. I have better things to do in here than call you, Juliet."

He was a liar. A cheat. A bastard. Traits she'd finally recognized by year eight of their marriage. But watching him closely now, she sensed he might be telling the truth.

"You haven't called to threaten me?" she asked. "Not yesterday? Not several times last week?"

"In case you haven't noticed, I'm in jail. I don't have a phone in my cell, I don't have access to a cellular phone, and as a rule, the guards don't let me roam the halls at two A.M."

"But —"

"You're a fool, Juliet. You were nothing before I discovered you and you'll be nothing again."

"I've gotten along perfectly fine without you."

"That's right. You and Nicole Palisade. God, I knew you were gullible, but I can't believe you haven't seen through her."

"Nicole's been there for me through everything."

"Nicole's been stabbing you in the back. If you looked at your so-called friend a little closer, you might find that *she's* figured out a way to call you at all hours of the day and make you believe it's me."

"That's a lie."

"Always true to your friends, right? How many people told you I was seeing other

women? How many people did you ignore?"

"I didn't want to believe it."

"You don't want to believe that Nicole's
a bitch, either." He laughed cynically. "I
thought you were the one who turned me
in to the Feds, but it was your good friend
Nic."

"She wouldn't do that."

"No? She was in love with me once.
Probably still is, and jealousy is a rather
ugly thing. She wanted to get even with me
for dumping her and taking you into my
bed."

"She got over you long before we got
married. She told me so."

"Poor gullible Juliet." He shook his head.
There was laughter in his eyes. "Haven't
you ever wondered how *Buzz* gets so many
good photos of you? So many good stories?
If you think Nicole has worked for you out
of the goodness of her heart, you're wrong.
She's done it to get back at you for stealing
me. For stealing the role of Amazonia."

Juliet felt as if she were being strangled
by this news.

"Does it really surprise you?" Garrett
asked. "She started writing stories while
she was playing your Amazonia sidekick."

"Why didn't you tell me?"

375

"Because the more stories Nicole wrote, the more popular you became. The more popular you became, the more money we made, and I do love money, Juliet. Money and women." He sighed, touching her hair again. "You were always my favorite. The only one I ever married."

Nausea hit her. The room was trying desperately to spin around her, trying to make her think she really had lost her mind, but she wasn't going to let Garrett or Nicole or anything else ruin her.

She gripped the edge of the table and pushed herself up. Again she wanted to slap him, but he didn't deserve her energy. Instead, she smiled, blew a big Dubble Bubble bubble, something she knew irked the hell out of him, and with hips swaying like a five-dollar hooker, flounced out of the room without bothering to say good-bye.

When she reached the inconspicuous Chevy she'd rented at the Santa Barbara airport, after flying south from Jackson, the tears began to fall. She'd thought all she had to do was face Garrett and the nightmare of her past would be over, but now she had to face Nicole, too.

But not today.

No, this time, she was going to think rationally and do everything the right way.

Chapter 22

Nanny #15 lasted a day and a half. Cole should have known that a woman who looked like Lon Chaney's werewolf wouldn't suit his needs. No woman would ever again be like Autumn.

Er . . . Juliet.

Hell, he needed to remember that that was the name of the woman he'd asked to marry him. A multimillionaire who'd accepted his proposal and walked out on him in the space of five minutes. Had that really been a week ago?

Hell if he knew why he had so much trouble keeping women around. Raven and half the people in town wanted to know the same thing, too. They especially wanted to know about Autumn Leeves, the darling of Plentiful.

He wasn't about to tell them the truth about Autumn. She'd have to tell them herself. If she ever had the guts to come back.

He was mad at her, mad at himself, and lonely as hell — and too damn busy and stubborn to do anything about it.

"Uncle Cole?"

He looked up from the notes he'd been scribbling about Hector's latest bout with another animal — a skunk this time — to see Holly sitting atop the once emaciated Newf. The dog stood on all fours, massive amounts of drool dropping from its chops, while patiently allowing Holly to brush the fur that was again showing some kind of sheen.

"Everything going okay?"

"Tinker Bell keeps slobbering on me."

"You wanted to keep her and take care of her. The drool is part of the package."

"I guess that means she shouldn't sleep in bed with me when she isn't sick anymore."

"It might be better if she sleeps on the floor."

"Do you think Rathbone and Lugosi and Karloff will mind her sleeping in my room?"

"At first, maybe, but they'll get used to her being there, and pretty soon she'll seem like part of the family."

"I was getting used to Autumn, too, and then she left." Holly sighed heavily. "She didn't even say good-bye."

That was his fault. He'd pretty much shoved her out the door when he said he couldn't believe her. Hell, they hadn't even had much of an argument; he'd been too hurt, too angry, and wanted her gone. God, what a fool he'd been. Besides the girls, Juliet had been the best part of his life.

Holly climbed down from the Newf and crawled into his lap. "I didn't think I would miss Autumn, but I do. Do you miss her, too?"

"Yeah. It was pretty nice having her around, wasn't it?"

Holly nodded. "Do you think she'll come back?"

She had so darn much in her other life, why would she want to come back? He didn't want her money, and he doubted she'd want to live without it.

But that's not what he told Holly. For her sake and for his, he remained positive.

"I hope she'll come back, honey. With all my heart, I hope we'll see her again."

Chapter 23

Juliet's hair had been stripped and bleached and pampered off and on for three solid days by the colorist who'd cared for her hair for the past five years. Rocco Toracelli had given her a bed in his Carmel beach house, plied her with mangoes and yogurt and seemingly endless margaritas while she cried her heart out and tried to pull her life back together again.

How odd that the only person she felt she could trust after fourteen years of racking up "friends" was the hairdresser who'd always looked at her with an air of disdain. Who could have known that he'd done that because he thought she was a snob.

"You want this Cole back, you go after him," Rocco said as he applied endless amounts of goop to her hair and then gave her a full body massage.

"I have one other problem to deal with

first. My so-called assistant and friend."

"Nicole Palisade is a bitch. I would have told you that years ago if you'd asked."

"Was I really a snob?"

Rocco had shrugged. "You never came in to the shop alone. There was always someone else with you, usually that Nicole, and she made a point of telling me that you had too much on your mind and were not to be disturbed. I figured you were a bitch."

God, she'd learned a lot from Rocco — like the fact that she'd been blind to so very, very much.

But no longer.

Fortified with every vitamin known to man, dressed in a knock-down, drag-out, skin-tight hot pink jumpsuit, brand-new Jimmy Choos, rhinestone sunglasses and a wad of Dubble Bubble, she pulled her newly-painted pink Mustang — which a friend of Rocco's had retrieved from the airport in Jackson Hole — into her very own Carmel driveway and swung her long legs out of the car.

Nicole, bless her treacherous, microscopic-sized heart, had taken up residence at Juliet's oceanside estate in Juliet's absence, a bit of information Rocco, who wanted to be a private detective, not a hairdresser, had gleaned from Juliet's gossipy neighbors. Juliet's staff had been let go, too, Juliet had learned. No doubt Nicole was pocketing the money set aside for the gardener, the chef, the housekeeper, and the poolboy.

Taking a deep breath, Juliet dropped her keys into her pink flamingo tote and strolled up to her own front door and rang the doorbell like an Avon saleslady anxious to sell the woman of the house a bushel of goods.

Ding dong.

Juliet heard the click of heels on the hand-painted Mexican tile. It was Nicole's familiar click. And right about now, Juliet imagined Nicole peeking through the peep hole to see who was at the door, groaning inwardly to see Juliet waiting for permission to enter her own abode.

The door opened slowly. Nicole wore a wide smile as if pleased to see her boss. "You've come home."

"Did you think I'd stay away forever?" Juliet said, walking into the house that now felt stuffy and cold.

"I didn't know what you'd do after that libelous article appeared in *Buzz*. I tried calling you at that saloon in Wyoming, but they said you'd stopped working there. I tried calling your cell —"

"I've gotten a new number."

Nicole frowned. "You should have called to tell me."

"And what would you have done with the information?" Juliet's voice dripped with animosity.

"What do you mean? I'd file it away for emergencies, of course."

"Or dial the number in the middle of the night, and when I answered . . . play one of those tapes you made of Garrett's conversations."

"You're not making any sense."

Juliet folded her arms over her chest. "I know about the tapes, Nic, thanks to a very clever private detective. I know about the phone calls and the photographer who's been following me around for years, and the articles you've written. Or should I say the lies you've written?"

"I'm your friend, Juliet. I've been here for the last couple of weeks making sure your life doesn't fall apart while you ran off and tried to figure out who you wanted to be."

"I know who I want to be now, thank you."

Nicole smiled in spite of Juliet's accusations. "Then our lives can get back to normal?"

"That depends on how you define normal."

A frown touched Nicole's face. "You're acting strangely, Juliet."

"Actually, you're the one who's been acting strangely." Juliet reached into her tote and pulled out an envelope. "In here I have all sorts of wonderful information about you, like your connection with *Buzz*, your involvement with a private investigator who specializes in bugging people's phone calls and meetings, and God knows what else. I also have pictures of you sitting in the middle of my bed drinking my champagne out of my best stemware while thumbing through a box of cassette tapes that, I should tell you, are now in my possession."

Nicole's mouth dropped open a second before she raced from the foyer, down the hall and into Juliet's bedroom. Juliet followed, then leaned against the doorjamb and watched Nicole search for the box that was now resting safe and secure on Rocco's kitchen table.

Nicole's shoulders stiffened. She turned and a slow smile touched her face. "How did you find out? Did Ben tell you?"

"Ben?" Juliet asked. Rocco hadn't mentioned that name.

"The so-called *National Geographic* photographer you've been chummy with. The man I recruited eight years ago to take photos of you. My lover."

Ben. The man who'd been trying to kick a bad habit. Who had an editor who wanted one kind of photo while he'd wanted to take another. The man who'd refused to believe the arms-dealer story in *Buzz*. He'd been following her, watching her every move, and masquerading as a nice guy — or maybe he was. Damn if she'd jump to conclusions like everyone else.

"Ben never mentioned you at all," Juliet said. "Someone else has been watching you for the last week."

Nicole's eyes narrowed. "Turnabout's fair play, right, Juliet?"

"That wasn't the reason at all. In spite of what I'd been told, I didn't want to believe you were the one writing the stories in *Buzz*. I didn't want to believe that you were out to get me."

Nicole laughed cynically. "Loyal to the very end, right?"

"I've been your friend, Nic. We trusted each other."

"You were never my friend."

"I took you everywhere with me. I —"

"If you hadn't stolen Garrett from me, I could have traveled the world on my own. I would have been rich and famous and a star."

"That's not true, Nic."

Juliet spun around at the sound of a familiar voice.

Ben stood behind her, silent and stealthy.

"What are you doing here?" Juliet asked, angry that she'd befriended him in Plentiful, after he'd spent years following her around with a camera.

"You've got every right to be mad at me," he said, smiling at Juliet. "But —"

"Ignore her, Ben," Nicole spit out. "Tell her you're here to see me."

A mixture of rage and untold hurt filled Ben's eyes, but he ignored Nicole's words, and continued to look at Juliet. "I wanted to tell you about me. Wanted to end everything, but sometimes addictions can be awfully powerful. And I was hooked on the worst thing possible."

"You didn't follow me here, did you?" Juliet asked.

Ben shook his head. "I just flew down this morning. Took me a long time to decide what to do —"

"What are you talking about, baby?"

Nicole's eyes were wide. Filled with fear. "And what did you mean when you said I wouldn't have been rich and famous if she hadn't stolen Garrett from me?"

"Garrett didn't love you, Nic. When are you going to understand that Garrett never loved anyone but himself?"

"That's not true. He loved me."

"No, Nic. *I* loved you. *Me.* For eight long years, but no matter what I did, it was never good enough."

"That's not true, baby."

"Yeah, it is." Ben tossed his cell phone to the center of Juliet's bed. "*That's* the phone you bought me so you could tell me what to do. So you could keep track of me while I kept track of Juliet. *That's* the phone that tied us together, because God knows you never wanted me close." He laughed bitterly. "I don't need it or want it any longer."

"You can't leave me, Ben. I need you."

"You need too much, Nic. And too much is never enough for you."

Nicole ran after Ben as he marched from the house. She stood just outside the doorway. "Don't go, Ben. If you do, it's over between us. Over, do you hear me?"

Juliet stared in stunned silence as Nicole begged and pleaded for Ben to come back.

"Please, Ben," Nicole cried. "Come back."

Juliet heard Nicole's sobs as Ben climbed into his car and took off. Damn it! She wanted to offer some comfort, just as she always had. "Can I do anything, Nic?"

"Haven't you done enough to ruin my life?" Nicole's face was filled with rage when she spun around, and then she laughed. "But just wait. Just wait. The next issue of *Buzz* will be on the streets to-morrow, and even if I do say so myself, it contains my finest writing yet."

Ben was right. Nicole needed too much, and too much would never be enough.

It took courage, but finally Juliet said, "Get out, Nic." She wanted to turn away, but she faced her, keeping the upper hand. "Now."

"You owe me a month's salary."

Juliet shook her head. "I owe you nothing."

"You can't get rid of me."

"Now that I know who's behind all the lies, all of the vicious gossip, I have the power to fight back." Juliet smiled. "In other words, you don't have someone help-less to pick on anymore, which, I imagine, takes away all of your fun."

Nicole's eyes narrowed. She might have

been thinking up another retort, but Juliet closed the door in her face and locked it behind her.

Juliet fought her tears. Fought the urge to collapse. She couldn't fall apart now, not when she had one more very important matter to deal with.

Chapter 24

"Well, well, well, when did Cole Sheridan become a drinking man?"

Cole looked up from the bottle of Moose Jaw he'd been nursing for nearly an hour to see Molly standing on the other side of the bar. He looked at his watch. "About fifty-two minutes ago. You would have known if you hadn't been hiding in your office."

"I was having a late-night snack with Floyd." Molly winked. "I fixed up a batch of the best hot wings this side of heaven, in case you'd like to try a few."

"Thanks, but I made peanut butter and jelly sandwiches for dinner."

Molly whisked her towel around on the counter, scrubbing at nearly invisible water spots. "I heard you had to fire Nanny #15."

"Actually, it seems Squeeze got out of her enclosure and slithered up the woman's thigh while she was sleeping on the sofa watching horror movies."

"That snake's going to be the death of you yet. Have you ever thought about getting rid of it since it seems to cause you so much trouble."

"She only scares off the people that have no business hanging around my place."

"She didn't scare off Autumn."

"No" — Cole took a swallow of beer — "that would have been me."

Molly plopped her elbows on the bar. "How'd you do that?"

"I asked her to marry me."

Molly's bushy brows rose. "Did you now?"

Cole nodded slowly. "Yep."

"I take it she turned you down?"

"Let's just say the proposal didn't go quite the way I'd hoped."

"Any regrets?"

"Far too many."

"You love her?"

"Yep."

Molly popped the top on a Moose Jaw and took a sip. "So how come you're not down in San Francisco trying to sweet-talk her into coming back to Plentiful?"

"Guess I was kind of hoping she'd come back on her own." Hell, he'd hoped that maybe, just maybe, she'd let him help her with whatever was troubling her because, damn it all, he loved her.

The Misty Moon's swinging doors burst open and Lillian, Ida Mae, and Mildred bustled across the peanut-strewn floor. "Oh, my word, you are not going to believe what's on the cover of *Buzz*." Mildred slapped the tabloid on the copper-topped bar right in front of Cole. "It's a good thing Scarlett's home in bed or she'd drop that baby right here and now if she saw this bit of news."

"What news?" Molly asked.

"Juliet Bridger's made the front page again."

Cole twisted the paper toward him. "What this time?"

"You'll be shocked to hear this as well, Cole. Juliet Bridger's not only consorting with a nefarious arms dealer," Ida Mae said, "but she's disguised herself and she's been hiding out right here in Plentiful."

Molly lifted her bottle of beer. "You don't say."

"I do too say." Ida Mae shook her head and tsked. "Would you believe our very own Autumn Leeves is that reprehensible thief Juliet Bridger?"

"And she pulled the wool over all of our

eyes," Lillian added.

"Wait a minute." Cole pushed away from the bar, away from his friends and neighbors. He thought about just walking out of the place because he didn't want to hear the negatives about Juliet, but spun around halfway to the swinging doors.

"You can't really believe that crap, can you?"

"I've been reading *Buzz* for years," Mildred said, "and it's always been *relatively* truthful."

"*And*" — Lillian said — "Autumn disappeared without saying good-bye to any of us."

"That wasn't done on purpose," Cole said. "Trust me. Something important came up and she had to leave."

"What could have been important enough for her to leave you high and dry with five babies to care for?" Ida Mae said. "God knows she probably flew off to the Mediterranean to give that hunky arms dealer a billion or so dollars."

"Come on, Ida Mae," Cole said, "do you really believe the Autumn Leeves who painted Joe's Gas and Bait pink with little fishes swimming all over it is capable of doing something like that?"

"Well . . . I don't know. She could have

been trying to fool us into thinking she was sweet."

"She could have skipped town when her wallet disappeared, but she didn't," Cole added. "She planted flowers at Joe's place. She served drinks here. She took care of my little girls and as far as I know, she never asked for a penny from anyone."

"Okay," Ida Mae said, "so maybe she was very sweet."

"She blackmailed Jim Foley," Lillian said. "Is that a good thing?"

"Blackmail's never good," Cole said, "but she — and the rest of you ladies — did it for a good cause. She saved my butt."

"And I'd do it again."

Cole spun around. His heart went into overdrive when he saw a blond bombshell standing just inside the Misty Moon.

Juliet strolled toward him and he couldn't miss the tears in her beautiful blue — not violet — eyes. She looked from one friend to another. "I know I lied to all of you. It was wrong, but to tell you the truth, I just didn't want to be Juliet Bridger any longer. I didn't want her fame, her fortune, or the gossip that surrounded her."

Cole wanted to go to her, but she was finally dumping bad history, telling him a lot of the secrets he'd wanted to know, and he was happy to listen.

Juliet smiled weakly. "If my car hadn't broken down, if Cole hadn't rescued me out there on the highway, I never would have stopped in Plentiful, but I'm glad I did. Because for the first time in as long as I can remember, I got to be the person I created, not someone created by the tabloids, or by a rich ex-husband, or a movie director. I didn't know if you'd like the real me and, whether you did or not didn't really matter. I liked me — everything except the lies. And I fell in love with everyone of you."

Her smile widened. "Especially you, Cole. And" — tears slid from her eyes — "I meant it when I said marrying you would make me the happiest person on earth. You probably don't want me back, but —"

"I do."

Amid cheers and whistles and Molly inviting everyone to a round of Moose Jaw on the house, Cole strolled toward Juliet and pulled her into his arms. "I love you," he whispered, gathering her close. "I don't care about your past. I should have told you that before, but I was hurt and angry —"

"And pigheaded," Juliet added, her smile radiating through her tears.

"That, too." Cole wove his fingers through her hair, keeping her close, where he'd always keep her. "I used to think my life was pretty damn good, but you — and the girls — have turned every moment into something special. And . . ."

A dozen smiling faces circled Cole and the woman he loved, listening and sighing at every word.

"Was there something else you wanted to say?" Juliet asked, her sweet lips whispering over his mouth.

"Just that I love you, and . . . well, I'll tell you a whole lot more once I get you alone."

And then Cole captured Juliet's pretty pink lips . . . and kissed her.

Epilogue

BIMBO AND BUMPKIN MARRY AT THE MISTY MOON

Mystery novelist Juliet Bridger married Dr. Cole Sheridan, DVM, in a private ceremony at the Misty Moon Saloon in Plentiful, Wyoming. Attendees included the couple's five adopted daughters, three sleuths, the chief of police, his wife, nearly every resident of the community (except Jim Foley, who, sources say, is suing the owner of the Misty Moon for peanut poisoning), three Great Danes, a drooling Newfoundland, Frankenstein, and Squeeze.

The newlyweds are also featured on the cover of this month's *National Geographic*, in the magazine's "Country Weddings" pictorial titled AND THEN HE KISSED ME, by photographer

Ben Monroe, formerly of *Buzz*.

> *Buzz* humbly apologizes to Juliet
> Bridger for statements made in an
> unsolicited article about arms
> dealers.